BALTHASAR'S GIFT

BALTHASAR'S GIFT

A MAGGIE CLOETE MYSTERY

Charlotte Otter

English edition first published by Modjaji Books (Pty) Ltd in 2014
PO Box 385, Athlone, 7760, Cape Town, South Africa
www.modjajibooks.co.za

Cover artwork by Angela Briggs & Justin Anschutz
Cover lettering by Jesse Breytenbach
Book and Cover Design by Monique Cleghorn
Editor: Karen Jennings

Set in 11 pt on 15 pt Minion

Printed and bound by Megadigital

ISBN: 978-1-920590-52-9 (paperback)
ISBN: 978-1-920590-56-7 (e-book)

For Elise Cooper, a shining light.

1

Tuesday, 7am

Sunlight glinted on the knife. It could have been a watch, or the carapace of a phone, or the shiny buckle of his belt, but it was a knife. She knew from the sly way he pulled its serrated smile out of his jeans pocket and held it against the woman's ribs. His accomplice looted the woman's moneybag, stuffed coins into a plastic bag. She bowed her head in penitence, as if the shame of being robbed in public was too much. Her legs wobbled. Only the knife's grimace kept her upright.

In the early-morning rush, they could slip the knife into her torso and no one would be the wiser. Only when the crowds had melted away to their offices, shops and fast-food restaurants, donned their work faces, uniforms and name-tags, would her prone and bleeding body be found. Maggie watched from the traffic, trapped by the crush of suburban sedans and minibus taxis around her.

'Stop them!' she yelled, her voice muffled by the helmet. No-one heard her.

The knife-bearer aimed a kick at the street-trader's stall and her wares – an incongruous mix of apples, oranges and baseball caps emblazoned with the logo of the local football team – scattered to the ground. His friend shoved her and she staggered and fell, her head hitting the pavement with a sickening crack that Maggie heard despite her helmet and the revving of engines.

Her scream reverberated in Maggie's ears.

The traffic light turned green and Maggie opened the throttle. She smelled petrol. She watched the thieves' heads bobbing through the wave of people on the pavement. She watched the red t-shirt and the yellow thread their way through the crowd, eyes down, not running, but moving at a pace. They wove with intent, heading for the taxi rank that would take them out of town and out of danger. Maggie trailed them, the Yamaha's engine grumbling.

They crossed Longmarket Street, Maggie's route to work. She should turn right, go and park her bike and head into the office for her daily duties, but the sweet adrenaline of petrol fumes and the thieves' swagger drove her after them. She revved again, and one turned his head. Wordless, he looked into her eyes. She narrowed them. He grabbed the other man's arm, pulled it. They ran. Maggie gunned the engine.

The men dodged pedestrians, side-stepped and weaved. They threw glances over their shoulders at the roaring bike and flung a right at the corner. The traffic light was green and she followed. There were fewer people here, and the men ran faster. She was going to lose them. The cross-streets that led to the city's lanes were approaching; they would duck into the maze and be lost forever.

She dropped a gear and the bike whined in response, but the gap between her and the men widened. They were getting away.

There was only one option. She turned the front wheel towards the pavement and heaved up the handlebars. It was quicker on the pavement. A man in a suit with a cell phone clamped at his ear yelped and pressed himself against a shop window. She was gaining on the men. She could see the muscles in their arms straining and hear their panting breath. A woman who had just parked her car screamed and flung the car door closed. In the rear-view mirror Maggie could see the blackened 'O' of her mouth.

The bike nosed the back of their legs. Their t-shirts were dark with sweat.

'Stop!' she shouted. They didn't.

She saw the opening to a parking lot. Both men turned and sprinted in. Maggie followed, but the men split. One ran back onto the street. The other – yellow t-shirt, the knife-bearer – climbed the wooden poles supporting the roof of the open-sided carport. He heaved himself onto the roof.

Maggie turned off the engine, hoiked the bike onto its stand, and followed him.

Hands greasy with creosote, she struggled to get purchase on the roof, but she angled one knee over the drain. She hooked her fingers under the tin roof tiles, already baking in the morning heat, and pulled herself up. The roof shook with the man's tread as he ran down the length of the carport. Maggie ran after him, the thump of blood in her ears.

He reached the end of the port and swung himself over a wall. She heard a gasp of breath as he landed. She looked down at the two-metre drop and the concrete floor below. The man pulled himself to his feet, but he was hobbling. He had injured himself.

She knelt on the wall, turned herself around, held on by her hands and slid down, her stomach scraping against the rough bricks. She felt the jolt in her legs as she landed, swung around and saw the man round the corner. He was in her grasp.

She sprinted across the empty lot and turned the corner after him. The knife grinned at her.

'Leave me alone,' the man panted, his fingers gripping the knife's handle. 'I don't have the money.'

Maggie felt a cold bead of sweat trail between her shoulder blades. She stretched her hands out towards him. 'Give me the knife.'

With her other hand, she felt in her jeans pocket. She had Mathonsi on speed-dial.

The pain slashed across her open palm, a line of blood gathered across the word tattooed on her palm. The four letters inked there were now blurred. She looked up and saw his teeth before he turned to run. A red mist gathered at her temples, her vision grew hazy with outrage. He wasn't getting away.

Sprinting behind him, she grabbed his arms and tackled him, ignoring the searing pain in her hand. He slid to the floor, his injured ankle giving way under her weight. Maggie could feel the steel of muscle in his arms as they wrestled. His legs flailed against hers. She pulled back her foot and aimed a kick at his ankle. He screamed. As he clutched his foot, she reached around and pulled the knife out of his jeans pocket. Pointing the man's knife at him, she pulled herself to a standing position, about to press Mathonsi's number on her cell phone.

Instead her phone rang. It was the boss.

'This isn't a good moment,' she told him. At her feet, the thief wriggled to a sitting position. Maggie thrust the knife at his chin and he winced. His eyes held the blank patina of desperation. He started inching away from her. She trod on his outstretched hand – he was not getting away. Her steel-capped Docs would make sure of that.

'It never is,' said Zacharius Patel. 'There's been a shooting. Possible murder. Get yourself to HIV House this minute. Ed's already on his way.'

'OK,' she said. A murder was bigger news than a knife-wielding thief. 'Just got something to tie up quickly.'

'Don't mess around, Cloete,' Patel said. 'Try and get there before the cops if you can. Once they have the scene sealed, the story's comatose.'

She grimaced and killed the call. She didn't need Zacharius Patel to tell her how to do her job.

Maggie grabbed the man's skinny wrist with her right hand, pain forgotten, and with her left ripped one of the laces out of her Docs. She hauled him to his feet, pushed him against a lamp-post and tied his hands behind his back and to the post. Then she called Mathonsi.

'I've left you a present,' she told the policewoman. 'On Carbineer Street. Round the corner from Prince Alfred Parking.'

In the lot she rocked her bike off its stand and pulled on her helmet.

There was no time to wash or clean her bleeding hand. She had to get to HIV House and fast.

It was an eight-block drive through the rush-hour traffic. As she signaled to turn onto the road, a minibus taxi with windows open, kwaito blaring and passengers crammed in five to a seat, hooted and swung in front her. She swore under her breath and the driver flashed her a two-fingered peace sign. The taxis ruled the road and anyone who thought differently risked a side-swipe. She couldn't afford that right now. Work was waiting.

Then the traffic light changed and pedestrians swarmed across the road in herds. She swore again. When her passage was free of human obstacles, she gunned it, blurring the buildings and shops on either side of her.

Turning right, she saw the crowd clustered at the AIDS Mission, known to the locals as HIV House. A scowling policeman guarded the gate and the barbed wire fence.

She was too late. Patel was going to be furious. Thief-chasing was not officially on her job description.

She ran towards the silent crowd, scouring it for Ed, and found his blonde head and broad shoulders with a practiced eye.

'Hi,' she said. 'Got here as quick as I could.'

'Not quick enough,' the photographer replied, camera pressed to his face. Ed had a way with images, not with words.

She could hear keening from inside the building. Someone lay on the stoep, covered in blood. The medics were already there, trying to revive the person, and it did not look as if they were succeeding.

Notebook in hand, Maggie turned to the middle-aged man next to her. He was short and rotund and had both hands over his mouth, eyes wide.

'I'm from the *Gazette*. Did you see what happened?'

'Hau, Miss,' he said. 'I heard the shots from my shop. I ran here and then I saw him, just lying there.'

'Alone?'

'No, the boss of HIV House –'

'Lindiwe Dlamini,' she said. The head of the AIDS Mission was well-known for her opinions on HIV/AIDS. She told anyone who would listen that the government was not doing enough to stop the epidemic.

'Yes, she was holding him in her arms and crying. The blood from his chest was pouring out everywhere, onto her clothes. Then the police came and took her inside.'

'Do you know who he is?'

'He comes into the shop for cooldrinks. His name is Balthasar Meiring.'

Maggie remembered the whispery voice. She'd been on deadline, fingers stabbing the keyboard, as she answered the phone, grasping it between head and shoulders.

'Ms Cloete?' He had an Afrikaans accent with an overlay of English, as if he'd been to an English-speaking school or university. It was similar to her own, except that she'd not had the privilege of university. The *Gazette* had provided her tertiary education; a Bachelor's degree in murder, rape and robbery, day after relentless day.

'Cloete.'

'Balthasar Meiring here, from the AIDS Mission. We've got a case coming up in the High Court next week that you need to attend.'

'Uh-huh.' She stopped typing to flick through her notes. There was the quote she wanted. She fired it into the story with a battery of flying fingers.

'Some local families who've lost relatives to AIDS have a class action suit against a doctor who sold them a fake cure. We're talking major damages.'

She stopped typing and looked out of the window at the tops of the oak trees in the Old Supreme Court gardens. 'Sounds like a story we'd cover. Listen, I'll pass it on to Aslan Chetty, my colleague on the health beat. What did you say your name was again?'

'Meiring,' he'd replied. 'Balthasar Meiring.' He paused, then persisted, 'But Ms Cloete, you cover crime and courts. I know your work. I want you on it.'

'Appreciate the compliment, but I can't muscle in on my colleague's beat.'

'Ms Cloete,' the voice grew more urgent. 'These are people who have been dumped on by life. They need someone on their story who actually cares about their fate. Someone with humanity. Not just the kind of journalist that chases headlines. I've been away a long time, but I was here in 1989. I know the lengths you go to.'

'I'll see what I can do.' She was used to getting calls from nutters who believed their story was headline news and she was practised at easing them off the phone. Also she didn't want to think about 1989. One taste of a jail cell had been enough for her. 'I promise you, we're onto it.'

'You're the one, Ms Cloete,' the man whispered.

She ended the call and finished her story under deadline. On her way out, she stopped at Aslan's desk and told him about the caller. He shook his head. 'I'll do my best Maggie, but you know what it's like.' She did know. Thanks to the AIDS epidemic and the government's apparent lack of interest in it, health was the busiest beat on the paper. After crime, that was.

Balthasar Meiring had wanted her on a story, and now he was dead, shot in broad daylight in front of the AIDS Mission. Damn. She should have listened to him when he called, gone to the court case. If she had, would he still be alive? Did someone have to die nowadays to get her attention?

She made her way to the policeman and showed him her Press card. 'Do you know what happened here?'

Few police personnel on a crime scene offered information, but sometimes she chanced on one who'd talk. She always asked, just in case, but this one barely glanced at her.

'Just a robbery gone wrong,' he told her. 'Phone police liaison for confirmation.'

That was the answer she'd expected. Thandi Mathonsi, the police liaison, briefed Maggie daily on crime stories big and small and replied to her myriad questions. Tall and clever, she had an attitude as sharp as her designer spectacles and knew how to keep a journalist's appetite for more satiated without stepping outside her political boundaries.

'Stop with the photos.' Reacting to some signal from within, the grumpy cop put his hand across Ed's line of vision.

Maggie shot a look at Ed, hoping he'd got something. He grimaced and let the camera fall against his chest.

The medics gave up. Death had won. They covered the body in a black sheet. The police would take over from here.

'Clear off now,' the charmer at the gate told the crowd. 'Party's over.'

People dispersed, shaking their heads. No one liked to watch a person die. Maggie grabbed the rotund guy before he could disappear and they retreated across the road to the shade of a jacaranda tree. 'I'm going to be writing this up for tomorrow's *Gazette*,' she told him. 'Can I quote you?'

'That's fine.' He spelled out his name and she repeated it to him, to be sure.

'Anything you want to say about Meiring?'

'Friendly guy, always had time to talk. He spoke really good Zulu.' He fanned himself with a copy of the *Gazette*, which he'd pulled out of his back pocket.

'Has there ever been anything like this here before?'

'No shootings.' He sucked his teeth. 'Not since the hijacking in December. Some robberies and lots of people in and out, but this is the first big trouble in a long time.'

'Did anyone you know see anything? The robber, for instance?'

'Nope.'

A second ambulance arrived, and a woman in a blue jacket with fluorescent stripes on the arms climbed out and made her way into the house. She stepped over the blood coagulating on the stoep stairs.

Maggie and Ed waited in the shade as the police removed the body. People said journalists drank because of the stress but Maggie thought it was boredom. She spent her life waiting: waiting for people to stop crying, waiting for them to come out of their homes so that she could door-step them, waiting for people to phone her back, waiting for court cases to stop being postponed, waiting for the police to formulate a statement so that she could get a story out, waiting for the news editor to check her story so that she could submit it to the subs and bloody well go home. No wonder they drank.

Her hand was starting to ache. The blood had dried in a ragged line across her palm.

Now, the ambulance assistant came out, holding a woman by the shoulders. Lindiwe Dlamini had folded in on herself, collapsed against the young assistant's body. Her white shirt was blotted red and her navy skirt was streaked with dark marks. Maggie crossed the road.

'Mrs Dlamini?'

She looked up, eyes thickened with grief. There were smudges on her cheek. 'I'm Maggie Cloete, from the *Gazette*. Can you tell me what happened?'

The ambulance woman scowled, but Lindiwe Dlamini stopped. Maggie held her breath for information, anything that would give her story an angle.

'We'll release a statement in due course,' Dlamini said. She pulled a giant black handbag close to her body.

'Was it Balthasar Meiring?'

The woman stood, poised to get into the ambulance, the assistant's blue-coated arm still guarding her shoulders. Maggie caught the faint nod before Lindiwe Dlamini climbed in. The vehicle drove off, leaving two cops conferring on the stoep, mynah birds squalling in the jacarandas, and a pool of thickened blood. Apart from his name, she still didn't have anything – no witnesses, no statement from Lindiwe Dlamini, probably no decent pics thanks to the shitty cop.

All she had was an aching hand and a nagging feeling in her gut that she should not have ignored Balthasar Meiring.

2

Tuesday, 9am

Back at the office, she ran her hand under cold water. Blood, both dried and fresh, washed down the plughole along with dirt. She patted her hand dry and wrapped the wound with toilet paper. The tattoo was fading again. *Lynn.* She would have to get it re-inked. And then re-inked a few years after that. Just so she would never forget.

She got a coffee – black, no sugar – and headed for the conference room where her colleagues sat ranged around the oval table, piled high with today's paper. The room smelled of coffee and ink, underlaid with the adrenaline of a new day on the front-line. After eleven years of crime reporting, she was still not tired of that smell.

Aslan winked as she slid into the chair next to his, but Patel gave her the hooded look. The news editor was small and sinewy, with a muscular brain to match. He had a series of foibles, one of which was punctuality.

'You were late in today, Cloete.'

She shrugged. 'I had a thief to catch.' She leant in and pulled a freshly-printed paper towards her. Yesterday's crime report – a six-car pile-up on the highway – was on the front page. Seeing her name on the paper's main real estate gave her a glow of satisfaction.

'And got yourself injured in the process.' He gestured to her amateur bandage.

'It's nothing.'

'Well, we're honoured that you're on time for conference. We're waiting with bated breath to hear more.'

Sally-Anne Shepstone, the arts reporter, giggled. Any men needing their egos propped up could rely on Sally-Anne to provide the service.

'Looks like a murder. Victim's a guy called Balthasar Meiring.'

'Motive?'

'Don't know. Cops at the scene seemed to think it was a robbery gone wrong.'

'Do we know anything about this Meiring?' Patel scratched the side of his head with a pencil. Life on the news desk, in thrall to six deadlines a week, a team of headstrong reporters and an editor bent on maintaining his status on the cocktail circuit, had speckled his temples grey.

'A little. He called me last week, about the fake AIDS cure case at the High Court.'

Patel frowned. 'He called you and now he's dead?'

She winced. 'Ja. I passed the case on to Aslan, but it's probably back in my beat now.'

'I'll try and find time for it,' Aslan ran a hand through his elaborately gelled hair.

'You said you were too busy.'

'That's before it became a high-profile murder case.' Aslan leaned back in his chair and gave Maggie the full benefit of his winsome white-toothed smile.

'Which, naturally, falls into my beat.' She folded her arms. Two could play the game. She'd taught him everything he knew about journalism; she wasn't going to let him encroach on her territory.

'Then let other pens dwell on guilt and misery.' Aslan, who had majored in English Literature, had a habit of quoting Jane Austen. She grimaced at him. She had never cracked an Austen and didn't plan to.

'Children, no squabbling.' Patel's voice shut them both up. He turned to Ed, 'Got any pics?'

'Some,' the photographer said. Sally-Anne leant in and whispered something in his ear. From the proximity of her lips to his ear, and the slight crinkling in the tanned skin around his eyes as he listened, it was evident that theirs had progressed beyond a professional relationship. Maggie turned the fist of her good hand inside her injured palm. What did he see in that superficial, simpering nitwit?

'Why only some?' Patel gazed at him the way a mongoose fixes on a snake.

'Cops weren't co-operating.'

'You'll have to visit the grieving family then. Rescue the story and get a photo of them looking devastated.'

Maggie fiddled with the toilet paper bandage. It was already starting to unwind. 'The police probably haven't done the next-of-kin yet. It only happened an hour ago.'

Patel rubbed his chin. 'Meiring,' he said. 'Could he be any relation to Lourens Meiring?'

Lourens Meiring was a local farmer who had received an incongruously light sentence over a decade ago for killing one of his workers. He'd pleaded self-defence and the apartheid criminal justice system had seen fit to give him less than a year suspended.

'Don't know,' Maggie said. 'Though one guy said Meiring spoke good Zulu. That could pin him as a farmer's son.'

'Check it out before you go. Cloete and Bromfield dismissed.'

They rose to leave.

'And Cloete?' Patel looked at his notes, not at her.

'Yes?'

'Nzimande's pressurising me for a strong lead today, so please pull this one together. No detours to chase bank robbers or beat up pick-pockets. I want a decent front-page lead out of this and some good pics.'

He gave her a twisted smile.

'Yessir.' She snapped her heels together and stalked out, Ed close behind. Zacharius Patel might be under pressure from the editor, but he didn't have to tell her how to do her job. She knew better than anyone on his staff how to bring in a story against the odds.

'I'm going to Archives to background check Meiring,' she told Ed. 'Get your gear and meet me at the cars.'

Ed sloped off to gather his cameras and she went to gather information. En route upstairs, she called Officer Mathonsi, who answered after the second ring.

'Hi Maggie.'

'Thandi, the guy who was shot outside HIV House this morning. Have you got anything?'

'Yes,' she said, stretching out the word as if she were stretching her arm for a file. 'Meiring. It's a Greytown family. Farmers. The team's notified them already. Father's on his way to ID.'

'What are the parents' names?' Maggie held her breath.

'Sanet and Lourens.'

She breathed out. Balthasar Meiring was the son of a trigger-happy right-winger who would not be pleased to see the local press on his doorstep, asking questions about his son's involvement at HIV House. Damn Patel for being right. Again.

Thandi gave her the address – a farm called Oorwinning out on the Greytown road.

'And my present?' Maggie asked. 'Did you find him?'

'By the time we got there, he was gone. Left nothing behind but a blood-stained shoe-lace. I presume it's one of yours?'

Maggie ignored the barb. Thandi Mathonsi could laugh all she liked, but the cops weren't doing enough to protect ordinary people. She said goodbye and, pulling off her untied, flapping boot, made her way up two flights of stairs to the Archives.

'Morning, Alicia,' she called and heard a rustle behind the stacks before Alicia emerged. She was dressed in shades of mauve to match her blue rinse and smelled of old lady's lavender perfume. She was the *Gazette's* longest-standing employee and regarded herself as the gate-keeper of information. She required special handling. She also had a medical dispensary to rival any pharmacy.

'How are you?' Maggie asked, blocking her nose against the sensory overload as the archivist leant on the counter and regarded her with mournful eyes. Stuck in the archives, two floors away from the action of the newsroom, Alicia believed that a polite enquiry about her state of health was her due. Without it, she wouldn't release information and information was what Maggie needed.

'I slept badly,' she said. Alicia had a predilection for bad nights. 'Bloody monkeys cavorting on the roof again.'

'Sorry about that.'

Alicia squinted at her. 'Got a problem with your footwear, chum?'

'Yes,' she said, putting the laceless boot on the counter. 'Do you have any spare shoelaces?'

'I do. Looks like you need a bandage for that hand too.'

Alicia opened a drawer, pulled out some antiseptic spray and doused the wound. It stung, but Maggie was grateful. She didn't need a septic hand. She pulled a bandage out of her pharmacopeia, wound it around Maggie's palm and then produced a shoelace, neon green.

'Now that we have got basic self-care out of the way, is there anything I can do?'

She made her request and laced up her boot as Alicia went off in a lavender mist to the Eighties section to find the file on Lourens Meiring. She returned bearing a yellow cardboard file entitled 'Meiring, Lourens' and subtitled 'Involuntary manslaughter, Afrikaner secession, Afrikaner Weerstands Beweging, AWB'.

Maggie sat at a desk, opened her notebook and took some notes on Meiring senior. He'd received nine months' suspended in 1986 for involuntary manslaughter. The victim was one of his farm-workers, a man called Pontius Ncube. She peered at a dusty photo of Meiring around the time of his court case; bearded, dressed in khakis and suntanned, he looked like a standard issue KwaZulu-Natal farmer. Just one with a murder charge around his neck.

'Thanks, Alicia,' she said, slapping the file back down on her desk. 'Time to go and face Mr AWB.'

3

Tuesday, 10am

Despite her throbbing hand, Maggie drove the Greytown road. As an artist, Ed needed to stare out of the window and admire the scenery, and she preferred him to do that when he didn't have both hands on the steering wheel. Since no *Gazette* car came with air-conditioning, they had the windows rolled right down. She wiped her sweaty brow as her t-shirt grew damp and stuck to the back of the car seat.

They spun over the soft hills leading east out of town. In the sky, a hawk spiralled over its prey. Ed aimed his lens and snapped a photo. A dam glinted to their left and she fantasised about the cool water, the delicious plunge from hot to icy cold, catching a glimpse of Ed's muscled thighs. She stopped. That was deep water, too deep for her.

There had been a time when she'd had intimate knowledge of Ed Bromfield's muscled thighs. She was a cub reporter, thrust from covering suburban crime into the middle of a bloody civil war, where daily battles broke out in the KwaZulu-Natal townships between Mandela's ANC cadres and the old guard Inkatha chiefs. She remembered teenagers lying on the ground as their blood leaked into the baked earth, women cut down with pangas as they hung their washing out to dry. She'd taken refuge in Ed's arms for a couple of months to try and forget the images.

In the years since, they had faded, but Balthasar Meiring's call last week had reminded her.

'Turn-off's here,' Ed's voice brought her back to the present. A creaking blue sign indicated Oorwinning farm.

She turned off the tarmac highway onto a dirt road, rutted and bumpy. The wattle trees of the Meiring's plantations marched like well-drilled soldiers over the hills. The wattles were invasive aliens grown for the leather industry, so this vast acreage of forest meant that Meiring was a wealthy man.

She smelled the cloud before she saw it in her rearview mirror – a farm bakkie thundering up behind them and trumpeting like a rampaging bull elephant. Maggie swerved to the side of the road and stopped as the vehicle sped past, filling the Toyota with dust.

Ed waved his hands in front of his face. 'Maniac.'

She spluttered and tried to catch a glimpse of the driver but the dust concealed him.

Winding up the window against another onslaught, she pulled back onto the road. It was a further six kilometres of forest before she saw the farmhouse. Its two-metre tall fence, topped with barbed wire, did not welcome or encourage visitors. To the right of the gate stood a buzzer on a stand, so she buzzed.

'*Ja?*' came a female voice.

'*Goeie môre*,' she switched to Afrikaans.

'*Môre.*'

'Is that Mrs Meiring?'

'*Ja.*'

'My name is Magdalena Cloete, from the *Gazette*, in Maritzburg. I am very sorry to hear the news of your son.'

Silence.

'Mrs Meiring, we would like to pay tribute to Balthasar – write something in the paper so that people know what an appalling tragedy this is. Can I come in and talk to you?'

She looked at Ed and held thumbs. The 'pay tribute' line usually worked.

She heard some offline talking, as if Mrs Meiring were conferring with someone. Her husband? Armed with one of his shotguns?

'Go away.' It was another voice on the line now. A male voice, crusty with emotion. 'We've just heard that our son is dead. Leave us alone.'

'Is that Mr Meiring?'

'*Ja.*'

'Mr Meiring, we are so sorry about your son's death. However, the more we know about him, the more we can help the police investigation. Catch his killer.'

Ed gave her the thumbs-up. Her line was working for him.

She heard a creak and watched as the iron gate swung open.

The house lay to the left, a large white single-storey building surrounded by a deep veranda and flanked by a large oak tree. Barking dogs accompanied them around the back of the house to a gravelled parking area. She got out of the car, but jumped back in when an alsatian snarled at her. The beast put its feet up on the door and tried to bite her through the window. This wasn't looking good. She glanced around for a farmer with a shotgun.

A woman, tall, with cropped pale hair, appeared. She pulled the animal by its collar.

'I'll just tie her up.'

When the dog was safely tethered, Maggie got out of the car.

The woman stood in the lee of her house, one hand crumpling her long shorts. They were stained with something.

'Mrs Meiring. I am so sorry about what happened.'

Her hand fluttered to her throat. 'My husband has just come back from town. He's ...' She stopped.

So the maniac on the road was Meiring, on his way home after identifying the body. Mrs Meiring pulled a much-used tissue out of her pocket and wiped her eyes. Maggie took the gap. 'If you don't mind, I would like to talk to you about your son, get some details, so that we can pay tribute to him.'

'That's fine.' The woman wrapped her arms around herself. She was starting to shiver. Shock.

'Can we come in? It's hot out here and we could do with a drink.' Mrs Meiring needed a drink, she thought. And a strong one.

'Follow me.'

They went into the house and found themselves in a kitchen, spotlessly clean and varnished. There were no signs here that death had interrupted the daily rituals of morning.

'The veranda is that way. Lourens is waiting. I will just get Cora to come and make some drinks.'

Mrs Meiring pointed to a long corridor. Maggie followed it, Ed behind her, into a dining room with tall French doors leading onto the veranda. She had time to notice the serried ranks of ancestors caught in sepia gloom on the dining room walls. The veranda overlooked a pleasant, well-maintained garden with abundant roses, a vegetable garden and a view of the distant Drakensberg spearing the sky. These were the mountains that the Meiring's ancestors and Maggie's had struggled over by ox-wagon to settle a new land. Aliens, just like the wattles. And surveying the mountains, his back to them, one shoulder leaning against a pillar, was Lourens Meiring.

'So the vultures have landed,' he said, turning and blowing a waft of smoke out of his mouth. He smoked an unfiltered brand, thick and narcotic. He looked much like the photograph she had just seen of him, except in the intervening years he'd grown a white Father Christmas beard that was yellowed around his mouth.

'Mr Meiring, we are so sorry for your tragic loss,' she stepped forward, bandaged hand held out to shake.

He dragged on his cigarette again and ignored the hand. 'Are you?' His eyes were an uncomfortable shade of pale blue, like the sky on a day that is going to be too hot.

Mrs Meiring joined them, with a younger woman in tow. Maggie could tell by her height that she was a Meiring daughter, but unlike her mother she had dark hair and her father's ruddy complexion. Both women flicked their eyes towards Meiring, waiting for him to take control. Instead, he inhaled on his cigarette and turned his back.

Mrs Meiring filled the gap. 'This is my daughter, Christabel. She lives nearby with her husband, Jannie, and their kids.'

Maggie looked at Christabel. 'I am sorry about the tragedy of your brother's death.'

She nodded. Her eyes and nose were red from crying.

'I am just hoping to get some details about him, to piece together a picture of who he was. Shall we sit?' she said, indicating the veranda furniture.

Christabel positioned herself close to her mother on the rattan sofa. Meiring remained standing. Maggie looked both women in the eyes. When Aslan was shadowing her, learning the crime beat, he'd called it her death face. He had been a natural at making people warm to him, flashing his teeth and crumpling his face with compassion.

'Mrs Meiring, tell me about your son. What was he like as a person?'

Sanet Meiring gave a half-smile. 'Very artistic. Loved painting, books, music. When he was little, he liked to help me in the garden. He had a lot of friends. When he came back from school or university, he always went off to visit them. We didn't see that much of him.'

'Did he live here?'

'No, he hadn't lived here for a while. He moved to London in 1990, after he graduated.'

'Where did he study?'

'Stellenbosch University. He got a very good BA.'

'What was he doing in London?'

Sanet sighed and turned her attention to the roses. Her face looked sleepy, as if she was ready to wake up and find herself brushing away a dream.

Christabel glanced at her mother and a frown played between her eyes as she answered on Sanet's behalf. 'He worked as an auxilliary nurse in one of the hospitals.'

Maybe that connected with his AIDS work. He had medical experience.

She tried to reel Sanet Meiring back in from her reverie. 'Mrs Meiring, when did your son return?'

'1998.' Christabel was still being her mother's mouthpiece.

'Why did he come back, do you know?' Maggie knew the statistics. Ex-pats who'd done eight years in London weren't likely to come back. They got used to the rain, learnt how to use the Underground and where to buy the best biltong. Why return to the land of sunshine and violent crime?

'He just missed home. That's a good enough reason, isn't it?' Lourens Meiring said over his shoulder.

'Yes, of course it is.' Conciliation was a useful tactic with the recently bereaved.

At that moment, a middle-aged woman in a maid's uniform appeared with a tray of iced water. She had a matching icy expression. She poured water and passed each person a glass. Maggie felt rather than saw her hover.

'Thanks, Cora,' said Christabel pointedly. Cora left.

Maggie sipped her water and tackled the biggie. 'Balthasar was shot outside the AIDS Mission. Do you know why he was there?'

Sanet's gaze would not unglue from her garden. Maggie watched as the woman's eyes followed a hadeda dressed in housewife brown peck its way across the lawn.

'We believe he worked there,' Christabel replied for her parents.

She noted the 'we believe'. Why the prevarication? 'How long had he been at the AIDS Mission?'

'He started work there as soon as he came back. July 1998.'

She felt a familiar prickle down her neck, that of a story starting to crystallise. She tried to meet Sanet Meiring's unfocused gaze. 'Mrs Meiring, isn't it a tragedy that your son has become another victim of South Africa's escalating crime, especially since he has only recently returned from overseas?'

'They know not what they do,' said Sanet. Her eyes lifted to the ramparts of the mountains, ranged in a semi-circle in the middle distance. 'Whether the courts and the police do justice or not, we take comfort that God's justice will be done. They will be judged in a heavenly court and will be found wanting.'

Maggie thought of the phone call, his whisper. 'Mrs Meiring, did Balthasar have any enemies? Is there any chance this wasn't a mistake?'

'No!' Christabel answered for her mother. 'He was much-loved, by everyone. How can you even say that?'

Maybe not that loved, Maggie thought. The man had a court case pending in the High Court. He didn't like someone, and there was a chance that someone didn't like him back.

'Do you have a picture of him we could use for the paper? We would return it, of course.'

Sanet dragged her gaze back to the people seated on the veranda. 'Yes,' she said. 'Let me find one.'

She got up and left the veranda. Christabel spoke to Ed. 'What are you planning to do with that? Take photos?'

'Only with your permission,' he said.

'Maybe you want a picture of Ma and me in the garden,' she said. 'In front of the roses she and he loved so much.'

'Ja,' said Ed, compliant. 'Good idea.'

'Where did Balthasar live?' Maggie asked.

'Somewhere in town,' said Christabel, eyes still fixed on Ed. 'We were never invited.'

'Did he live alone?'

'You know, Miss, my brother was a very private person. You can't find things out from someone if they do not want to tell you. You can't just invade their private life.' Her lips formed a hard line.

Maggie heard the hum of a vacuum cleaner from inside the house. Even when death came, houses needed to be cleaned, the daily battle against dust fought. Why had Balthasar Meiring never invited his family to his home? What was the cause of the bad blood between them?

'Do you have an address, a telephone number?' She would phone the house with the hope of finding someone to give her a better picture of Balthasar. Listening to his family felt like listening to people describe someone long-dead.

Sanet returned, bearing two photographs. One was of a schoolboy, anxious and spotty. The other was of a family group, at least ten years old, judging by the clothes they were wearing. Balthasar, tall and thin with a shock of pale blonde hair, stood next to his mother. Maggie tried to connect him to the quiet man who'd called her, to the body she'd seen that morning. As usual, the mental leap it took to link a living person to their corpse was almost too great. She gave up.

'Who's that?' she asked instead, pointing to a woman next to Sanet and Christabel. She was as tall as both women and resembled the daughter in looks and colouring.

'My twin, Claudine. She lives in Durban,' the young woman said. 'Oh God, Ma, Claudie. We have to tell her.' Her face collapsed: their time was up. The storm clouds of grief were about to burst.

'I just need one quick photograph.' Ed stood up. 'Mr Meiring ...?'

The dead man's father ground his cigarette out on the floor and shook his head. Ed ushered the two women to the rose-garden, where

Sanet stared at the camera with glazed eyes as if focusing on her heavenly court. Maggie watched as Christabel plumped her hair for the photo. On the veranda next to her, arms crossed and face inscrutable, Lourens Meiring watched too.

In the kitchen, she prised both photographs from Sanet, promising to return them the next day by courier. She asked for Balthasar's home telephone number, which Christabel scribbled down.

'Could I phone later in the day to speak to Mr Meiring?' she asked, as Christabel shepherded them to the car. 'Maybe he'll have something to add.'

'No!' Sanet, standing in the doorway, awoke from her trance. She glared at Maggie, who felt cold, despite the heat. Having been ignored by Meiring's mother for the past twenty minutes, she was shocked by the tempest of emotion.

'It will be too much, too much for him and us! It already is. Just go away and write your piece. Say he was a good son and we loved him. Say that we take comfort from God and that we hope, we only hope …' her voice broke '… that He will accept our son in Heaven, and not condemn him. He was such a good, good boy. I will never know how it went so wrong.'

She bent her head into her daughter's shoulder. Patting her mother's back, Christabel gestured for them to go as if flicking away flies. They climbed into the car accompanied by the alsatian's growls. Maggie turned the car in the parking area, and as she did so Cora came out of the kitchen, carrying a bucket. Her face was immobile under its knotted doek as she watched them down the driveway. Through the open car window, Maggie heard the hadeda griping in the big oak.

They drove along the dirt road, bumping over the potholes. Dust flew in the open windows, filling her mouth. As she drove, she watched the mountains recede and fought down an urge to swing the car around and drive towards them. There the air would be cool and refreshing, not tinged with heat and death as it was down here in the valleys.

'That was rough,' she said, as they flew past the wattles on the way back to the main road. 'Did you get the feeling that they hardly knew him?'

Ed pulled a chamois out of his pocket and began cleaning his camera lens. 'Don't know. They're in shock. Probably not themselves.'

Ed was right. They'd interviewed countless grieving families over the years. There was no telling how people would behave in the light of murder. 'Seems to me they were somehow estranged.'

Ed put the chamois back in his pocket and leaned his arm on the open window, staring at the wattles rushing past. 'Bit like you and your lot.'

She bit back a retort. In his homespun, irritating way, Ed was right. She had grown up amongst people like the Meirings. But when children became adults, they saw their parents with fresh eyes. Perhaps Balthasar Meiring couldn't accept his parents' devotion to their God and had distanced himself. She knew that feeling only too well.

She had to punish Ed for being right.

'How are things with you and Sally-Sue?'

Ed winced. He probably imagined it was a still a secret. 'Her name is Sally-Anne. You know that.'

'She's an idiot and you know *that*.'

'She's not,' Ed said. 'She's a great girl.'

If you liked going to hairdressers and lunching and attending the ballet, then Sally-Anne was a great girl. She had lasted precisely two days as a crime reporter, had staged a nervous breakdown, collapsed at her first murder scene and begged Patel to reassign her to arts. She didn't have the bottle for news, the sap.

Ed stared out of the window, while Maggie pushed away thoughts of him and Sally-Anne. She thought about Meiring's stony monosyllables, the blank daughter and Sanet's incursions into dreamland. Were they really mourning his death? Or was their true pain that in life Balthasar Meiring had pushed them away?

4

Tuesday, 5pm

She wrote the final words of the Meiring story and pressed 'Submit.'

Patel wasn't going to be impressed. After dropping Ed, she'd gone to the address that Mathonsi had given as Balthasar's home – a rambling place in the leafy suburbs – where she buzzed and halloed, but no curtains flickered, no heads popped up in windows and no one let her in. The place was a tomb.

Later, she tried Balthasar's home number, but it just rang. She called the Mission, but they were on answering machine. She tried the fourteen C. Meirings listed in the Durban phone book, but had no joy in raising Balthasar's other sister. Veering close to deadline, she wrote the story, using a bit of license with the quotes and including Lourens Meiring's 14-year-old crime. That judge might have let him off the hook, but she wasn't going to. She didn't like killers. Even if their crime had taken place a decade and another government ago.

Five minutes later, Patel called her to the news editor's desk. It was a large island in the middle of the *Gazette*'s open-plan office, centred precisely so that he could keep an eye on everyone from the reporters to the subs. They were all in shouting distance.

Patel liked his team to stand at his desk like schoolchildren while he read their copy. He took off his reading glasses and peered up her. 'Bit anodyne, this, Cloete. No weeping girlfriends? No shocked colleagues?'

'Ja, I know. I'll follow up with the Mission tomorrow. They weren't answering calls today.'

'But the pics are excellent. Ed did a great job of planting the mother and sister in front of the roses.'

'Yes didn't he?' How nice for Ed to get accolades.

She returned to her desk minus accolades and kicked one of its legs for good measure. Aslan leaned over from his terminal, where he'd just finished writing up his story for the day.

'I have a high respect for your nerves, Maggie. And what your nerves need is a drink.'

'I can't tonight, Aslan,' she said. 'For once, I'm not in the mood for alcohol.'

'Then how about a curry? We can either do Mrs Chetty's finest or I'll treat you to Thai at China Sam's.'

She was tempted. Aslan's mother cooked the meanest lamb curry outside Durban, and the Thai green curry at China Sam's was not bad, but it had been a long day.

'I'll pass tonight, Aslan. I'm going home to run some bubbles, nibble on bonbons and read *Sense and Sensibility*.'

He snorted with disbelief.

'More likely you are going to take the Chicken and go rampaging in the plantations with your motorcycle crew.'

'Never on a school night,' she told him. Chicken was her nickname for her bike – a 1998 Yamaha XT 350 – and Aslan was the only person who knew this. She had confessed after a long night of beer with vodka chasers and now he held the knowledge like a dagger over her head.

Aslan blew her a kiss and headed off. She slung her backpack over her shoulder and grabbed her helmet from under her desk. She wouldn't hit the plantations tonight – there was rain in the air and she was in no mood for mud – but she would blow away the sweat of the day by screaming up the highway to Hilton and back. Some good healthy lorry-dodging was in order.

She headed out, waving goodbye to the night subs who were settling down for their shift. The Chicken waited for her in the parking lot. The bodywork shone and she could already feel the engine growl underneath her and hear the throttle as the bike roared up the highway. She wanted the sting of petrol in her nose and the blood-rush of ducking and weaving between slow-moving trucks, dangerously overloaded taxis and speeding cars.

Then her cell rang. Swearing, she pulled her helmet off and rifled in her backpack.

'Cloete.'

'Magdalena Cloete?' The voice was Afrikaans, gravelly.

'Yes. Who's this?'

'Lourens Meiring. You keep away from my family, you understand?'

'Just doing my job, Mr Meiring.'

'I have some things to tell you. Some things about the death of my son. Things his mother and sisters don't need to know.'

She waved goodbye to her evening run. She was back on duty.

It was a short spin from the office to the Church of the Vow, where Meiring wanted to meet. The streets were emptying, as minibus taxis gathered passengers to take back to the townships and the mynahs tried to drown out the kwaito rhythms emitting from each vehicle with a sunset cacophony of their own. The last of the street vendors packed their goods away. Thunderclouds gathered on the hillsides around the city and the streets smelled of rain.

She rode past the City Hall, its clock tower piercing the sky with a tall Victorian finger. The Church of the Vow was a low-slung farm building with a modest Cape Dutch gable instead of a steeple. Meiring's white bakkie was parked outside and the farmer stood propped against the cab, arms folded, his crossed legs encased in khaki knee socks.

'*Kom*. I want to show you something.'

Maggie's eyes took a second to adjust to the cool darkness of the church. They walked to the front, Meiring's calves stomping their conviction before her. He stopped at the pulpit, an imposing affair made of dark wood that reached to the rafters.

'Before I say anything, I want you to look at this.'

He pointed to a sign on the pulpit that read '*God is liefde*.' She looked. 'This is what we believe. God is love. Before we talk about death, or murder, or who did what to whom, I want you to know this.'

'Uh-huh,' she said.

'And not only believe, but practise. We practise the love of God, every day.'

Had Meiring's victim, Pontius Ncube, noticed Lourens Meiring practising the love of God?

'My son, Balthasar, was killed today.' He turned to Maggie, and she saw that grief had carved the lines on his face even deeper.

'I am sorry.' She wanted to get out of the church with its breathy darkness and dusty past. Years of Sunday enforcement, listening to bearded men tell her how to live her life while her legs and back grew numb on the hardened pews, had done that to her. She had been a patient child, but she was patient no longer. 'I'd prefer to talk outside.'

They found a bench facing the street and Maggie sat and flipped open her notebook. She stretched the fingers of her right hand and felt the answering stripe of pain in her palm. The heat of the day had not ebbed; her shirt was damp again and she looked forward to putting on a fresh one.

Meiring remained standing. His face twisted. 'He came at me with a knife.'

'Balthasar?'

'No, Ncube. We had argued about money. For three months in a row, he had asked for an advance on his wages, and once again he asked for an advance. I said I couldn't keep giving him loans against his salary and he attacked me with a knife.'

'You shot him,' she said.

'I did, but it was self-defence.'

'You shot him in the stomach.'

According to the court report, Meiring had instructed one of the other workers to pull Pontius Ncube, who was spouting blood, under a tree and give him a drink of water. Then they went back to work. Two hours later, Meiring radioed for an ambulance, which took another hour to arrive. By the time it did, Ncube had died.

'The Ncube family have been threatening me. They still want reparations, even though I paid them R10 000 in 1986. They say they have no livelihood, that I took their wage-earner away.'

Meiring stood with his hands in his pockets, looking down at her. This was the first time today he had looked her in the eye. The man was opening up to her, in a way he had refused to do on the farm. What had she said into the intercom earlier? 'The more we know, the more we can help the police investigation.'

'Do you have proof of the threats – letters or tapes of phone-calls?'

'No, they were verbal.'

'Any witnesses?'

'Yes, my son-in-law, Jannie. He was working for me then.'

'How does this relate to what happened today?'

'I believe the Ncubes hired someone to kill my son. To make it look like a robbery. They are a vengeful people.'

'Who? The Ncubes?'

'No, the Zulus. They are a vengeful people, full of anger.' His forehead glistened with sweat and he pulled a spotless white hand-kerchief out of his pocket and wiped his face.

It was a feasible scenario. A family, enraged and grieving, might take revenge by killing Meiring's son. In her notebook, she wrote 'Ncubes?'

Meiring slumped onto the bench next to her. 'I am truly sorry for what I did. I acted in the heat of the moment. You must believe that I have spent the last fourteen years regretting what I did that day.'
She saw tears gathering in the corners of his eyes.

'I have asked my God for forgiveness, but I cannot forgive myself.'

Repent and you shall be forgiven. Ask and it shall be given to you. The words which allowed people to turn their backs on their mis-deeds, allowed them to hand over responsibility to a ghost and move on with their sinful, selfish lives. She rubbed her palm.

Meiring wiped his eyes on the long sleeve of his work-shirt. 'And now my son is dead. He has not set foot on the farm for ten years. The place of his birth, his land.'

'When did you last see him?'

'On 5 March 1990. I will never forget. It was the day he left for London. We fought. He rejected our ways, the church, the land, our belief in self-determination. He said the only way South Africa would succeed as a country was with a democratic government. I believed, I still believe, that minorities need to be protected. He said those days were over. I said some things I regret.'

Meiring twisted his hands. They were red and sun burnt, flakes of skin peeling away at the point where his wrists met his shirtsleeves.

Thunderclouds above them darkened. The rain was on its way. Maggie stood up, helmet in one hand.

'I must go, Mr Meiring. Thank you for your time. If you haven't already, then mention your suspicions about the Ncubes to the police and they can follow them up.'

This time he didn't look at her. His eyes were cast down to his hands. 'The funeral is on Thursday, at his school chapel. 10am. You may come. If you choose.'

She left Meiring on the bench. The man was suffering, in pain. But he had once killed a man in cold blood. She didn't know if she should trust him or run a mile.

5

Wednesday, 9am

The Meiring story was front-page lead. It gave her a kick to be in pole position. Then she checked out her colleagues' positions in the daily rankings – all the *Gazette* reporters wanted their names up in lights and competed to get them there. This was not a job for little egos.

Her thrill was short-lived. Aslan had the top of the op-ed page to himself, with an intelligent, well-written piece on growing AIDS denialism in the government. When a glossy Joburg magazine had head-hunted the *Gazette*'s health reporter at three times her salary, Aslan had applied for the beat. With his flawless two-year performance as Maggie's number two on crime, he was a dead cert for the position and, of course, he got it. As she read his article, her front-page lead lost its sparkle.

She'd only ever had one op-ed piece, last year, when she'd exposed the mayor of Howick for using rate-payers' money to fund his stable of shebeens and whorehouses. There were parts of Howick where she was *persona non grata* and other parts, those that were now actually getting electricity and water thanks to the sudden surprise injection of cash to the city's coffers, where she was fed the best home-brew and the choicest chicken walkie-talkies. Her investigative work mattered to Howick; she just wasn't sure how much it mattered to her bosses.

All they wanted from her were daily headlines and free, on-the-job training for the rookies. Aslan had been the best of the lot – an empathy king who could hold a weeping mother's hand as she produced a cherished photograph of the victim, pat a hijackee on the back as he told of his beloved four-series being wrenched from him at gunpoint, make tea as a suburban duchess mourned her lost canteen of silver and her grandmother's diamond ring.

He also had a strong stomach, an essential quality for crime reporting that Sally-Anne had lacked.

'Good story, Aslan,' Maggie clapped the health reporter on the back as she sat down next to him at morning conference.

He beamed at her. 'So what's going on with the Meiring story? Did Meiring just have bad luck? Wrong place, wrong time?'

'I'm not really sure,' she told him. 'But I'm going to find out.'

'I know you will.'

The door closed behind Patel, who chewed gum as Maggie briefed him on her meeting with Lourens Meiring. Unlike his reporters, the news editor didn't drink alcohol and never touched coffee. His worst vice was spearmint chewing gum.

Patel rubbed his nose as he listened to Maggie, then dismissed Meiring's contentions with a wave of his hand. 'Waste of time. We've had a lead story out of it and it's clear there's nothing more there. If Thandi Mathonsi's got no big crime stories for you, then go and dredge something up at the Magistrate's Court.'

She sighed. The High Court was where the state tried its big cases; treason, murder and rape. The Magistrate's Court had jurisdiction over everything else, so it was full of bottom-feeders, petty criminals and the desperate. Not a nice place to spend the day. Shopping for stories there was joyless, but it was worse if she got there late. Unless she collared the prosecutors early and quizzed them about their caseloads before they went into court, she would miss out on the juicy stuff and end up with tat.

She stood her ground. 'It's worth sticking with the Meiring story, Zacharius. It's a high-profile murder.'

'Only high profile to a particular demographic. For most people in this town, it's just another crime story.'

'I think there could be more to it, Zacharius.' She thought of the two women at Oorwinning, unable to piece together a clear picture of Balthasar Meiring for her, of Lourens Meiring and his tears. 'I want to pursue it.'

Patel laced his hands together and leant on the conference table. 'I appreciate your ambition to get the story behind the story, but our role here is to report the news. If the police tell us this is a robbery gone wrong, then that's what we report. If they find the guy with Meiring's blood on his hands and cell phone in his pocket, that's what we report. We will report what they say, and only what they say, even if you get a call from outer space telling you that Balthasar Meiring was killed by aliens.'

He looked around the conference room for affirmation of his wit and Sally-Anne provided it again, with an obsequious smile. Maggie slouched back in her seat and folded her arms.

'You're the crime reporter, Cloete.' He always called her Cloete when he was angry. 'You want to turn this into some kind of investigation, I can see that, but that's the cops' job. Your job is to report crime. And let's face it, there's enough of that going on to keep you busy.'

She waylaid Patel after the meeting. 'Zacharius, cut me some slack. I want to investigate this further. You yourself said the story was too anodyne.'

He led her back into the conference room and shut the door. 'Your job is to bring in the daily crime stories, Maggie. There's no budget on this paper for an investigative reporter and we don't have the time or the resources for you to be chasing your instincts all over the province.'

'Zacharius, it's so weird. The father told me he hadn't seen his son since 1990. They had never been to his house, hardly knew what he did. I can't put my finger on it yet, but something's not right.'

The news editor walked to the window and stared out. The venerable oak trees in the Old Supreme Court Gardens across the road waved their branches at him. He turned and shared their wisdom with her. 'Maggie, I see what's going on here. Meiring was a renegade Afrikaner just like you, alienated from his family just like you and he cared about the unfortunate masses of this country just like you do. You identify with him.'

He unwrapped a fresh piece of gum and put it in his mouth. 'And you feel guilty for not responding to him when he called you.'

'Crap, Zacharius. It's nothing to do with that. I'm just asking for some leeway.'

'Leeway denied.'

'You're censoring me! Whatever happened to press freedom?'

He chewed. 'I am censoring you, Cloete. I decide how to allocate resources and I decide what's relevant and what's not. And my decision when it comes to the Meiring story is that you'd be wasting resources if you followed it.'

'And if I did on my own time?'

Zacharius Patel's jaw tightened. 'Just keep your nose clean and report what the cops tell you.' He walked to the door without looking at her. 'And that's an order.'

She stared after him, enraged. She really, really didn't like being given orders. If he had been courteous about it, maybe she would have listened. But telling her to stop was like issuing a challenge. Something she couldn't resist. Patel could throw his insubstantial weight around as much as he liked – but she was still going to find out more about the Meiring murder.

Back at her desk, she called HIV House and a man told her they'd be issuing a press release later in the day.

'What was Balthasar Meiring like?' she asked.

'I'm sorry, I've been told to say nothing more. Wait for the release.' He put the phone down.

She tried her list of phone numbers and still couldn't raise anyone. She called Officer Mathonsi, who gave no credence to Meiring senior's theories. 'It's just a robbery gone wrong, Maggie, no more, no less.'

'Are you following up with the Ncube family?'

'No, Meiring's accusations are too absurd.'

Maggie sighed. Patel was closing down on her and the cops were closing down on Meiring.

It was time to head for the courts. As she made her way there, she saw a gaggle of kids around a busker, and stopped to watch. His juggling gathered squeaks of delight from his rapt audience. Maggie's attention was drawn more to his biceps and a pair of arresting green eyes.

'Got some money for the performance, Miss? A small token of appreciation?' he yelled as she walked away.

'Some people have real jobs to do,' she shouted back. She wasn't throwing her hard-earned money after a trickster. Plus her blood was still boiling after Patel's put-down.

A scraggly palm tree outside the Magistrate's Courts rustled at her as she walked in.

'Not you too,' she told it.

The corridors of the courts were cool and empty of everything, including hope. It was a place where desperation seeped from the walls. Since she couldn't raise any prosecutors, she court-hopped until she found a case that could make a half-decent story, and spent the day listening to a lorry-driver who'd overturned his truck on the N3 after a pit-stop for a bottle of cane try to justify the level of alcohol in his blood.

She submitted the story to Patel who passed it without comment. He didn't even look at her. Was the news editor sulking? She was just about to go home and seek comfort in a ten-kilometre jog, when Aslan came over to her desk brandishing a fax. He had the misfortune to sit next to the whining machine.

'Here's something about the story that isn't,' he said. He'd witnessed Patel chastise her in news conference that morning. 'I presume you're ignoring orders.'

'Not me. I am the world's most obedient crime reporter.'

Aslan raised his eyebrows and went back to crafting compelling words about cancer research.

She read the fax. It was the press release from the AIDS Mission, complete with a statement from Lindiwe Dlamini.

'We would like to pay tribute to our colleague, Balthasar Meiring, who was tragically killed outside our offices yesterday. He was a dedicated volunteer, who gave willingly of his time, his medical expertise and his love to tend to people with AIDS (PWAs) in our province. The service that the AIDS Mission provides in visiting PWAs in their homes, helping with palliative care and taking those who need transport to their local clinics, will be poorer without Balthasar's commitment, gentleness and determination to help those too ill to help themselves. He will be sadly missed.'

There were the usual condolences to the family, a notice about tomorrow's funeral and then this: 'To celebrate the life of Balthasar Meiring, his colleagues at the Mission will be holding a remembrance service on the premises on Saturday at 3pm. All welcome.'

Balthasar Meiring had wanted her attention when he was alive and she had not given it to him. The least she could do, now that he was dead, was pay him the compliment of going to his memorials. Even if it meant defying her boss.

6

Wednesday, 10am

Today's *Gazette* lay on the passenger seat of the car. He reached over for the newspaper, unfolded it and read the front page.

'Manslaughter' Son Killed in Shooting
by Magdalena Cloete, Crime Reporter

A thief shot and killed the son of Lourens 'Manslaughter' Meiring outside the AIDS Mission in Loop Street at 7.55am yesterday, before fleeing with the victim's cell phone and wallet.

According to police, 31-year-old Balthasar Meiring, a volunteer AIDS worker at the Mission, disturbed a robbery when arriving early for work yesterday. The thief shot him four times in the chest and he died on the scene.

Meiring senior was convicted of involuntary manslaughter in 1986 in the shooting of Pontius Ncube, and served a nine month suspended sentence.

Spaza shop owner, Godfrey Mhkize, said he heard shots outside the Mission early yesterday. 'I ran there and saw a woman, who I think was the Mission head, Lindiwe Dlamini, holding a man who was lying down. There was a lot of blood and I was not sure if he was still alive.'

Mhkize said the murdered man had patronised his shop. 'He was always friendly and spoke excellent Zulu.'

Dlamini was not available for comment yesterday, but police confirm that she was the first to arrive on the scene and found Meiring lying on the veranda of the AIDS Mission with four bullet wounds in his chest.

Meiring, a graduate of Stellenbosch University and a former Goodwill College pupil, only returned to South Africa eighteen months ago after living in London for nine years. His parents own a farm outside Greytown.

'We trust the police and the courts to do justice for our son,' said his mother, Sanet Meiring yesterday. 'We take comfort that God's justice will be done.'

His sister, Christabel Breedenkamp said, 'Our family was so happy to have Balthasar back in the country. Our hearts are broken that he has been taken from us after such a short time.'

According to his mother, Meiring was a renowned art-lover and gardener, who had many friends. 'He was a good son and we loved him,' she said.

Meiring, who was single, leaves behind his parents and his twin sisters, Christabel and Claudine. Police appeal to witnesses to come forward. Please contact police liaison, Officer Thandi Mathonsi, on the police action line.

He folded the paper and tossed it back onto the car seat, sniffed and looked out of the window. The suburban street was quiet. He heard the distant sound of a dog barking. People here had small yappers that squeaked every time a leaf rustled or big beasts that lay like sleeping lions in the sun all day long but would rip an intruder's throat out.

The house was on a corner. He kept his car hidden behind a screen of bamboos. From there he could keep watch. The nearby houses languished behind tall trees, planted for privacy, so no home-owners came walking down their driveways to monitor him. In this part of town, people got nervous when strange cars parked in their street for a long time. In other parts of town, they would go unnoticed until someone needed a new set of tyres.

Gates, guards, electric fences, chicken wire, cameras, shards of glass embedded in the top of concrete walls. People here kept themselves in and others out. He gave a short laugh, empty. The rich were in prisons of their own making, while the poor walked around in freedom.

A drop of sweat trailed from his hairline down his temple and he flicked it away with one finger. He rolled up the car window, turned the key and switched on the air conditioning. He took a cooldrink from the cubbyhole, pulled the tab and slugged. He needed the sugar hit, but it was lukewarm. Disgusting. He opened the window and threw the can out. It bounced off a rock between him and the house and landed behind a canna.

It was so hot. Nothing made him feel cool anymore. He switched the car off again.

There was someone there.

Through the fence he could see the old lady making her way across the gravel from the house to some outbuildings. She was carrying rubbish bags. She stopped, rested, then picked them up again. He watched her disappear, heard the clanking of bins. She walked back across the gravel, stopping once to adjust her doek.

His mother wore a doek when she was sweeping, to protect her hair. She'd send him out into the veld to play. 'Shoo, shoo,' she'd say. 'Go away.'

He'd run to the koppie, to check his dassie traps. Mostly they were empty. Underneath the koppie was a cave, his safe place. He'd hide there on days when his father drank too much, feeling the cool rocky floor under his cheek.

Once he fell asleep to the sound of rain. When he woke it was night and the rain had stopped. The earth was damp and muddy under his bare feet and the night sky milky with stars. His mother met him at the doorway, her finger on her lips.

'Father is sleeping,' she said.

He lay on his blankets and watched the clouds return. They swept in, covering the stars and the moon. The moon tried to shine through the clouds but they swallowed it. He wanted to be a cloud, to grow big and strong so that he could squash Father.

The next morning he overslept and Father took out the sjambok. The whip's leather mouth whistled in the air before it bit him. He held his breath, squeezed his eyes shut and clamped his lips closed. The bites from the whip flayed the old ones that his father had already put there. The old bites and the new ones bled together.

Had Balthasar Meiring felt the bites when the bullets went into him?

He picked up the newspaper and turned the page.

7

Thursday, 10.25am

She waited in the Goodwill College chapel for the funeral service to start. Here she was in a church again. Compared to the modesty of the Church of the Vow, everything here was expensive, from the perfumed people to the stained-glass windows to the limousines parked outside. An elite school for boys, it had so much damn money that it could afford all-white buildings that required yearly repainting. Nothing but the best for the country's future leaders and captains of industry.

At conference, she'd told Patel she was going to the High Court to cover the fake AIDS cure case. Aslan said that he had made time in his diary for it, but Patel came down on her side.

'Maggie has an interest in the Meiring story and this lead came directly from him, Aslan.'

Aslan pouted. Although he relished the status that came with being health reporter, the op-eds and the interviews with senior scientists and doctors, she suspected he missed the cut and thrust of crime. There wasn't all that much adrenaline in reporting on hospital statistics.

Patel had news at conference: as of next week, a new rookie, Jabu Sibiya, would be shadowing Maggie. Lucky it wasn't from today, she thought, since Patel expected her to be in court and here she was sitting in the hushed chapel, waiting for Balthasar Meiring's funeral to start. It wouldn't do for Jabu Sibiya to witness the senior crime reporter's complete recalcitrance. Not on his first day, anyway.

She sighed and looked around her. In this chapel, the rows faced each other instead of the altar. She was seated halfway up on the right, from where she could see the Meirings at the front. Lourens Meiring wore a suit and Sanet wore something diaphanous and black. Christabel sat beside her twin, Claudine. Next to them sat a sun-reddened young man, with an infant in his arms and a small girl tugging his jacket. The family all carried Bibles. Meiring had his slung in one hand like a farm implement, while Sanet clutched hers to her chest.

Why had they sent their son here? Rich liberals from Johannesburg and Durban favoured schools like these, not Afrikaans farmers obsessed with minority rights.

She cased the crowd. There was a tall elegant couple in black opposite, wearing the kind of clothes that could feed a family for a year. In deference to the funeral, Maggie had broken with her summer uniform of black t-shirt, cut-off jeans and short Docs, but her linen pants and top felt lacklustre in comparison with the beautiful pair's designer wear. She shifted and pulled at the pants. They were itchy and uncomfortable.

A small woman dwarfed by a giant hat walked in, recognised the couple, deposited kisses on each set of cheeks and started to cry. The taller woman patted her and whispered in her ear. They both reached into their handbags and pulled out cell phones, which they switched off. A second man joined them. She knew him. He was Dumisane Phiri, a lawyer who had won last year's local election on an ANC ticket. He kissed the women and shook hands with the man.

Then he spotted Maggie and his face grew grim. It was like watching a mask fall away. She had covered a case of his two years before, where he'd defended a teacher accused of demanding sexual favours in exchange for end-of-year exam success. The teacher got six years, Maggie got big headlines and Phiri got a red face. But that was no reason to grimace at her; lawyers had to accept that journalists would cover their cases and report them in the newspaper whatever their outcome.

A whooshing of robes down the aisle announced the school pastor. He bent over the Meirings, taking Sanet's hand. Then he took position near the coffin, the doors of the chapel slid closed and music began to play. The service was underway.

'... this good man taken from us at the height of his power, in the summer of his years, cruelly wrested from us by those who know not what they do. We thank God for his life and we ask God to comfort his family, Lourens, Sanet, Christabel and Claudine. We ask God to guide the hands and minds of the police as they seek out the perpetrators of this terrible deed.'

Claudine did a reading. 'But I said to you that you have seen me and yet do not believe. Everything that the Father gives me will come to me, and anyone who comes to me I will never drive away; for I have come down from heaven, not to do my own will, but the will of Him who sent me.'

'And this is the will of Him who sent me, that I should lose nothing of all that He has given me, but raise it up on the last day.'

'This is indeed the will of my Father, that all who see the Son and believe in Him may have eternal life; and I will raise them up on the last day.'

It was the last phrase that triggered it. A memory clean as a knife, of Lynn and her mother's funeral. The fat priest droned on about Lynn's heavenly rest and her tears froze with rage on her face. Breaking sixteen years of enduring sermons in silence, she got up, faced the people who had shunned Lynn and her mother while they were alive.

'They are dead! When will you people get it? They are gone forever! Gone!'

Then her legs stopping working and she fell and Ma and Pa pulled her up and dragged her out of the church to a chorus of tuts and 'Shames'.

That night was the one and only time Pa used a belt on her. He said he had to beat out the devil that had caused her to shame herself in God's house.

She heard weeping from the front row and looked to see who it was. Sanet and both the sisters. Glancing back at the seats opposite she caught the eye – green – of another man. He stared at her, an amused grin on his face. Then he winked and she knew: it was the juggler from yesterday, looking a lot less down-at-heel in a dark suit. She ignored him and tried to push down the feelings of fear and loss.

Would the Meirings find comfort in the words? Would they run screaming from the church? She looked towards them. Mr Meiring stared at the roof of the chapel, his face carved in granite like the mountains near his farm, while his wife dissolved behind a handkerchief.

After the reading, a burly man got up to deliver the eulogy. He had cabbage ears and the kind of neckless head produced by years of playing rugby. The priest described him as 'former headboy of this school and a dear friend of Balthasar's'. Unsettled by the amused green eyes across the aisle, she had not caught his name. She gave herself a mental slap and tried to concentrate.

Cabbage Ears kept stopping to blow his nose and wipe his eyes. He also mumbled. She took notes, gathering that at school Balthasar had been artistic rather than sporty and that he'd loved music and theatre. At university Balthasar had introduced Cabbage Ears to his 'darling wife' – at this an immaculate head of blonde hair sitting near the Meirings simpered - and then had followed his dream and left for London. There his life had 'not been easy' and he'd had 'very personal experience of how difficult it can be for someone living with AIDS'. Later Balthasar had returned to South Africa wanting to share this experience and help those 'too sick and immobilised by the disease to help themselves.'

The speaker raised his eyes and looked to the congregation. 'Balthasar Meiring was a true friend, a gentle, humble man who saw the humanity in others. We have lost the biggest, best and kindest heart I have ever known.' She made sure she got these words down.

Then he broke and the priest patted him on the back, easing him back to his place next to the blonde.

A last prayer and the service was over. Cabbage Ears, Dumisane Phiri, the elegant man opposite, the juggler and a couple of others went forward as pallbearers. She was relieved that the juggler was on the other side of the coffin from her.

Outside in the sunshine, the heat of the day pressed down on her. Within seconds, she was layered with sweat. She watched Phiri in a grip with Cabbage Ears. They both looked at her, and the rugby player seemed to be pacifying Phiri, who then turned on his heel and flung himself into his sleek black sedan.

Meiring came over and offered one of his large hands. She shook it.

'Thank you for coming, Miss Cloete. We appreciate it.' He looked tired, beaten, and as he walked back to his family she felt a shard of guilt at playing up the manslaughter angle in her article. She pushed it away. Her duty, as Patel never tired of pointing out, was to sell papers.

The green-eyed juggler appeared at her side. 'Friend of Balthasar's?'

'No, from the *Gazette*.'

'The gutter press.'

She grimaced. The *Gazette* was a modest provincial paper, hardly a tabloid, but his comment drove the shard deeper. 'Were you a friend of his?'

He indicated the elegant guy in the expensive gear. 'He was at school with Paul and me.'

'You were at school here?' The white buildings glistened around them.

'Ja. Very convenient for our parents. Packed us off to boarding school so that they could get on with their real interests.'

People were climbing into their cars, ready to follow the hearse to the cemetery in town where the Meirings planned to bury Balthasar in the family plot. Maggie would be trapped in the cortege. She was going to be hideously late for court.

'Any chance of a lift?' The juggler tried to look winning.

'Don't you already have one?'

'I'll just let him know I have a better option.'

She watched him walk away. The juggler was dark where his brother was pale, and he didn't have the latter's burnished prettiness. His face was lumpier, less honed, but on the other hand, he did have the biceps and those laughing green eyes. He returned, self-satisfied.

'Before you get in my car, you'd better tell me your name.'

'Spike Lyall.'

'Maggie Cloete.' They shook hands.

'Ouch!' she winced.

'Sorry, I didn't see the bandage,' Lyall said. 'Is that a battle wound?'

'Comes with the territory.' She reversed out of the parking space and trailed the cortege down a tree-lined avenue.

Well-shod schoolboys in uniform walked along the road carrying their book bags from one mansion to another. The privileged few. An emerald cricket field, manicured to within an inch of its life, arced away to their left. Outside the school gates they passed cows in a field and two barefoot children at the side of the road, dressed in rags and chewing sticks of sugar cane. They waved to the cortege. Of all the people in all the cars, she and Spike Lyall were the only ones who waved back.

'How did you cope with all this?'

'What do you mean?'

She pointed to what they had just left and then to the two kids. 'The wealth inside, and the poverty outside.'

'We shut our eyes,' he told her. 'Didn't you?'

'I didn't go to a school like this.'

He raised his eyebrows.

'So tell me about Balthasar Meiring.' She had given him a lift; he owed her information.

'Will I make headlines if I do?'

'Off the record then.'

Lyall stared out of the window. The Toyota hugged a road that wound through farmlands and plantations. Here they were pines, but they were still aliens, still making money for unscrupulous farmers. To the right, the land swept like a carpet all the way to the Drakensberg. The rolling hills, the few dark patches of natural forest and the shine of water looked peaceful. But this had been Balthasar's turf, his stomping-ground, and he would have seen beyond the bucolic harmony to the disease that had the province in its grip.

'His relationship with his family was troubled.'

'Lourens Meiring said so. He said they'd fought.'

'Their politics were different, but it was more than that. Balthasar had a lover in London. A Brit, called Stephen. They couldn't accept that he was gay. They wouldn't hold the funeral at their own church, so it had to be here at school.'

She frowned. 'Was Sanet part of this?'

'Oh, she was worse. She came to London once to see him. After the accident.' Spike turned towards her and she could sense his eyes on her face. She felt her skin respond to his glance. There was something about this man that made her body react.

'We were all in London, Balthasar, Paul, me. I was on a gap year and they were working. I managed to roll Paul's car one night. Balthasar was in the back. He fractured his leg in a whole lot of places, and went to ICU. She came to see him.'

'Sanet left the farm?' She found this hard to imagine. Her image was of a woman tied to the land, to her duties.

'Yes, it was a big deal. Then Balthasar told her about his lover and she walked out. Took the next plane home. She stayed in London for a whole twelve hours.'

They were off the highway now, tracing the cortege's path through town to the main municipal cemetery.

'Where's Stephen now?'

'He had HIV and developed AIDS. Balthasar nursed him until he died.'

She remembered Cabbage Ears' words. *Someone living with AIDS.* Why didn't he mention how hard it was to say goodbye to someone dying of AIDS?

'When did he come back home?'

'Soon afterwards. Steve left him money to help South Africans with AIDS. That's when he went to work at the Mission.'

'But he still didn't see his family?'

'He saw Claudine. He couldn't forgive his mother for her rejection. He said she put her beliefs before her family.'

'And his father?'

'Their differences were political. Balthasar couldn't take the whole minority rights thing.'

She put on the indicator and turned into the cemetery lot. She parked the Toyota and stared through the windscreen, both hands still on the steering wheel.

'So now he's dead. His father reckons it was a revenge killing for the Ncube murder.'

'No,' said Lyall. 'I don't think it was that. But I don't think it was just a robbery either.' He lifted his eyebrows and the corners of his mouth turned down.

'A hate crime then? Someone didn't like the fact that he was gay?'

'Not that either.' The juggler sighed. 'One thing you should know about Balthasar – there was no grey. It was all black and white. If you weren't on-side, then you were invisible to him.'

'And this meant?'

'That he made a lot of enemies. He wasn't scared of speaking out.'

Mourners moved in solemn groups towards the graveside. Spike Lyall pulled the door handle and turned to look at her over his shoulder. There was something solemn and lovely in his eyes that made part of her stomach turn over. 'Thanks for the lift. You going to come to the grave?'

'No, I must head back to work.'

She climbed out of the car and watched him go. She didn't like cemeteries any more than she liked churches. She was happy to steer clear.

She turned to get back into the car, but a shadow fell across her body. She lifted her arm to shade her eyes. It was Phiri.

'So it's Miss Magdalena Cloete, of the *Gazette*.'

She nodded.

'I'm going to ask you to leave now. For the sake of the family. You've done your business, but now you can let them grieve in peace.'

'And if I don't?' Here it was again: a man trying to tell her what to do.

'I could ask you nicely.'

She held his eye. He was a good-looking man, who no doubt got attention from women, and was used to adoration and obedience in various combinations. She shrugged her shoulders and refused to budge.

His eyes narrowed. 'Or I could phone your employer. Jabulani Nzimande is a good friend of mine.'

If her editor found out she was at a funeral instead of doing her job in court, he could fire her within the hour. She should leave, but her stubborn streak kicked in. 'I have every right to be here. Lourens Meiring invited me.'

He removed his backside from the Toyota and moved closer to her. Dumisane Phiri was trying to intimidate her but she wasn't going to let him. She put her hands on her hips.

'How did you know Meiring?'

Being defiant in the face of authority was how she'd got, and kept, her job. She wasn't going to stop for Dumisane Phiri.

He raked his fingernails through his close-cropped hair. 'We were at school together.'

'You were at Goodwill?'

'Yes, Miss Cloete, black boys can also go to private schools.' He rummaged in his pocket, presumably for his cell phone. 'Now get out of here, before I call Jabu.'

'I'm going,' she said, 'but only because I have a court case to get to. Before I do, tell me off the record, what you think happened to Balthasar?'

'A tragic case of a robbery gone wrong,' he said with the rictus of a grin. 'A typically South African fate, don't you think?'

Putting on his sunglasses, he strode away to join the rest of the mourners, checking once over his shoulder to make sure she was leaving. Balthasar Meiring's death might have been a mistake, but threatening her was a mistake too. Dumisane Phiri was going to learn that by trying to head her off, he'd only intrigued her more.

8

Thursday, 12pm

Ernie Gumede, keeper of the *Gazette*'s stable of ancient cars, didn't remove his eyes from the picture of Miss February in the men's magazine he was flicking through when she handed him the keys to the Toyota. He merely grunted. She had to hold thumbs that Patel was too busy worrying about today's front-page lead to check the requisition records. If he did, he'd see that she'd taken a car when she should have been in court. Ignoring orders and wasting resources were two infractions guaranteed to send the news editor's blood pressure through the roof.

She trotted past the City Hall, just as the clock chimed twelve and scattered a flock of doves roosting in the clock tower. They flapped into the ice-blue sky, wings thrashing, and then settled back down in their perches, ready to be surprised again in an hour's time. Maggie had Balthasar on her mind. He had asked her to cover this court case and she was curious to find out why.

The High Court smelled better than the Magistrate's, a mixed perfume of anxiety and floor polish. She found the courtroom and entered with a bow, sitting in the spectator's benches. As she cased the court, she mused that, for once, she was appropriately dressed. Over the years, various judges had given up objecting to her wearing jeans and shorts in their courtrooms.

The two advocates stood below the judge's dais, listening while the Honourable Khanyi Sithole spoke tersely to them. Maggie didn't know the advocate for the families, a lanky white guy, but she knew Errol Mdunge, who nodded when he saw her. Mdunge liked getting his name in the paper, and he made sure he kept the press sweet. Dr Schloegel sat on the accused's bench. He had accessorised his mustard suit with tan shoes and spiky rectangular spectacles. He had fleshy, pursed lips that looked self-satisfied and he kept his eyes fixed on his lawyer, whose sartorial taste was infinitely better than his.

She turned to look at the families, all dressed soberly for court in shades of black and navy. She also saw a couple of crisp-suited gentlemen in designer sunglasses, which suggested that they wanted to hide and be noticed at the same time. One had tribal scars on his cheeks, a practice which had died away everywhere but in the most rural communities. The other, a white guy, was built like a brick shithouse. There was something familiar about him, something that made her flesh creep.

Before she could work out how she knew him, the courtroom rustled into action, and the advocate for the families called his witness, Mrs Nhlangulela, to the stand. She looked anxious and tired. Under his gentle questioning, her story emerged. Her son discovered he had HIV, which rapidly developed into full-blown AIDS. In desperation, when Dr Schloegel came peddling his vitamin cures, known as Schloegel's Herbals, they bought these instead of trying to scrape together the money for antiretrovirals. Schloegel assured them that the vitamin preparations should be taken daily, and also recommended a healthy diet with lots of fresh, preferably organic, vegetables.

'Mrs Nhlangulela, for how long did your son take Schloegel's Herbals?' he asked.

The court translator spoke to Mrs Nhlangulela in Zulu, listened to her response and replied, 'Four months.'

'And in those four months, how much money did the family spend on vitamins?'

'R4000.'

'Was this money you had saved?'

When she heard the question, Mrs Nhlangulela raised a clean handkerchief to her eyes and wiped away tears. Unable to answer, she shook her head.

'Mrs Nhlangulela, the court needs to hear how you came by the money to buy the vitamins.'

The translator leant in close and conferred with the distressed woman. 'We borrowed it from a money lender,' he replied.

'And why did you not spend that money on antiretrovirals?'

'We were told they made people more sick.' This rumour had gone from a whisper to a rumble. If the government didn't trust the medication enough to make it universally available, then people didn't trust it either.

'And how long after he started the course of vitamins did he die?'

'Four months.'

'Mrs Nhlangulela, how old was your son when he died?'

'He was thirty-one.'

Maggie scribbled notes. Half an hour into Mrs Nhlangulela's testimony, Judge Sithole called the lunch recess.

Maggie went to her favourite cafe, the Mooi Boy, where the plastic tablecloths matched the plastic cheese in her toasted sandwich. She chewed and fumed. It was hard to understand why the government wouldn't make antiretrovirals available when they could halt the progress of AIDS. Someone like Benjamin Nhlangulela could still be alive, working and supporting his family. Instead, he had died and his family was in hock to township moneylenders.

She walked back to the courts. Under the eaves of the City Hall, she caught sight of the two courtroom thugs in close conference with an older, heavily-built man, dressed in a snappy suit. Her neck prickled – it was Lucky Bean Msomi, the town's biggest crook. She knew him from his trademark crocodile-skin brogues, his corpulent belly and his air of owning everything – and everyone – in sight. She hovered in the doorway of a jeweller's, pretending interest in a display of diamond engagement rings as she kept a discreet eye on them.

Msomi was not just a big fish, he was a shark and she had been on his trail for two years. Eighteen months ago she'd lucked on a guy in local government who was prepared to talk. He'd told her that Msomi was using government property for his own purposes. Instead of road-work equipment, certain storage units belonging to the provincial administration were piled ceiling-high with coffins. By stockpiling them, he kept coffin prices artificially high.

She nurtured her contact for months and just when he was prepared to bring her documentation to show Msomi was paying someone in government for his storage facility, the guy vanished. Disappeared. Swallowed by the shark. At the same time, Msomi started sending his thugs in one of his many black BMWs to lurk outside her apartment building. She got the message: the bottom-feeders were watching her.

Now Maggie watched them. Msomi clapped the twosome on the back and then, waving to someone inside the City Hall, climbed into a BMW that had been waiting for him. His underlings made their way back to court, and she followed, prickles coursing up and down the tendons of her neck. Could Schloegel and Msomi be working together? The German fed people an expensive cure that wouldn't kill them, but didn't stop their deaths. Msomi, a well-known money lender with tentacles throughout the greater Maritzburg townships, would then loan the families money to pay for funerals – in his coffins, using his hearses, with his contacts at the cemeteries – and then charge them fat interest rates on their loans.

That afternoon she took notes as witnesses – a brother, a sister and a grandmother – told the same story over and over, that of a family member in the final stages of AIDS and a last-ditch attempt to save their lives by scraping together cash to buy Schloegel's vitamins and additional products (creams, health bars and massage oils, branded a hopeful green and white), all to no avail. The victims lived for three months or four, and then died of AIDS-related illnesses.

'Snake oil,' she wrote in her notes, underlining the phrase three times. The final stroke of her pen slashed through the paper to the next page. 'Bastards,' she wrote underneath.

Judge Sithole called the day to a close and Maggie left, the slippery tiles beneath her worn smooth by thousands of feet. She was glad to leave the smell of anxiety behind her and take some deep breaths of humidity and taxi fumes instead.

While she wrote the story and wiped the grime of court from her brow, Aslan Chetty, still immaculate in his lovingly pressed jeans, came swinging over. She ignored him. She had to get the bloody thing done. He perched on her desk and tapped his fingernails on her terminal until she was forced to acknowledge him.

'What?'

'How much fun was your day?' He batted his eyelashes.

'Appalling. Let me get this done, and then let's go for that curry you mentioned.'

Aslan nodded and went off to bend someone else's ear. She submitted the fake AIDS cure story, which endured Patel's scrutiny unscathed and then gathered Aslan.

En route to China Sam's, he complained that his day had comprised a series of non-starters and he had no chance of a byline tomorrow. Aslan loved having his name up in lights. His parents loved it even more: Mrs Chetty cut out every story he wrote and collected them in a scrapbook which she brought out for visitors. So far, Mrs Chetty had filled seven books.

'Nothing for Mama's book today, then?' Maggie asked as they sat down and ordered drinks. Aslan drank sweet white wine and she had a Castle with a vodka chaser. He was no drinker, while she, on the other hand, most decidedly was.

'Nothing. What a crap day.'

They glanced at the menus for show, but ordered their staple meals: a three-chilli green Thai curry for her and Szechuan beef for Aslan. China Sam's menu was nothing if not eclectic. Its furnishings were the same – a Chinese lantern here, Indian miniatures there, a picture of a minaret. Anything east of Cairo would do, both in decor and the kitchen.

While they waited for their food, she told Aslan Balthasar Meiring's story, leaving out the fact that she'd attended the funeral that morning.

'I don't know much about Meiring, but neither do his family or friends. They all seem guarded.'

'Well I can tell you something,' said Aslan, eyes sparkling, as the waiter brought them their meals.

'What?'

'Have you met my Auntie Meeta?' Aslan asked with all sincerity, but since each of his parents were one of seven children, she really couldn't keep up with every single one of his aunties, uncles and cousins.

'Nope.' She knew the genealogy would follow.

'She's my dad's oldest sister. You know, Rovindra and Jeff.'

Rovindra and Jeff she did know. These cousins of Aslan's were bhangra artists who had taken Pietermaritzburg by storm at Christmas.

She and Aslan had been to their concert, which was so successful that they were now planning a Durban and North Coast tour for Easter, taking in Stanger, Ballito and even Empangeni. They were big and getting bigger.

'Auntie Meeta's their mother. Anyway she told my mother who told me that until a week ago Balthasar Meiring visited her neighbour, Youvashnee Chalik, on a regular basis.'

He stopped to let that sink in. 'Mrs Chalik is a renowned herbalist and spiritual practitioner. People come from far and wide for her preparations.'

She sipped her beer. If Balthasar had been visiting a herbalist, could this mean he was seeking a cure for something? Or maybe he visited Mrs Chalik for spiritual solace.

'Would she talk to me?' She forked her curry and rice casually, not wanting Aslan to see how eager she was.

'Mrs Chalik would talk to anyone who is friendly with Auntie Meeta and her lovely sister-in-law, Mrs Prevathi Chetty, mother of the famous reporter Aslan Chetty.'

She loved this about Aslan: like his mother, he actually believed he was a local celebrity. 'Could you arrange it? Before conference tomorrow?'

'Watch me.'

Aslan embarked on a series of cell phone calls, during which he appeared to talk to all forty-three of his first cousins and at least five aunties. He set up her appointment with Mrs Chalik for 8am the next day. She was so grateful that she paid for his meal.

As they walked arm-in-arm out of China Sam's, he said, 'Fancy checking out the talent at Crystal's?'

This was Aslan-and-Maggie-speak for Aslan flirting with all-comers and her watching. After today's funeral and the harrowing court testimony, she needed the entertainment.

Crystal's lay around the corner from the office, settled between a liquor store and a supermarket. It was neither chic nor hip, just in convenient walking distance. Colonised by the journalists, the younger lawyers and some of the graduate students, it was a place where the music was not so loud that they couldn't talk, but loud enough that if they wanted to get stupid and dance they could. Also, the drinks were cold.

They settled in their usual corner, with a view of the bar and the dance floor. She wrapped herself around a vodka and soda, while Aslan nursed a sparkling water. Soon they were joined by half the newsroom, including Sally-Anne and Ed. The arts reporter clambered all over Ed like a creeper, arms around his neck and one leg dangled over his, while the photographer drank his beer and impersonated a rock. Her suspicions were confirmed. How long would this latest relationship last?

'So, Mags, how's it going with the AIDS Mission murder story?' asked Sally-Anne, voice dripping with sugar.

Maggie looked stony. No one called her 'Mags', especially not people currently sleeping with Ed.

'Not going at all. Story's gone dead.'

She plinked her fingernail against her glass, keeping half an ear on Aslan's conversation and trying not to watch Sally-Anne twine her fingers in Ed's hair.

'Well, they're a funny family, aren't they?'

Maggie gave her a look that said explain yourself, minion. When Sally-Anne didn't respond to that, she said, 'What do you mean?'

'I knew Claudine and Christabel at school. They stuck together, you know, didn't mingle. I don't think boarding school agreed with them. After a couple of years that father of theirs turned up in the middle of term and removed them.' She sighed. 'I'll never forget his safari suit. I think they went to day school in Greytown after that.'

'You could have mentioned this three days ago, when I was writing the story.'

Sally-Anne trilled a little laugh, and patted Ed's broad shoulders. Maggie fought the urge to slap her. 'Oh, I didn't want to stray onto your territory, Mags. You're the crime reporter; I'm just the arts correspondent.'

She said 'arts correspondent' in inverted commas, as if it were something Maggie would disparage. She was right, Maggie did disparage the arts, but only when they were covered by someone as vapid and duplicitous as Sally-Anne Shepherd.

'Oh!' the arts reporter shrieked. 'There's Jackie!'

She rushed off, presumably to greet one of her ridiculous girlfriends. Maggie pictured them in the bathroom, jumping up and down and sharing lipsticks. She slugged her vodka, and watched Aslan charm one of the waiters. If there was no one else around, Aslan would flirt with a pole. He was adorable enough that the pole would probably go home with him.

He slid a fresh vodka in front of her.

'Mood enhancer? You're looking a bit grim.'

She grunted and listened to Aslan gossip to Ed about the office. Growing bored, she cased the room and saw Sally-Anne hanging around the neck not of a fluffy blonde clone, but of Spike Lyall. She blanked her face to hide the fact that her heart had lurched directly into her belly and was flopping around there.

He was not alone. The entire post-funeral party had walked in with him. They were in various stages of disarray and looked as if they were celebrating, not mourning. Spike Lyall tried to shake off the enthusiastic puppy that had attached herself to him. He managed to disentangle her, pecked her on the cheek and she sauntered back over to the journalists' table looking pleased with herself.

'Know him too?' Maggie said.

'Yes, I was friends with him when I was at school,' Sally-Anne replied. 'We were also together at university. He's gone back now and is doing his PhD and some teaching.'

Maggie took a few deep breaths.

'You knew Spike Lyall at school? The same school Balthasar Meiring went to? Don't tell me you knew him too?'

'Yes, but only vaguely,' she re-draped herself over Ed. 'He and Jack's brother were three years ahead of us.'

'I thought his name was Spike.' She gripped her vodka glass.

'That's just a nickname from schooldays. His good friends call him Jack.'

It was the 'good friends' that tipped her over the edge. That and the vodkas that Aslan had been feeding her.

'You withheld information from me.'

'What information, Mags? I hadn't seen Balthasar for thirteen years.'

Sally-Anne looked wide-eyed and innocent, the look she used to good effect on Zacharius Patel. Maggie wanted to wipe it right off her silly face.

'You could have helped me get access to the sisters, more background information on him from his school friends. You deliberately scuppered my story.'

'Oh please, Maggie.'

It was beginning to dawn on Ed and Aslan that she and Sally-Anne were having issues. Her finger pointing at the arts reporter was their first clue. Her raised voice was their second.

'A story is only dead when you have investigated all possibilities. You denied me access to some of those possibilities. I'm telling Patel tomorrow.'

'Oh for God's sake. You're just being petty.'

'Let's talk then.'

She grabbed Sally-Anne by the arm and frog-marched her out of the bar. The arts reporter looked frightened. As they passed Spike Lyall, he reached out an arm to his friend.

'Sally-Anne? Everything okay?'

'Fuck off, *Jack*,' Maggie growled, lending the name as much invective as she could muster. 'We're working.'

9

Thursday, 11pm

In the car park, she let her victim go. The cloudless night sky was washed with stars. Out of habit she looked for the Southern Cross, but it didn't provide its usual anchoring comfort. She shivered in her sleeveless linen shirt.

'Where's your car?'

Sally-Anne led her to her Mercedes convertible, a present from her father when she started work at the *Gazette*. Mr Shepherd didn't want his precious daughter driving all over KwaZulu-Natal in the paper's rickety pool cars. At first, Jabulani Nzimande had objected to this priority treatment, but after Sally-Anne spent a cosy half-hour with him in his office, flattering him and promising to pay her own petrol bills, he had relented.

Having escaped the crime beat, Sally-Anne now chauffered herself to the ballet and to opera in fitting style. Maggie sniffed the car's box-fresh smell and smoothed its leather seats. Ed and Sally-Anne probably went for dates in this car too. Was she the kind of woman who would ask a man to drive her? If Maggie ever owned such a fabulous piece of machinery, she would never let anyone else drive it.

The thought of Sally-Anne and Ed together in the convertible brought her crashing back. She turned to the woman sitting next to her.

'Tell me everything you know about Balthasar Meiring. Don't leave out any details, even if it was just school gossip. I want to know it all.'

Sally-Anne stared through the windscreen, and talked without looking at her.

'Balthasar was gay.'

She sighed. 'No shit, Sally-Anne.'

'It was an English-speaking private school. He struggled to fit in. He was gay, Afrikaans and arty, not interested in playing rugby or going to parties to meet girls. He kept to himself.'

'But not that much of an outsider. They were all at his funeral.'

As she said it, she wanted to kick herself. Here she was, declaring to her enemy that she had flouted Patel's orders. She glanced at Sally-Anne, who was checking her mascara in the mirror and didn't appear to have noticed.

'They went on to university together,' the arts reporter said, dragging her attention away from her own reflection. 'Paul, Balthasar and Francois Bezuidenhout.' That was Cabbage Ears' real name. She recognised it now - he was the scion of a wealthy KwaZulu-Natal businessman and was now running his father's empire. The kind of person who appeared on the *Gazette*'s business pages, signing deals and licking bottoms.

She thought of another outsider who'd been at Goodwill. 'What about Phiri? How did he fit in?'

'He was in the first rugby team along with Paul and Francois.'

'Phiri didn't play soccer?'

Sally-Anne turned to her with disdain. 'There is no such thing as soccer at Goodwill College. They played rugby in the winter and cricket in the summer. Even Dumisane Phiri. He made sure he fitted in.'

So Phiri was a politician, even then.

'How come you know so much about Goodwill?'

'Our school was their sister school. We did plays together, had socials, went to watch their rugby matches. If they were interested in someone in the hockey team, they came to watch our matches.'

This was a world Maggie didn't know. Her Afrikaans state school threw girls and boys together in one loud, fervent, ideological mix. The only thing it shared with the likes of Goodwill was the obsession with rugby. Her brother Christo's sport.

'So the sisters were at your school. What were they like?'

'Oh, they were just weird. I wasn't a boarder, but my friends told me they would kneel to pray before getting into bed at night, and they would walk around arm in arm singing hymns in Afrikaans. I think they were teased.'

'You think?' It was not hard to imagine Sally-Anne as a schoolgirl. She would have been leader of the coolest clique, wearing the right clothes, going to the right parties and getting off with the right boys. 'Come on, Sally-Anne.'

'Okay, they were teased. We made fun of them – their weird hair, weird clothes, weird family.'

'So they didn't finish school there.'

'No, they didn't. They were called out in the middle of a Maths class and told to pack their bags. Their father was waiting for them in a bakkie. They were gone in forty minutes. Later we read about the murder.'

'Anything else?'

'No. Can I go now?'

'Ja.' Maggie got out of her car. 'But if you mysteriously remember something about the Meirings in the night, make sure you tell me tomorrow. You weren't a crime reporter for very long, but you do know that any information helps a story.'

'Please tell Ed I've gone home. Tell him I'm exhausted.'

Sally-Anne drove off. She didn't look smug or self-satisfied anymore. Unfortunately, though, Maggie had not been able to tease anything useful about Balthasar Meiring out of her.

Back in the bar, she relayed the message to Ed, who was chatting to a waitress and did not seem bothered. Photographers were fickle. Taking stills all day meant they didn't have long concentration spans.

'What are you staring at?' Ed turned to Maggie as the waitress removed a tray of glasses.

'You.' After a couple of vodkas too many, her body had forgotten that she was no longer sleeping with Ed. She examined the forearms that were leaning on the table near hers. Just under his tanned skin with its dusting of golden hair, those arms were threaded with muscle. Like the rest of his body. She lifted one hand, about to stroke the arm nearest to her.

'Stop, Maggie.' He was looking at her gently. 'Don't. You know I'm seeing Sally-Anne now.'

She looked up into his blue eyes. 'You usually make an exception for me.'

He laughed. 'I know. But I want it to work this time.'

Ed had wanted it to work with her, so badly, but she'd thrown him out after a couple of months. She couldn't take the neediness. The one person who needed her was in a mental institution and the other one was dead. She didn't like being needed. But when Ed was between girlfriends or fighting with one, he'd been known to buzz her doorbell late at night. And she'd been known to let him in.

'Sleep tight, Maggie,' he said and left.

Aslan had found a new group of people to charm. She watched him, all flashing eyes and gesticulating hands, making the people around him laugh. She ordered a fresh vodka from a waiter and sipped it.

In order to not think about Ed's tanned arms, she thought of Balthasar and his history. He'd stood up to his right-wing father and his pious mother, so he'd been a misfit in his family. He'd been a misfit at school too. She could relate to that. Her high school had been a tough-as-nails scrabble of white-knuckled, scrape-kneed, buzz-cut, Bible-reading Afrikaner Nationalists from the roughest part of town. And if you happened to think that apartheid was wrong and that Noah's Ark and Adam and Eve were nothing more than lovely fairy tales, you were likely to get beaten up. Daily.

It hadn't been a bad training-ground for crime reporting, she thought ruefully. At least she'd grown a thick skin and learnt not to trust anyone. But what her school hadn't given her was the sense of self-importance that Balthasar's friends seemed to have. Cabbage Ears, the one Sally-Anne called Francois, had the large smile and arrogant presence of someone used to being accepted wherever he went. It was something they all shared. They walked the planet as if they owned it and the very special air that they breathed.

Maggie felt no such ownership. She felt lucky to have a job and a roof over her head, just enough money to pay her bills and Christo's. Her little brother joined the army with the same stupid enthusiasm with which he flung himself into a rugby scrum; total disregard for danger and the potential for injury. Back then, white boys had a compulsory two-year stint protecting South Africa's borders from whichever twisted threat the Nationalists dredged up to cast fear into the white community's hearts. In the eyes of her family, Christo was a hero, keeping them safe in their little Pietermaritzburg beds from Communists, ANC guerrillas and, naturally, the omnipresent Libyans.

They took him to the drill hall on a hot January morning. It was stuffy with testosterone, sweat and tears, as mothers and girlfriends hugged their boys for the last time, pressed photos and letters into their hands. Christo tolerated Ma's hugs, Pa's handshakes and backslaps.

'Next time we see you, you'll have a number one haircut and will have forgotten what it's like to wear mufti,' said Pa. Christo laughed, but his eyes slid away to the others. He was ready to join the big adventure. Maggie, who had just started work as a general factotum in the *Gazette*'s HR department, felt the sting of envy. She'd have liked to be climbing onto a big truck and putting Pietermaritzburg behind her for a bold new life.

They drove to Ladysmith six months later for his passing-out parade from basic training. Maggie sat in the back of Pa's Ford and watched the Drakensberg get closer. The yellow winter grass stretched for miles, slashed by black gashes where farmers had burnt firebreaks. The Berg rose up through the windscreen, the walls of Giant's Castle forming an impassable barrier.

The family was allowed three hours with him, for which time Ma had spent four days cooking, her natural tendency to over-cater gone berserk. There were boerewors rolls, a melktert, two cold chickens, a banana and pineapple salad, potato salad, beetroot salad, Christo's favourite peppermint crisp tart and a tin full of date biscuits and rusks. They sat in the orange and white striped folding-chairs that Pa had hauled out of the boot, manfully trying to eat their way through Ma's giant buffet. Christo was thin and ate little.

Ma, sensitive to the core, kept pressing food on him until Pa finally snapped, '*Los hom uit, Annatjie, hy's nie honger nie!*'

'Food's lekker, Ma,' said Christo, conciliatory, as he shredded his roll with his fingers and chewed on a piece of boerewors as if it were gum. After wiping his hands, he brushed a phalanx of imaginary crumbs off his spotless uniform.

Then he told them: he was being posted to South West, from where he and his squad would patrol the Angolan border. Good news for a patriot, bad news for a teenager showing signs of mental strain. Pa was proud though; he pumped Christo's hand up and down, trying to inject his boy with the fervour he'd need to kill people.

When it was time for them to leave, Christo took the tin of biscuits but refused everything else. After giving Ma a brief hug and Pa a handshake, he adjusted his beret and walked off to rejoin his commando, his tall skinny figure a khaki spike in the yellow grass. On the way home, Maggie stared through the back window at the receding mountains, and thought of her brother's hand, brushing and brushing away the crumbs in his head.

She swept aside the old bitterness. Tonight she felt bitterness on Balthasar's behalf. With friends like these, out partying on the night of his funeral, who needed enemies?

Francois Bezuidenhout approached her. 'You're Maggie Cloete? From the *Gazette*?'

'Yes.'

'You were at the funeral today.' She nodded. No point in denying it. The man had seen her there.

He leaned his arms on the table-top, where Ed's had just been. 'Dumi told me he chased you off. I'm sorry if he was harsh – we're all under stress right now.'

'Funny way to show it,' she pointed to the group. Francois' blonde wife was dancing with Spike, Spike's brother and his wife were snogging, and the little woman, who she'd seen that morning in the giant hat, was leaning up against Dumisane Phiri.

'Phiri, for example, isn't he married?'

Bezuidenhout sighed. 'They both are. I'm going to have get her out of here before they do something stupid.'

'Before you do, tell me one thing,' she said.

He nodded. 'Sure.' She could see he was making every effort to be amicable, to make up for Phiri's earlier behaviour.

'Why did the Meirings send him to Goodwill? Surely it was too liberal for them?'

'It is a church school, so they knew religion would be covered.'

'That can't be all.' Out of the corner of her eye, she could see Aslan making his way towards her through the crowded bar.

'I think he questioned them and they couldn't take it.'

'But they brought the sisters home. After the murder. Why not Balthasar?'

Bezuidenhout shrugged. 'Maybe they thought the girls needed protection, but Balthasar could stand on his own two feet. Who knows what goes through people's heads?'

'What's going through my head,' she said, skin thinned by vodka, 'is why you're all here. You buried your friend today, and you're all out partying. I think it's disgusting.'

He gave her a big-eyed sincere look. She could tell why he'd been head-boy. 'It's been a rough few days. Some people cope by withdrawing, others go out and have one drink too many.'

Aslan came over before Maggie could tell Bezuidenhout what she thought of his coping mechanisms. 'I'm off to get my beauty sleep. Need a lift?'

'No thanks, I'll get my bike.'

'You've had too much to drink, Maggie.' He bent forward and whispered, 'You're in a state of *complete* inelegance.'

All she wanted was to get on the Chicken and open her throttle up the highway, far away from Crystal's, from work, from Balthasar's unappealing friends. She even wanted to get away from Spike Lyall. He was one of them. The only person in that crowd she wanted to talk to was Balthasar and unfortunately, he was dead. When he'd wanted to talk her, she had not been prepared to listen. She gave in to Aslan and let him lead her towards the door.

Someone stopped her before she got there. 'Maggie.' It was Spike.

'Where are you going?'

'Home,' she told him. Lyall's face dissolved and reformed and it dawned on her that she was swaying. 'Far away from you and your bloody awful friends.'

She staggered out of Crystal's and let Aslan drive her home.

10

Friday, 6am

Her head thudded. Her mouth felt as rough as sandpaper and tasted worse. She pulled herself to a sitting position with difficulty and slugged some water. The only way to fight pain was with more pain, so she pulled on some shorts and her running shoes.

At first, the road was wide, liberally sprinkled with houses on either side, but at the top it narrowed. To the right was a gulley that ran for several hundred metres. Thanks to the February rain, it was clogged with trees and bush, an acid green jungle. Mist rose up from the gulley, hot and sweaty. The pain in her head grew worse. A couple of vervet monkeys shouted insults at her from the top of a tree. She flapped her hand in front of her face to stop bugs from diving down her wind-pipe.

She focused on the road and the rhythm of her feet. She had to go through the pain and beyond it. Back home, a scorching shower completed the chastisement. Then she caught a taxi to work where she collected the Chicken and headed for Northdale.

Youvashnee Chalik owned a modest house, painted turquoise, with orange and green neighbours. She parked the Chicken in the drive and admired the statue of Buddha that dwarfed the tiny front garden. Suburban Pietermaritzburg loved eastern spirituality, but with every third housewife buying reflexology kits and incense burners and setting themselves up as gurus, she didn't know if Mrs Chalik would be fake or the genuine article.

Now she stood on Mrs Chalik's doorstep, ready to find out what the healer knew about Balthasar Meiring. As she stepped up to knock, the woman opened the door. Dressed in a sari one shade paler than her house, with a bindi on her forehead and henna patterns on her hands, Mrs Chalik was the epitome of calm. She was definitely not hungover. Maggie had aura envy.

Cool air glanced off her skin as she stepped inside and received Mrs Chalik's delicate handshake. Maggie followed her down the tiled corridor, lined with blue shelves upon which a variety of Buddhas sat in happy repose, to a sitting room, where the woman indicated for her to sit. The room smelled of nutmeg and cinnamon.

'You are here about Balthasar Meiring,' Mrs Chalik said, sitting down opposite Maggie.

'Yes, I've been covering the story. I am trying to find out more about him.'

Mrs Chalik shook her head and sighed. 'Such a tragedy. I've been in terrible shock since I heard, not sleeping.'

She saw people in shock every day. Few of them looked as composed and elegant as Mrs Chalik.

'What do the police say?' The woman smoothed her sari over her knees. The fabric was shot through with silver.

'They're looking for a thief with blood on his hands and Balthasar's wallet in his pocket. Chances that they'll find him are minimal.'

Maggie watched her for a reaction, but she remained composed.

'Killed for a wallet and a cell phone,' Mrs Chalik said. 'What kind of world do we live in?'

She didn't want to bemoan the sad state of the world. 'I believe he visited you.' Maybe Balthasar had felt at home here amongst the Buddhas. The peace of the room was even making Maggie less edgy.

'Yes. We had much to talk about.'

She stayed silent, hoping Mrs Chalik would fill the gap. She did.

'I admired him for rejecting his background. He couldn't understand how his family and friends, people with all that wealth, didn't share some of it with the needy. He was an AIDS crusader and he wanted everyone else to be.'

Having met Balthasar's family and seen his friends in action, Maggie could understand his impatience with them.

'Did you only talk?'

'No. I made an ointment for him, a herbal preparation for people with AIDS. It's used specifically to soothe the skin of those with herpes and Kaposi's.'

Kaposi's Sarcoma. She knew from Aslan's articles that this tumour affected people with AIDS, usually as lesions on the skin, but also in the mouth, the gut and the respiratory tract. It appeared once a sufferer's immune system caved in.

'Something special, the ointment?'

'I like to think so.' She gave a half-smile.

'What are the ingredients?'

'That is Balthasar's secret. But there were some very special herbs that only I could source for him. Then I would make it up in large quantities, he would collect it and deliver it to various people he took care of.'

She interlaced her fingers and laid them in her lap. She looked satisfied, but Maggie had more questions.

'Did Balthasar charge people for the ointment?'

'Oh no!' Mrs Chalik looked horrified. 'He provided it as part of his service as a volunteer at the AIDS Mission.'

'Did he pay you?'

'That seems like a very rude question, but if you must know, he paid me for the ointment. He didn't pay for the cup of tea and the friendly conversation.'

She had chinked the aura. Mrs Chalik was growing irritable. She would have to irritate her some more – she'd thought of Herr Doktor Schloegel. It was a long shot.

'Aren't there a lot of other AIDS products on the market? Could someone have felt aggrieved that Balthasar had a free product?'

Mrs Chalik folded her arms and pursed her lips. 'I have no idea.'

'Do you know about Schloegel's Herbals?'

'I do.'

'Then explain something to me. What's the difference between his products and Balthasar's?'

'My dear, Dr Schloegel claims that his concoction cures AIDS, which it clearly cannot. Balthasar's lotion merely alleviates some of the symptoms. There's a world of difference.'

Mrs Chalik rearranged her sari. Outside in the street, a car squealed its tyres. The noise was like metal on the sponge of Maggie's brain. Northdale had woken up.

'Did Balthasar Meiring have AIDS?'

The healer drew herself up to her not very full height and her nostrils disapproved of Maggie. 'That is not a question we ask. You should know that.'

She was right; AIDS disclosure had become an incendiary issue. People had died for going public with their status. Maggie used the silent trick again.

'As far as I know, Balthasar Meiring was perfectly well.' Then she pursed her lips.

'What's your main line of work then? Making preparations?'

'I am a herbalist, my dear, and a spiritual healer. I believe in the mind/body connection, so I strive to heal both the soul and its physical manifestation. Many people are blocked emotionally so they come to me for assistance.'

'Was Balthasar blocked?' She had to ask. She hoped the answer would be enlightening.

'No.' She smiled. 'Balthasar was one of the most highly evolved human beings I have ever had the joy to meet. He operated on an elevated spiritual plane. I felt honoured to have been able to help him. And to call him a friend.'

She leaned forward. 'I don't mind telling you, dear, that I think he is helping me. From the other side.'

Maggie didn't mind the spiritual mumbo-jumbo; it made a lot of people happy. But she didn't want to hear how Balthasar had reached out to Mrs Chalik across the veil. That was a little too much for her to stomach. However, maybe Mrs Chalik had special insight into the murder that no-one else had.

'Do you think it could it have been a hate crime?'

The woman drew back. 'I don't know what you mean.'

'Mrs Chalik, it was common knowledge that Balthasar Meiring was gay. Could someone have killed him for that reason alone?'

'I have no knowledge of that kind. Surely not in this day and age?'

Hate crimes did happen. People only needed to read the newspaper to know that. But Youvashnee Chalik clearly liked to keep her world perfumed and sanitised.

Maggie slapped her knees. 'I'll be off then.'

Mrs Chalik swayed to her feet, took a step towards her and took her hand in one of her hennaed ones.

'My dear, you are most severely blocked. I would recommend a thorough course of colonic irrigation. If we could clear some of your physical passages, it would make a path for wondrous spiritual growth.'

She wasn't letting anyone, not even the fragrant Mrs Chalik, anywhere near her passages. She promised to send her best regards to Aslan Chetty and left.

Back at the office, she glanced at the paper and noted that the Schloegel's Herbals story had made page three. In conference, Patel turned his steely glance on her. 'What's on the agenda, Cloete?'

She told him that she would be covering the fake AIDS cure case again. She didn't tell him that she'd visited Balthasar Meiring's personal herbalist that morning and found out that he was bankrolling a soothing skin cream made of mysterious herbs for KwaZulu-Natal's AIDS survivors. Neither did she mention she'd be attending his memorial service at the AIDS Mission the next day. Maggie and Zacharius Patel were operating on a need-to-know basis. These were things he didn't need to know.

On her way to court, her stomach reminded her that she'd ignored breakfast and she stopped in at the Mooi Boy for a salad roll. She ate it on the run. Down one of the lanes, between a ladies' underwear shop and a store selling model aeroplanes, she saw Spike Lyall. He was juggling, this time for a woman and her small daughter, both of whom were entranced. She increased her pace, hoping he hadn't seen her, but she heard footsteps coming after her.

'Maggie! Wait.' The guy loved punishment.

She kept walking. 'I've got to get to court. I can't stop.'

'I'll walk with you.'

She said nothing and he joined her. He wore a t-shirt and long baggy boardshorts and she noticed that he had nice legs. That didn't mean she wanted to talk to him.

'You were quite upset last night.'

She stopped and turned on him. 'I don't know why Balthasar's friends were out on the town having a big party on the day of his funeral. I thought that was weird. Sorry if you don't agree with me.'

He smiled. 'I do agree with you. I know it looked weird.'

'And what's this juggling thing about, anyway? There's no money in it. You're just showing off.' She wanted to wound him.

Spike Lyall laughed. His green eyes flashed.

'I do it to meet women. I met you.'

'You met me at a funeral.'

'Yes, we met there but I saw you in the street first.'

By now, they had arrived at the High Court. 'I'm going in now,' she told him. 'I've got a court case to attend.'

'Can I come with you?'

'No, you cannot. Go and juggle for some teenagers or write your PhD or whatever it is you do with your time. Some of us have work to do.'

'You've done your research.' Spike smiled.

'No, just my job.'

She turned on her heel to avoid Spike Lyall's self-satisfied face and went through the gates to the High Court. Before putting her back-pack through security, she looked over her shoulder. He had set up his juggling on the pavement outside, next to a gogo sitting on a red tartan blanket with a basket of oranges for sale. The old lady clapped her hands and exclaimed in delight. He had wasted no time getting another woman's attention. A minibus taxi called 'Smooth Operator' stopped to drop off passengers outside the court complex. The moniker was more than appropriate.

A thrill coursed through her when she saw that Lindiwe Dlamini was in the courtroom. She wanted to hear her voice. This was the woman who'd worked with Balthasar Meiring every day, who'd admired his gentle bedside manner. She'd also cradled his dying body in her arms.

On the stand, Dlamini confirmed her name, her position as head of the AIDS Mission and that, as part of her work, she had visited two of the families – the Nhlangulelas of Imbali, who had testified first yes-terday, and the Ntombelas from Willowfontein. She was an imposing woman, not tall, but quiet and dignified. Her stance at the witness box was confident and she met the advocate's eye and answered his questions succinctly.

'I visited Benjamin Nhlangulela at home in Imbali in May last year. He was very weak. His family told me his CD4 count was low and that he had a high viral load. They could not afford antiretrovirals, but they had invested some money in a vitamin cure sold by Dr Schloegel, who assured them that it would boost Benjamin's immune system and help his body to fight the disease. I told Mrs Nhlangulela that HIV can infect active immune cells and that any preparation or pill that claims to boost the immune system could increase the spread of the virus, not stop it. However, they told me that the man who had sold the pills to them was a doctor, who had convinced them that the pills would work.'

Lindiwe looked at Mrs Nhlangulela, who had buried her head in her hands, with shimmering compassion. Maggie wondered how she could maintain that, working day after draining day with a ruthless epidemic. How did AIDS workers prevent themselves from getting fatigue? How were they able to see each case as an individual one and not as a statistic?

'Mrs Dlamini, when did you next visit the Nhlangulela family?' he asked.

'A month later, in June.'

'And how was Benjamin then?'

Lindiwe looked at him as if she were trying and not succeeding to squash something inside her. 'He had died.'

Mrs Nhlangulela sobbed. The sound made the hairs on Maggie's arms stand up.

After Lindiwe's testimony, Judge Sithole called a recess for lunch.

Maggie followed Lindiwe out, and waited while she talked with the Nhlangulelas. She had her arm around Benjamin's mother and the older woman leaned in on her, just as she had leaned on the medic who'd escorted her from HIV House on Tuesday.

'Mrs Dlamini, can we talk?' she said after Lindiwe said goodbye to the family.

The woman pulled herself up tall. 'I have nothing to say that's on the record. And I won't speculate about the murder.'

'I only want to ask a few questions about Schloegel. Come, I'll buy you lunch.'

They walked out of the courthouse into the midday humidity, Lindiwe clutching her giant black handbag like protection. Maggie glanced to see if Spike Lyall had conquered more grannies' hearts, but he had deserted his turf for somewhere more productive. She began to sweat and craved a cold drink, preferably one with bubbles and alcohol in it. Up the road from the courts lay a complex of shops, with cinemas and a hotel. It contained a few boutiques of the kind Sally-Anne Shepherd might patronise – small, expensive, with snooty owners – and a big chain restaurant called Guido's that would sell her a steak and a beer. There would also be air-conditioning.

Settling into a booth, Maggie ordered a Castle and a rump steak, and Lindiwe ordered iced tea and a plate of chips. While they waited for their food, Maggie tried to sound her out. 'So these products, Schloegel's Herbals, how widespread are they?'

'They're everywhere.' Her dark eyes met Maggie's. 'He's got an impressive sales mechanism set up.'

'How, though?' How could a German guy, who couldn't speak Zulu, muscle his way into the townships?

She rumpled the sides of her mouth. 'Contacts.'

'So someone in the township is helping him sell his AIDS cure?'

'Yes.' Lindiwe glanced away.

She thought of the thugs in the designer spectacles huddled with Lucky Bean Msomi outside the City Hall. 'Msomi?'

'That's not a name people throw around lightly in this town, Miss Cloete. I really don't want to talk about this. Not here, not now.' She gathered her copious bag and got up. 'I'm just not ready to talk yet. Sorry to waste your time and your money.' She left.

Maggie took a large gulp of beer and tackled her steak. While she chewed, she thought about Lindiwe Dlamini and wondered when she would finally decide to talk. She kept batting Maggie away.

She sighed and reviewed her notes. There was a front-page story in the Schloegel material. No one liked a quack and no one liked a quack making money out of people with AIDS. After finishing the steak, she ate Lindiwe's chips, then pushed the plate to one side and stared around the restaurant. Guido's was buzzing with lawyers, civil servants and office workers all enjoying their lunch.

She caught sight of a familiar face closeted in a dark booth in a corner of the restaurant. Dumisane Phiri was deep in conversation with a man in a black suit. He hadn't noticed her. Curiosity piqued, she made her way to the Ladies', so that she could walk past them and see who had engaged Phiri's attention. As she pushed open the door to the toilets, she turned and looked back. She didn't know the man, but he had a hard face.

In the Ladies', she washed her hands, ran them through her hair and examined her reflection. She was not one for vanity, but it was important to check she didn't have any mushroom sauce on her chin or steak strands between her teeth. Should she stop and talk to the two men? Or should she drop it, and observe them incognito?

Opting for the blunderbus technique, she left the loos and greeted Dumisane on her way past. Irritation washed his face when he saw her.

'Miss Cloete.' He put his hand up to his companion, as if indicating that this wouldn't take long.

'I've just had a great steak and I'm fine, thanks,' she said, although he hadn't asked. 'You?'

'Good, good.'

She looked at the other guy. His little eyes were bloodshot, and he looked as if his coffee wasn't quite the stimulant he was after. He glanced back at her and then buried his nose dismissively in the mug. He wore a grey Italianate suit, the kind that South Africa mass-produced, with the designer's label still sewn on the cuff.

Dumisane, born politician, couldn't ignore social nicety. 'Maggie, this is a business associate of mine, Vincent Ndlela. Vincent, this is Maggie Cloete from the *Gazette*.'

Ndlela offered his hand for her to shake. As their hands met, one long, pointed fingernail grazed the new scab that had grown on her palm. She whipped her hand back, trying not to wince.

'Do we know each other?' she asked.

'Don't think so,' he said, returning his attention to his empty coffee mug. 'I know your work.'

She turned back to Dumisane. 'I'm over at the High Court today. Some German quack's been peddling fake AIDS cures all over Eden-dale and Imbali, and the families of five dead customers have instituted a class action suit. Lindiwe Dlamini has just testified.'

Ndlela stiffened. He put the coffee mug down and wiped his face elaborately.

'Well I'll leave you to it,' she said. Dumisane bid her a polite, if not sincere, farewell, but Ndlela stared at her. She could see the intelligence in his cold eyes, and a shiver ran through her. If she ever bumped into him alone in a dark alley, she would have to have her fastest running shoes on, or be armed with a very large gun. Preferably the latter.

Back in the courtroom, while she waited for the afternoon session to kick off, Maggie wondered why Dumisane Phiri chose to hang out with a nasty type like Vincent Ndlela. Surely it would be more appropriate for an up-and-coming politician to rub shoulders with his City Hall colleagues?

In the Schloegel case that afternoon, Lindiwe told of visiting the Ntombela family numerous times, and watching as Elsie Ntombela grew steadily weaker despite the infamous vitamins. Three months after starting the course, she died.

Judge Sithole, keen for her weekend, called an end to proceedings before Schloegel's lawyer could get stuck in. On the way back to the office, Maggie's cell phone rang.

'Cloete.'

'My name is Mbali Sibanyoni.' It was a child's voice. She spoke English with a Zulu accent.

'Yes?'

'I am Balthasar Meiring's daughter.'

11

Friday, 4.30pm

'His daughter?' She stopped dead on the buzzing Friday afternoon street, her phone pressed against her ear. The crowds surged around her, bumping against her with their shopping bags and to avoid stumbling, she had to brace her legs.

'Yes, his daughter. I need to talk to you. But not on the phone.'

She ran to the office, heart doing wild zigzags inside her chest, and knocked off the day's story in under ten minutes – a record. Then she took Zacharius Patel a caffeine bribe and told him she was leaving early. He furrowed his brow and nodded. Within thirty-five minutes of receiving the call she had flung on her helmet and flown out of the office.

Mbali said she would meet her in Wylie Park, on a bench near the Athlone entrance. The park was near her school, she said. Maggie had run past it that morning. A dog walkers' paradise by day, it made a home for druggies and muggers at night. Even though it was five in the afternoon and still light, she didn't want any kid hanging about there on her own, so she gunned it.

Balthasar's words rang in her head as she opened the Chicken's throttle up Old Howick Road. 'Someone with humanity, someone who cares for the victims.' That level of involvement had got her into trouble at work more than once. Both Patel and his predecessor, a lugubrious Zimbabwean called Bert Townsend, had warned her to back down.

'Jeez, Maggie,' Bert would say, scraping his comb-over back into place with nicotine-yellowed fingers, 'the verb is report. You are a reporter. It's not your job to get in there and get your hands dirty.'

She resolved to be cool and professional, a promise she made frequently to herself and to her editors. Still, as she rocked the Chicken onto her stand on the grass outside the gates of the park and walked in, her heart was racing.

Thunderclouds loomed like dark palaces in the sky, towering edifices of air and water. The sweat that had dried on her back while she drove penetrated her t-shirt again. This damn humidity had to break.

She found the bench and Mbali. Dressed in shorts and a t-shirt, she seemed well cared-for and healthy. She looked about ten years old.

'Hi. I'm Maggie Cloete.' She spoke quietly, aware that the child had lost the man who she called her father only four days ago.

'Hi.' The child stared into the middle distance and swung her legs. 'My dad got killed.'

'I know,' she said. 'I'm really, really sorry.'

'He was my second dad. My first dad died too.' Mbali kept her eyes trained on her swinging legs. 'He was sick.'

She knew what that euphemism meant. AIDS.

'How about your mother?'

'She died too.'

'I am so sorry, Mbali.'

The child looked at her for the first time. 'Why do you keep saying sorry? You haven't done anything.'

'I know. I'm just sorry that you have this sadness.'

'We didn't go to the funeral.' Tears pooled in her big brown eyes.

'I went. They said some wonderful things about him.'

Mbali began to cry for real. She put her arms around her. She understood that feeling of desertion; knew it in her bones. Mbali cried and cried, Maggie's black t-shirt soaking up her tears. The dark green leaves of the azalea bushes rustled and she could smell rain.

Mbali looked up at her and said, 'Can I come home with you?'

'What about your own home?'

'Nkosazana wails all the time and I don't want to be there.'

She skimmed the possibilities. Here was a link to Balthasar, a living link, not some ghostly recollection of a hazy boy. Mbali had something to tell her and most of all, she wanted the child to trust her. Also, a storm was on its way. The bamboos down near the stream were spitting like snakes.

'Okay, here's the deal. You can come home with me for two hours if, and only if, you phone home first and tell them you're safe and will be back by 8pm.'

She handed her the cell phone and she dialled a number, had a rapid conversation and then turned and said, 'I'm ready.'

Lighting crackled over them, followed by a boom of thunder. Mbali grabbed her hand.

'You realise I don't have a car,' she said as they ran towards the gates, tree branches lashing each other. 'I have a motorbike.'

Mbali managed a brief glimmer of a smile.

She placed her helmet over the child's head and drove home, praying she would not bump into any cops on the way. It would not do for the *Gazette*'s chief crime reporter to be caught driving without a helmet and with an under-age child riding pillion.

They parked in Maggie's underground parking spot, just seconds before the cloud palace opened and dumped several kilotons of water on greater Pietermaritzburg. She noticed that Mbali was shivering and as soon as they got inside the sixth-floor flat, she gave her one of her jerseys to put on. It came to her knees, but she still quaked.

She tried to think what she could do to stop her shaking and then remembered Ma's panacea for all ills. Milk and honey. She warmed some milk in the microwave and stirred in honey. Mbali sat on the sofa, knees tucked right under the jersey, sipping the milk.

'I'm so tired,' she announced when she finished the drink.

'Mbali, didn't you say you wanted to talk to me?'

'I do, but can I sleep first?' As she put her head down on a sofa cushion, her eyes closed.

Maggie had a bath. She sunk her head under the water. The sound of water throbbing on her eardrums was not soothing. Something in Mbali's eyes reminded her of Christo; a vulnerability, a sense that the world had let them down. Christo had lasted two months on the border. He went AWOL and when the army found him, living rough on Durban beachfront, he declared he'd become a conscientious objector. He was given a six-year sentence and put in a Pretoria jail.

Ma took to bed with the shame and could not be moved. Pa came to visit Maggie at the *Gazette* during her lunch-hour. Over a plate of Spur chips, he told her he was taking Ma to the South Coast.

'It's a permanent move, meisie. I think the change will do her good. We'll find a new community and start over.'

'You're dumping us,' Maggie said. 'Me and Christo, just like that.'

'No, meisie, not you. Just this town. We can't show our faces in church here anymore.' He didn't mention his son. He put his hand over hers, but he was already craning his head for the waiter so that he could pay the bill. The way his scrawny neck hung out of his shirt collar reminded her of a tortoise. One that would retreat into its shell at the first sign of trouble.

Maggie refused to talk to either of them before they left town. Last she heard, they had set up home in Scottburgh, but she had no forwarding address, no phone number.

One day she received a call at the office.

'It's Jon Hammond,' the voice told her. 'From the End Conscription Campaign. There's been an appeal against maximum sentences for conscientious objectors. Your brother's coming home.'

She met Christo at the bus station. She hadn't seen him for two years and she was looking out for a tall, thin, blonde teenager. The man who climbed down the stairs of the bus was overweight, unkempt and shaking. He hugged her and said, 'I need a drink.'

Christo's downward spiral was fast. He woke her night after night with his roaring nightmares, which he denied in daylight. He got a simple job as a teller at a supermarket, but complained to the boss that his colleagues were talking about him and raiding his till. When he was fired for a physical attack on another staff member, he stayed home drinking. It was when she woke one night to find his hands around her neck, eyes purple with anger and fear, that she realised he needed help.

The noise pulled Maggie out of the bath. She grabbed a towel and ran dripping to where Mbali lay. The child wailed and tears ran down her cheeks.

'Mbali, wake up.'

The child shook herself out of her dream and looked at Maggie, whose wet feet had made a trail of footsteps on the carpet. She looked stunned and then, as consciousness returned, realised where she was.

'You're all wet.'

'Yes, I was having a bath. Wait here while I get dressed.'

She went to her bedroom and put on some jeans. When the rain stopped, it would be hot again and she would want to be in shorts, but now she needed denim armour.

'I'm just going to make coffee,' she called to Mbali and went into the kitchen. She switched on the kettle. It was Friday afternoon. She should be at Crystal's with Aslan, drinking vodka and watching him flirt, but instead here she was making coffee while a child waited for her in her sitting room. She stared out of the kitchen window and watched as the rain came to a halt. After a brief pause, freshly-washed birds started singing. Don't get involved, she muttered to herself as she poured boiled water over instant coffee granules.

Whatever you do, don't get involved.

She put the spoon in the sink and glanced out of the window. A black BMW with tinted windows came to rest near the pavement outside the apartment block. Someone rolled the window down and she could see the glint of sunglasses. Phiri had a black BMW, but then so did Lucky Bean Msomi. Anyone who thought he was anyone in Pietermaritzburg drove a black BMW.

She poured Mbali a glass of water. Out in the street, the BMW still lurked. She flicked the driver the finger and banged down the blind.

Back in the sitting room, Mbali said, 'I need to tell you something.'

'Let me just get my notebook.' She grabbed her backpack from its place at the front door. She sat on the sofa next to Mbali, coffee mug resting on the table in front of them.

Mbali turned to her. 'I want to tell you about Balthasar.'

'And I want to hear all about him,' she said. She explained that as a journalist, she wrote down what people said. She asked Mbali to introduce herself and then speak slowly and clearly.

'I am Mbali Sibanyoni,' the child began. 'I am eleven years old. My sister Grace is four years old. My brother is seven and Mondli is nine years old. My other brother Sbusiso died when he was five. He had the same thing as my mother and my father.

'First my father got sick, and then he died. Then my mother got sick, and I stopped going to school so that I could look after her. Then she died. We were alone. We were scared. People in the village didn't like us.'

'Why not?'

'They thought we would make them sick.' AIDS denialism again. Even though most of the villages in rural KwaZulu-Natal were rife with HIV, people couldn't admit it. They took their fear out on the smallest and most vulnerable.

'I had to take care of my sick brother and my baby sister. My other brothers stopped going to school. They went into the bush, trying to find food for us. Some neighbours gave us food. Our village, near Shongweni, is a very poor village. Some days we ate grasshoppers and drank warm water to fill our stomachs. If we had bread, we mashed it with water and gave it to Sbu, because he was the sick one.

'Then one day, Balthasar came to our village with the AIDS woman, Mrs Dlamini. They were visiting another sick man in the village. I ran to Mrs Dlamini, and I begged her to come and see Sbu. She came, with Balthasar.

'When I first saw him, I laughed. He was so white and thin. His hair had no colour. He wore a long white shirt over white trousers, and his legs were so long, he looked like a praying mantis. When he came into our house, he had to duck his head.'

'What was he like?' She was starting to put some flesh on Balthasar's misty figure.

'He was nice to us. He boiled water and gave Sbu a bath in bed. He washed all his sores and put some special cream on them. Some of them he bandaged. He washed Sbu and he talked and we listened. We had never heard a white man speak such good Zulu. While he talked, Mrs Dlamini said she would go to get us food.

'She came back with a whole sack of maize and some beans. She brought us new jeans to wear. She even brought us takkies and fleeces.'

'How did you feel?'

Her face lit at the memory. 'We were so happy! Happy to have nice warm clothes and some good food to eat. She told me we shouldn't eat all the food in one day.'

Maggie winced.

'Then Mrs Dlamini and Balthasar went outside and had an argument. She came back in and said that people from her organisation would try to look after us. She would tell a friend of hers called Brenda Tshabalala who lived in the village to visit us and help us. Then Balthasar came in, carrying more food. He said to hide it, because we didn't want people to steal it. He also said he would be back soon. Then they left.'

'Did he come back?'

Mbali looked at her as if she were stupid. 'He came all the time. We were glad when he came because we didn't like Mrs Tshabalala. She was always cross and had a loud voice.'

Her voice grew softened. 'One day, something bad happened, to Grace, and she had to go to hospital. Balthasar took us home, to his house, to keep us really safe. We were happy to go with Balthasar because he was nice to us and he always brought us food and treats.'

'What happened to Grace?'

'I don't want to say.'

She left it. She would push a grown-up for information but not this multiply-bereaved kid.

'We drove a long way, all the way from our village into town, until we got to his house. When we got there, he said that me, Grace, Sbu and the boys, we would be his children now. He became our father. We were very happy. Our father had died, our mother too, and we had no one to look after us.

'Two weeks after Grace came out of hospital, Sbu died. We were very sad that our little brother had died. Balthasar promised that if any of us got sick like Sbu he would buy the muti we needed to get better.

'Four days ago, he got up early and went to work. Then the AIDS lady, Mrs Dlamini, phoned to say someone shot him dead. We have just been sitting there, at home, not knowing what to do or where to go. Nkosazana won't let us go outside the house or answer the phone.'

'And you didn't go to the funeral?'

'No. That made us sad. Mrs Dlamini said she is coming tomorrow to fetch us for his other funeral.'

'Who looks after you now?' she asked, praying that there would be a good answer.

'There is Nkosazana, but she is very old. She doesn't know what to do. She keeps crying and saying, 'My baby is dead.' Claudine came once with food, but then she went again. There is a nurse who comes during the day to look after the sick ones, but Balthasar used to look after us at night.'

'How many sick ones are there?'

'Busi, Joyce and Msizi. Balthasar says Grace is our miracle baby because she still hasn't fallen sick.'

'Who are the other three?'

'They are Nkosazana's grandchildren. Their parents died too.'

Maggie struggled to take this all in. Balthasar had set up an orphan-age for children, some with AIDS, in his home, and had made no contingency plans for the eventuality that he might turn up dead. Now there were seven children and one elderly adult who needed looking after.

'Mbali, why did you call me?'

The child looked up at Maggie. 'Balthasar told me to. He said if anything bad happened to him, we must phone you.' Then she buried her head in her hands.

Maggie stood up, then sat down again. Her guts churned. Balthasar had believed that she would somehow take care of his orphans. She hadn't listened to him the first time, but she was going to have to listen to him now. She had no choice, damn him.

'Let's take you home, Mbali.'

At Balthasar's house, Mbali hopped off the bike to open the security gates with a key she had in her pocket.

Turning her head over her shoulder, she said, 'Will you come in and talk to Nkosazana?'

Maggie teetered on the abyss. On one side was professional distance, the kind her news editors had counselled her to adopt. She could see the figures of Zacharius Patel and Bert Townsend waving to her and shouting, 'Don't, Maggie!' On the other was a pair of dark imploring eyes. Mbali tugged at her hand.

'Okay, okay,' she said. 'I'll come in.'

12

Friday, 8pm

She parked the Chicken on the gravel driveway next to a yellow Golf while Mbali locked the gate behind her.

'Whose car is this?'

'Balthasar's,' the child said. 'Sipho brought it back.'

A typical red-brick Pietermaritzburg Victorian, the house had a green roof. The front door peeled black paint and above it a wisteria vine clambered unfettered. Mbali led her to a side-gate on the left, which turned out to be the kitchen entrance. A fence covered with tumbling jasmine divided this house from its neighbour. They walked past a covered scullery area, now disused, but where turn-of-the-century servants would have gathered to gossip and work.

Mbali unlocked the kitchen door and the sound brought feet hurtling down the corridor towards them. An old lady flung herself at Mbali and covered her with noisy sobs.

Maggie knew a smattering of Zulu, but she couldn't follow the torrent of words flowing from the old woman. Mbali received the attentions, then gently shook her off.

'How are the babies?' Mbali asked, in English.

'Sleeping,' the woman replied, wiping her tears with a tissue she produced from a pocket. 'Msizi wouldn't eat, but the other two had some pap. I changed them and now they are all asleep.'

She looked at Maggie. 'I am Nkosazana. Who are you?'

'I'm Maggie Cloete. I write for the *Gazette*. Mbali asked me to come and see if I could help you. I am really sorry about what happened to Balthasar.'

The tears began to flow again and this time Nkosazana didn't bother to wipe them.

'It is terrible, terrible. Such a good man, a kind man, looking after the children of other people, and now he is gone and we do not know what to do.'

'I'm going to find the others,' said Mbali, apparently deciding that, having brought Maggie to the house, her job was done. She ran down the corridor of cracked black and white lino, leaving just the echo of her feet.

'Can I make you some tea?' Nkosazana asked.

She didn't want tea. Having heard Mbali's story, she thought vodka was more in order, but she didn't want to insult the woman's hospitality so she followed her into the kitchen. Large but antiquated, it sported a small, ancient-looking stove, a fridge floating in swamps of water that someone had tried to stem with back issues of the *Gazette* and a single metal sink. There was also a small washing machine with a cracked plastic casing. Balthasar hadn't gone in for the latest in labour-saving devices.

Without asking, Nkosazana spooned three teaspoons of sugar into Maggie's cup and stirred them in. She didn't take sugar, but this wasn't the moment to argue. Nkosazana sat herself down on a chair next to her.

She sipped the tea. The sugar made her teeth ache and she tried not to wince. 'Tell me about Balthasar.'

Nkosazana looked grateful, as if she were dying to talk. 'My baby. I worked for his family for many years. Before the madam had the twins she had to lie down. She couldn't look after her baby son, she was too sick, so he became my son. I carried him on my back when he needed to sleep, fed him when he was hungry, bathed him when he needed to be clean. Then the twins came and she had no time for him, so he stayed mine. He grew into such a funny, skinny little boy. I called him my monkey. He always wanted to be on my back. I would still carry him when he was three, four years old. Except when the master was there.'

'Balthasar's father?'

'Yes, he didn't like it. He said I made him into a baby, that Balthasar should be running barefoot around the farm, shooting and trapping things.'

'He didn't do that?'

'No, he didn't like killing animals. He liked to be at home, in the kitchen with me, or in the garden with the madam. When the girls got big and went horse riding, he would still stay home with us, reading his books. Oh, he loved his books.'

'Were you still working for the Meirings when Pontius Ncube was killed?'

'That was a terrible time.' Nkosazana shook her head slowly from side to side. 'I knew the Ncube family, and I knew the master had killed him and I still had to go to work every day and see him. I hated him so much then. It made me sick to see him, that he could shoot a man and leave him to bleed to death. I decided I would leave, but I couldn't leave my baby there alone with the master. I waited until Balthasar went to university and then I left too.'

'Lourens Meiring says the Ncube family might have shot Balthasar in retribution for the killing of Pontius.'

Nkosazana leant forward and said in a whisper, 'They didn't. They know he was not like his parents.' She sat back. 'Anyway, he used to go down to the kraal to play with Pontius when he was small. They were friends.'

Maggie sat back, trying to take it all in. A stripe of ants walked in formation towards the sugar bowl and Nkosazana covered the bowl with a crocheted doily weighted down with small yellow stones. Then she got up and put her empty mug in the sink.

'Do you want to see the children?'

She had a moment of panic. Did she want to see the children? Couldn't she just say her goodbyes, slip out the back door and retain her professional indifference?

She started up the black and white corridor. Her instincts – the ones she usually listened to when there were rubber bullets to duck, a crowd of protestors turned nasty or a slime-ball fraudster started lying in the dock – screamed at her to head for the back door. She ignored them and followed Nkosazana. The walls of the corridor were utilitarian white. She focused on them to wrestle back the panic.

Nkosazana stopped at the first room on the right. 'This is where the girls are.'

She took a breath and looked in. The tiny room had just enough space for a bunk bed and a cupboard. Mbali waved at her from the top bunk, where she had tucked herself under the covers. She gestured for her to go in.

'That's Grace,' she whispered, pointing a finger to the sleeping form in the bunk below. Maggie bent down and glanced at the small dark head on a pillow. Grace's lashes rested like butterflies on her cheeks and she had her thumb tucked between her lips. Part of her wanted to stroke the child's cheek, but she resisted. Again she had the vertiginous sense that she was teetering on a cliff – one that she really, really wanted to fall off.

Nkosazana beckoned her from the door. She waved goodbye to Mbali and left the room.

'Grace is HIV positive,' Nkosazana told her as she walked up the corridor. 'Balthasar pays for her drugs, and she hasn't developed any AIDS symptoms yet. He says she's our miracle baby.'

Maggie noticed the present tense. 'And Mbali?'

'Mbali is fine. She was born before her father caught the virus and gave it to his family.'

She stopped at the next room. 'This is where the boys are. Mondli and Lungi.'

Nkosazana opened the door and she glanced in. Dark and slightly bigger than the girls' room, it also contained a bunk bed. She tiptoed over. No one lay in the bottom bunk, but when she looked at the top one, she saw two heads on the pillow.

Nkosazana had followed her in. 'That's Mondli against the wall. He's eight and his brother is six. Lungi hates sleeping alone, so he always climbs in with Mondli. They are both well.'

Lungi had curled up on his side against Mondli, with one arm thrown over the bigger boy's chest. Mondli slept with an arm above his head and his cheek resting on top of Lungi's head. At that moment, her heart cracked wide open. Her chest tightened and she had to focus on her breathing – slow and deep, slow and deep.

She hoped the darkness would hide her panic from Nkosazana.

'Now I'll show you the sick-room,' the old woman said. The corridor opened up into a wide room. It had a skylight high on the right, through which she saw the night sky. This open space in the middle of the house helped her breathe again. Nkosazana turned left, through a set of double doors to some kind of small anteroom, and paused in front of a door.

'These children in here are my grandchildren. Their parents are dead. I looked after them all alone in my house at Midmar. Then Balthasar came to find me last year, and offered to take us here. I was so happy – to be with him again, and also to have help. It is hard, when you are old, to look after children who are so small and so sick.'

She turned a doorknob and entered the room. With the help of the night-light, Maggie could see there were three beds and two cots. Two beds lay empty. 'Sometimes Balthasar and I sleep here, when the children are really bad.'

Nkosazana led her to the only bed with an occupant. 'This is Busi. She is five and the oldest of these children.'

She gasped. Busi was smaller than Grace. She was a wisp of a person. 'Busi's HIV turned into AIDS a year ago. She has TB too. Her TB drugs are not agreeing with her AIDS medication, and we are watching her very carefully. The doctor adjusted her ARVs and she's coming on Monday to see if it has made any difference.'

She nodded. Nkosazana was well educated in the language of AIDS, a disease that made medical experts out of ordinary people. She watched Busi in her sleep. Her chest rose and fell rapidly as if she were fighting for breath. While she watched, one of the little children in the cots started crying, a ragged, scratchy cry that she felt all the way down her arms. Nkosazana began stroking and shushing the child back to sleep. When the child would not be comforted she sang. It took Maggie a moment to realise she was singing in Afrikaans, a lullaby that she knew:

Wieg nou my baba tussen takkies so sag.
Net maar die windjie hou oor jou wag,
Kyk wat gebeur as die takkies swaai,
Met bubu en al sal die wiegie draai.

Nkosazana turned as she joined her at the cot. 'It's the song Balthasar sings them. Joyce loves it.'

She looked at Joyce. She wore a nappy and a t-shirt and scratched at some sores on her scalp. Maggie saw that much of her body was covered with big lacerations that oozed.

'How old is she?' she asked.

'Two and a half.'

No expert on babies, Maggie thought she looked little over one.

'Is that Kaposi's?' she asked. Nkosazana nodded, then took some lotion from a glass jar on the table next to Joyce's cot and began rubbing it into her skin. The lotion and the gentle motion soothed her and she went back to sleep.

'Is this Balthasar's special lotion?' Her meeting with Mrs Chalik had only been that morning, but already it seemed a lifetime away.

'Yes.'

'May I?' She opened the jar and sniffed the contents. She couldn't tell what herbs were in the ointment, but it smelled good. The panic that had been rising since the boys' room began to ebb away and she felt calmer. She walked to the second cot. A tiny creature lay there, naked except for an enormous nappy that dwarfed his twig-like limbs.

'This is Msizi. He is eleven months old. He has diarrhoea and we can't give him his medicine until the tummy gets better.'

Nkosazana sat suddenly on one of the spare beds. She looked up at her, 'So much death. Sickness and death. Death and sickness. And I am just so tired. These children need help and all they have now is me. Old, tired Nkosazana. I don't know if I can carry on.'

She looked grey and exhausted, near collapse.

'Have you talked to Mrs Dlamini at the AIDS Mission?'

'Oh, she is very nice. She has been to see us. She is sending a car for me and the children to come to the memorial tomorrow. She says she will try to help us, but that these children have more than most. They have food, shelter, drugs and doctors. Lindiwe's job is to care for those who have nothing.'

That would be the NGO line, the one Lindiwe would have to espouse.

Nkosazana led her back down the passage. Outside the kitchen, she clasped her arm.

'I am scared, Maggie. I don't know what the future is for me and the children.' Maggie rubbed her shoulder just as she'd rubbed Mbali's. 'He had an argument with someone last week on the phone. He was shouting and very angry. Later he told me not to answer the phone, that there were bad people around.'

This shone a new light on things. Who would Balthasar be arguing with and why? What bad people? 'Who was it?'

'He wouldn't say.' Nkosazana's broad face fell in on itself.

'What about Balthasar's parents? Can they help?'

'Those people!' The old lady found the energy to fill the two words with invective. 'They talk about God and about love, but they don't care.'

'And Claudine?'

'She helps us, but she lives far away in Durban so she can't come here all the time.'

Maggie told her she would see her the following day at the memorial service and made a mental note to ask Lindiwe who Balthasar could have been arguing with – when Lindiwe finally deigned to talk to her.

As she rode home, she decided on her course of action. It was not her job to look after Balthasar's children and Nkosazana; that role belonged to his family. She wondered what would happen if a busybody, maybe an interfering journalist, broke the news to Sanet and Lourens Meiring that they had four adopted grandchildren living in Pietermaritzburg, four kids who had been orphaned twice and who could do with some love and care. Would they find it in their Christian hearts to help them?

13

Friday

Still he watched the house.

It was old and big and stood on a large piece of land. That man had had money. He'd come back from the UK with a suitcase full of pounds to spend on the needy and the *deserving*. All that money, being spent on people who were going to die. But that man hadn't cared about keeping things tidy. There were weeds growing out of the pavement in front of the house, knee-high grass inside the fence and a shitty yellow Golf in the driveway.

A woman in white buzzed at the gate in the mornings and was let in. She left again before dark. The old woman lived there with the children, some that were well and went to school every day and some that were sick.

Now that that man was gone, they were alone at night. There were no guards, no dogs, no burglar bars on the windows. He'd been fearless. Or stupid.

The house was full of sickness and death. Full of children being kept alive by expensive drugs that that man had bought with his pounds. Sick children burning with a virus that was killing everyone, burning into their blood like poison so that they could never get better.

They said that monkeys brought the disease. He thought it was the exiles. People like that man who came back from overseas with pounds in their pockets and the virus in their veins, bringing their evil to the innocent.

His father said he was a bad boy. Evil, he'd say through the gaps in his teeth.

Every time, the whistle in his father's mouth echoed the whistle of the whip in the air. Then he would run, all the way to the koppie, the blood cooling on his back.

Even his own mother thought he was bad. If she thought he was good, she would have stopped his father from whipping him.

She'd been too scared. She let him push her at night. He watched the big man push the small woman into the bed, his teeth whistling. There was another sound then, a grunt from deep down in his stomach. She made noises too, like the dassie he once caught in the trap. It had nearly pulled its leg off. He put his hands around its neck to stop the squeaking.

The other children said he was bad too. They didn't want to play with him. When they walked home from school, kicking up the dust with their feet, he trailed behind them.

Only one person liked him. A small girl. She sat on the edge of the big open place where all the children played. He saw her, drawing patterns in the dust with her finger. Silently he joined her, made a pattern too.

'Don't play with him,' said a big girl, standing over them. 'He's a bad boy, a bully.' The big girl had a trail of mucus running from her nose to her lip. He tapped the little girl's shoulder and pointed at the slime trail. The big girl huffed off and he and the little girl laughed.

They met after school. She wanted to play baby games and he played them with her. He didn't mind. He showed her the koppie where the dassies played. She liked his cave and she liked running races. She was fast, not as fast as he was, but good for a girl.

He couldn't run like that anymore. Sometimes he struggled to walk. When he climbed stairs he had to rest halfway. At night, he lay waiting for sleep.

The cough sent him to the clinic. 'Pneumonia,' the nurse said.

He went home, got into bed and turned his back on his wife.

The pneumonia went away, but he stayed weak. His body, once full of muscle and power, grew full of weakness.

'Do you want to test?' the nurse asked.

He scratched his shoulder, where a new sore grew. Death sat there on his shoulder, gibbering like a monkey and showing its teeth. He had done things to make that monkey go away, but even the darkest things brought it back. It was his new companion, death, and it waited for him.

That man had known too. Tall, wearing his white robes and his do-good attitude like a badge of pride, he'd known, found out what the dark things were. Instead of leaving it to rest, he'd snuffled around in it like a dog at a carcass and came up stinking.

He'd warned that man, told him to stop, but he had not. He had stoked his anger. He was gone now, along with his ideas about truth, saving people and giving hope.

He took long breaths, went still, waited. Anger was a fire, but sometimes that fire had to burn quietly. When the time came, he would stoke the fire again, add coals, twigs and branches. The fire would burn strong, he would be transformed into a man of action again. A man of action was decisive, strong and powerful, but his power came from waiting, choosing the moment when the fire burned most brightly, and then, only then, acting.

The house remained quiet. No one came and no one left. When the usual afternoon thunderclouds grew in the sky, he started the car and it purred away.

14

Friday, 9pm

As she rode the escalator to her floor, she flipped through her notebook to find the Meirings' home number. It was time they heard the truth.

She walked to her front door, poised to get inside and call them, but as she put her hand out to unlock it, she stopped. Pinned to the door with a single red tack, and wafting in the slight breeze of the evening, was a note. She ripped it off and read the wonky hand-written capitals, 'Hands off the AIDS children bitch. Their going to die anyway.'

Someone didn't care about spelling. Either that, or English was not their first language.

It grated her. She had spent so many long hours perfecting her English, learning its intricacies and complexities. Bert Townsend used to send her copy back to her, printed out and riddled with red. She made the painstaking corrections, put the apostrophes and the commas in the right places, and resubmitted her copy. Her hands shook as he read, lips moving and free hand tidying his comb-over. Then the thumbs up across the room. 'That's my girl.'

Bert had been proud of her. She'd been a lackey in the HR department until he'd seen her promise and nurtured her, against his editor's wishes. She was the only reporter on the paper without the backing of a university degree. She was still the only one, still the bloody misfit.

Inside the flat, she dialled Balthasar's parents. Would Bert approve of what she was doing now?

'Meiring.' Lourens Meiring sounded a little blurred, as if he'd been enjoying a couple of evening brandies.

'Maggie Cloete here. From the *Gazette*.'

'*Goeienaand.*'

'Mr Meiring, I have been doing some investigating –'

'You spoken to the Ncubes yet?' His harsh voice rasped in her ear. 'Because the police keep telling me that they have nothing to do with the case and I know, I just know, that those people wanted to get their revenge. Mathonsi won't listen to me. Just tells me to wait for the police investigation.'

'I'm not phoning about who killed your son, Mr Meiring. I'm phoning to tell you that he has left behind a family, an adopted family, who you might want to meet.'

'A family?'

'Yes, Balthasar adopted a family of AIDS orphans who are all living in his house in town. He also has a second family there – Nkosazana and her grandchildren. Some of the children are very sick with AIDS, some are close to death.'

'Nkosazana,' he whispered. 'What is she doing there?'

'Balthasar invited her. He wanted to help her look after her grand-children.'

There was silence, followed by footsteps and the sound of a door being closed. Meiring returned.

'The children need help?'

'Well, there seems to be money, Mr Meiring, but Nkosazana is old and very tired. She doesn't have the energy to look after all those sick children,' Maggie said.

'Miss Cloete, I have a problem,' he said. 'My wife – her beliefs prevent –'

He was struggling to express himself. She used her silent trick and listened to him breathe. Eventually, he found the words.

'She believes that homosexuality is a sin. And that God has sent AIDS to those who have sinned.'

'But these are innocent children!' She was tempted to bash her head against the wall. Instead she rested it. Tried to think cool thoughts. 'They've done nothing to deserve being ill.'

Meiring sighed. 'Believe me, Miss Cloete, I understand that.' His voice was quiet now, very clear. The brandy mist had faded. 'But there's nothing I can do about my wife's prejudices.'

She made one last attempt. 'Well, in case you want to meet them, there is going to be a memorial service tomorrow at 3pm at the AIDS Mission. The children will be there.'

'Goodnight, Miss Cloete.' He put the phone down. She guessed that was a no.

She went to the fridge for her emergency supply of vodka and took one shot standing. Then she poured another, sat down and chucked that back. She shivered. The world was full of unpleasant people, people who thought they could intimidate her and prevent her from doing her job by plastering notes to her door. And other people who hunkered down in their bunkers refusing to take responsibility for anything beyond their manicured gardens and perfect homes. The vodka iced her throat and then burnt her gullet.

Ice to fight the fear, fire to metabolise the anger.

Floating only a very little, she grabbed her house-key and went next door to her neighbours. Grant Baxter, purveyor of underwear to all well-upholstered Pietermaritzburg ladies, lived there with his mother Dorothy in a flat as full of knick-knacks and ornaments, frills and furbelows, as hers was empty. She had a monk's cell to their lady's boudoir.

She knocked and Grant answered, holding a glass of sherry. His thickly gelled hair had escaped its moorings and listed into his eyes. Maybe it had been a rough day in the knickers trade.

'Hi Maggie, how's it hanging?' She knew it tickled Grant that a short-haired, jeans-wearing, motorcycle-riding crime reporter lived next door. He enjoyed thinking of her as his butch neighbour.

'Not great,' she told him. 'I'm being intimidated by a bunch of idiots and they left a note on my door tonight. I wondered if you'd seen anything.'

'No, darling, I've only just got in. Let's go and ask Mother.'

She followed him in. She didn't socialise with Grant and Dorothy, but she did look after their ancient cat William when they took their annual two-week summer holiday to Shelley Beach over Christmas and New Year. She followed their strict instructions to come in every evening, spoon some disgusting cat food out of a tin, clean the litter tray and put down fresh water. William ignored her, but gobbled the food, drank the water and took a copious poo as soon as the fresh kitty litter was down. She was nothing to him, merely the slave that replaced his humans for a brief period. He couldn't give a damn about her, that cat.

Grant led her into the sitting room where Dorothy sat ensconced in her pink armchair with the TV blaring, also sipping a sherry. Elegant in a dress, as always, she had her hair sprayed into a rigid silver helmet and a face full of concrete make-up that even long after the start of cocktail hour had not started to slide. William sat on her lap and he didn't open an eye to greet Maggie. Ungrateful devil.

'Hello darling.' She waved with her free arm but made no effort to turn down the TV.

'Hi Dorothy.'

'Maggie's had some disturbance next door, Mother,' said Grant. 'She wants to ask you a question. Sit, Maggie.'

She obeyed, sitting next to Dorothy in the matching armchair. The grande dame gave her a quick glance, but couldn't bear to tear her attention from the TV, where a game show host was trying to persuade a contestant that he was very happy to win a giant teddy-bear rather than the R20 000 prize-money.

'Some guys came round to my flat this afternoon, Dorothy. Left an anonymous note. I wondered if you'd seen anything.'

'A anonymous note?' Dorothy swung her gaze from the TV to Maggie and gave her sherry an attentive sip. Now retired from ladies' upholstery, she spent her mornings playing bridge with three other retirees in the block, afternoons in front of the soaps and blurry evenings with Grant. Her life was dull and she lived for intrigue.

'Was it a love letter, dear?'

'No, an unpleasant letter, one that made me very angry.'

'Oh.' Her gaze flickered TV-wards. Maggie had lost her. She was only interested in romance.

'Did you see or hear anything, Dorothy?'

'No, dear, I'm sorry I didn't.'

If there had been any noise, Dorothy would not have been able to hear it anyway over the blare of her TV.

'Sherry, Maggie?' Grant trilled from the kitchen, where she presumed, judging from the clattering and the smells, he was preparing his and Dorothy's TV dinner. 'Sorry we don't have any beer.' He chortled to himself.

About to say no, she thought of going back to her flat right then and being alone with AIDS orphans and murdered parents and righteous Christians and goonish crime lords and anonymous unschooled fuckwits trying to order her about. Against her better judgment, she said yes.

Seven sherries, two game-shows, one made-for-TV movie and a surprisingly good pasta later, she staggered the very short distance home. She couldn't wait to fall onto her lovely clean cotton bed sheets and sleep until day.

There on the door, not wafting like the first since the night had turned into a stolid block of airless humidity, hung a second note in the same wobbly letters.

'Scared now? Running? Leave the AIDS kids alone and youre fine. Mess with them and we do this ...'

Below the note, the idiot had taken an over-ripe tomato, smashed it against her front door and then smeared it so the entire bottom half of the door was painted with red juice and seeds. The remains of the tomato lay on the doormat.

Alert again, she ran downstairs. She saw no one in the reception area, so pushing open the door, she went outside to case the parking lot. Empty. She walked up the driveway to the road, sherry throbbing at her temples. The night pressed humid air down on her and she saw nothing. The person who thought they could intimidate her had gone. In the sky, clouds obscured the stars and there was a bitter slice of moon.

15

Saturday, 10am

On Saturday mornings, she usually went to visit Christo, but with a sherry hangover and the two notes that were spewing hate at her from the hall table where she'd dumped them the night before, she didn't have the energy to go first thing. Some days she could handle the results of what the last government had done – started a border war and sent white teenagers drunk on adrenaline and fear to terrorise their neighbours – and some days she couldn't. Instead, she put on her jogging gear and went to drive out the sherry toxins with a run.

She took a route uphill, past the girls' private school where Sally-Anne Shepherd had learnt to arrange flowers and whack hockey balls and become an upstanding member of provincial society. Skills Maggie didn't have and would never need.

Zacharius Patel and his boss Jabulani Nzimande didn't care if she could play a fine game of tennis or make small talk at a dinner-party. Day after relentless day, she had to find the biggest story and report it in such a way that sales and circulation remained good. Granted, being the only paper in town, the *Gazette* had no competition, but even so, if sales figures dropped below a certain number, Patel would grow twitchy and start talking about retrenchments. It was the journalists' responsibility to keep those numbers high. What she resented was Patel telling her which stories to cover and how to do it. She had a finely tuned instinct and she liked to listen to it.

On the way back down the hill, she picked up the *Gazette* at the tearoom, as well as some bacon and eggs. Her hangover demanded a fat fry-up.

After showering and washing up the breakfast things, she read the paper and noted with satisfaction that the AIDS fraud case had made the front page. Aslan had a diabetes story on page three. He'd be seething, and she considered calling him, but decided to leave him to sleep in, as he liked to do on Saturdays. She scoffed at Sally-Anne's film review of *The World Is Not Enough*, noting with something approaching pleasure that she'd called Bond's BMW Z8 a Z9. On Monday, she'd remind Ed to sub his girlfriend's copy.

Then she drove to Kitchener Clinic, buried deep in the leafy suburbs and surrounded by tall trees and rose-gardens so that its rich neighbours could pretend they were looking onto a lovely park and not a private mental institution.

She waved to the receptionist as she went in. 'Is Christo in his usual place?'

'Yes, Maggie. He's waiting for you.'

She saw her brother's heavy figure on the wooden bench. No longer able to drink, he had taken refuge in food. He'd love one of Ma's groaning buffets now, she thought, giving his back a brief massage in greeting. She pulled a Peppermint Crisp and a giant packet of salt and vinegar chips out of her backpack as she sat down next to him. Christo ripped the chip packet open.

'I was thinking about the one time we were on night patrol,' he began without preamble, jaws chomping. 'The enemy shot down one of our planes. They went to the wreckage and took out the two survivors. Point-blank range. Execution-style. We were told to capture and expedite.'

The smell of salt and vinegar overpowered the delicate aroma of the nearby roses. She could feel the heaviness of another storm gathering in the air. February was like this: heat, storm, brief respite, heat. It could go on for weeks. It took resilience to keep going in the oppressive heat, just as it took resilience to listen to Christo's never-ending stories.

'We took seven that night. Took them back to camp, made them dance around the fire. Then we each had a turn to kill one. Mine was very young, same age as me.' Christo scrunched up the empty chip packet and passed it back to her. He peeled open the chocolate bar, took a huge bite.

'I didn't execute him from behind. I shot him from the front, so that he could see the barrel of my weapon in his face. Afterwards, the Lieut gave us tequila.'

He turned to her, a big grin crossing his face, teeth smeared with chocolate. 'Tequila, man! We were on the border, in the middle of bloody nowhere. Where did he find that stuff?'

'I don't know, Christo,' she said. 'I just don't know.'

'Amazing, hey? Jeez, we got so shit-faced that night.'

Christo's doctors had told her that her job was to listen to his war-stories, no matter how gruesome, and not show any response. The effort of not responding always made her angry, and, shortly before three, she told her baby brother she had to go.

'Cheers,' he said, wrapping his arms around himself and not looking up as she left.

The city centre hummed with Saturday shoppers carrying glistening bags full of summer bargains from the fashion palaces on Church Street, gangs of teenagers flirting with each other, pavement hairdressers giving people their weekend dos. Radios blared, taxis hooted and added to the chaos by swerving across lanes, risking the lives of their passengers and all pedestrians. She dodged one self-styled 'Road Warrior' and swore. The driver leant out of his window and winked at her. 'Calm down.' Was this a message from the universe? Or had all the town's taxi drivers ganged up to irritate her with their insistence on her remaining serene and tranquil?

She drove past the City Hall just as it struck three, and heard the muezzin's counterpoint calling the faithful to prayer at the mosque just around the corner from HIV House. She parked, yanked her helmet off and ran a hand through her hair. She walked down the short garden path and, hearing singing from the back, made her way around the house. The little garden was completely full, with a standing choir and a row of dignitaries facing packed rows of chairs. She quickly found herself a seat at the back and sat, listening to the beautiful choral voices singing a Zulu hymn.

The rhythm and melody of the hymn twined in two strands that joined and separated in a pattern well-known to most of the crowd, who sang. She remained silent, remembering the other service for Balthasar, in a 100-year-old stone chapel with English hymns and shiny, top-of-the-range limousines.

After the hymn, the crowd sat and Lindiwe took her place at a small podium. She wore a black coat. She spoke clearly and her voice carried around the garden without a microphone. Maggie took out her notebook. She might never write this up as a story, but she wasn't going to take that chance.

'Welcome, comrades, friends and family of our dear brother Balthasar. We are here today to mark his tragic passing.'

Lindiwe took a deep breath and allowed her eyes to scan the crowd. Maggie felt sure she caught her eye.

'In an NGO like ours, we are accustomed to death. We see it every day, feel the seed of it in many of the people we meet. We are even accustomed to tragic death, seeing fathers and mothers cut down in the prime of their lives, seeing children orphaned and the elderly left to do the work of the young.'

She heard sobbing from the front row, where she thought Nkosazana and the children were.

'We are used to it, but we do not accept it. That is why an organisation like the AIDS Mission exists, why international churches pay us generous sums, why we give our time gladly and freely to those who labour with HIV and AIDS – because we do not accept. We do not accept that our people, so newly free, are being enslaved by a virus, we do not accept that young people should be allowed to die and we do not accept that this virus should be allowed to spread unchecked. That is why we work here, why my colleagues and I get up every morning and come to work – because we do not accept.'

There was a cheer from the first couple of rows and a collective nodding of heads.

'Balthasar was one who did not accept. He saw AIDS on a personal level. After nursing and burying his beloved Steve in London, he came back here, to South Africa, his homeland, to help his people. Balthasar knew how AIDS infects a body, how much suffering that causes, as the body loses strength and is victim to opportunistic infections. He knew how much pain and loss of dignity that can cause.'

There was a rumble of thunder and Maggie looked up at the sky. The afternoon storms usually came later in the day, but there was a cloud up there seven times taller than her block of flats and it was planning to open on the crowd.

'Instead of running away and hiding from HIV/AIDS, Balthasar came home to face it. He came home to face it in a country where people are too poor to afford ARVs and the government does not provide them, a country where the disease is still considered a mark of shame, and a country where people are too scared to take the test so they keep spreading the disease, turning it into a galloping epidemic.

'Balthasar Meiring was a brave man and a kind man. He was also a generous man, using his own car and his own petrol to visit the dying in outlying villages. He never questioned the distance, time and cost it took to visit someone, and he happily went to wherever he was called to spend time and lavish care on the sick.'

She didn't know what made her turn around at that moment, but she looked behind her. Standing at the corner of the house, stone-faced and inscrutable, was Lourens Meiring. He listed to one side, shoulder grazing the red brick wall. She got up and wordlessly led him to the spare seat next to her own. Lourens gave her a brief glance, which she presumed was a grateful one. She was pleased to see him there – her plan had worked. After the ceremony, she would introduce him to Mbali and the other children.

Lindiwe looked up at the crowd. She was a great speaker. Maggie knew from watching her in court the previous day that she was confident in a public capacity. What hadn't dawned on her then was that her experience probably came from speaking at funerals.

'Balthasar Meiring walked the talk. He visited the sick, drove people to their clinics, delivered food parcels, gave people bed baths, listened to them. Some carers are good at tending to the body, but Balthasar did that as well as tending to the person. He gave people back their humanity, by taking them seriously, listening to them, and trying to meet their needs. He was a superb and gifted carer.'

Next to her, Lourens Meiring gave a deep sigh.

'In his personal life, Balthasar was also dedicated. He made a home for seven orphans from different families. One family of children had lost both parents and was being cared for by their ten-year-old sister, Mbali. Another family was in the care of their *gogo*, Nkosazana Mbanjwa, who despite her age, was looking after a baby and two small children with AIDS.

'And now he too – this dedicated, kind, selfless man – is gone from us.'

There were sounds of weeping from the front.

'We have lost a worker and the children have lost a father. Again.'

Lindiwe shook her head.

'In this country, we have more than one virus. We also have the virus of crime. I want the journalists here today to note that crime doesn't only infect the wealthy at the gates of their big houses. Crime is everywhere, in the townships, on the streets, in small houses and large ones. It is a virus, like HIV, that we must fight.

'Crime has taken Balthasar Meiring from us, from his family and from his children. He was killed for a cell phone and a wallet. For nothing.

'I speak directly to the government when I say give us the drugs to fight AIDS and a well-trained, well-paid police force to combat crime. Give people jobs, houses and clinics so that they don't have to turn to crime. Bring light to the dark areas, so crimes don't happen there. Heal our country, so that we don't have to lose another person like Balthasar Meiring to the crime epidemic.'

She stepped away from the podium and the crowd got up as one to cheer. They ululated and people hugged each other. Then a short guy stood up, walked to the podium and asked for quiet. He was wiry with energy.

'My name is Sipho Nkosi. Balthasar told me once that this was his favourite song. If you could stand with me, listen and hold him in your hearts as I sing.'

She had heard the hymn hundreds of times, first when it was part of the struggle's litany of liberation songs and now, since it had become the national anthem, at every rugby and football match she ever watched – *Nkosi Sikele iAfrika*. They'd sung it in jail too, the detainees of the apartheid state. She hadn't known the words then, but she'd learnt them as her cellmates sung the hymn night after night.

Shutting her eyes, she let it wash over her, first Sipho's voice and then more, as, one by one, each person joined in, their voices knitted together in song.

Before the hymn was over, lightning flashed and the skyscraper above town opened, flooding the garden. People grabbed their belongings and ran for shelter inside the Mission. In the melee, she lost Meiring. She started to head in, but she saw Sipho frantically stacking chairs and went to help him. They made piles and dragged them under the cover of the back stoep. Then they stood there, panting, dripping, and listening to the sounds of people talking inside.

'Thanks,' he said, lighting a cigarette. 'You're from the *Gazette*, right?'

'Yes, and I went to the other funeral. Seems to me Balthasar Meiring had two lives.'

'No. He only had one life, this one,' Sipho pointed a thumb at the Mission behind them. 'He left his other life behind him years ago. It's just that his people couldn't admit it.'

She heard the whoosh as Sipho dragged on his cigarette. 'They wanted him to stop his work here. The mother didn't approve of it.'

She watched the rain fall. It was no gentle mist. It thundered into the ground, dented it.

'And he refused.'

'Sure he did. He had a crusade. He wasn't going to listen to anyone, especially not them. It made him even more determined to carry on with his work.'

She followed Sipho inside and wandered through the warren of offices, walls plastered with posters about HIV and AIDS. She hoped she'd find Lourens Meiring with a bevy of grandchildren on his lap, but there was no sign of him.

He had done a runner. The coward.

Nkosazana perched on an office chair, a cup of tea in her hand, talking to a woman. She greeted Maggie. 'This is Brenda Tshabalala. Brenda is from the same village as Mbali and the children.'

'Do you also work for the Mission?'

Brenda's eyes flickered between Maggie and Nkosazana. 'I'm not an employee. The Mission trained me to work in my village as a lay AIDS counsellor.'

'Did you know the Sibanyonis when they lived in the village?'

'Oh yes. Such a tragic case,' she sighed. 'Five kids struggling to survive alone. It was a good thing when Balthasar took them. Especially after Grace –' She stopped.

'What happened to Grace?' she asked. The hairs on her arms rose. She watched the women share a glance. Between them, they were silently deciding whether to take her into their confidence or not. 'Will someone please tell me what happened to Grace?'

Brenda lifted her arms and dropped them at her sides. 'She was raped.'

'Oh Christ,' she whispered. For a brief second, the room went blurry. She could hear quiet voices around her, but they felt distant, as if through a thick curtain. She brought herself back and asked, 'What happened?'

'No one is sure,' Brenda said. 'Mbali went to get medication for Sbu from the clinic. She had to walk there and was gone all day. Mondli and Lungi were supposed to look after Grace, but they were playing outside and lost sight of her and she wondered off. Hours later they found her, hurt, bleeding, down near the river. She would have died, but Balthasar arrived for one of his visits and took her to hospital.'

'Who did it?'

'We don't know.'

'Did anyone report it?'

'Yes, Lindiwe did. The police came to the village, asked a few questions, left again. We heard nothing after that.'

She fell into the nearest chair. It was hard to imagine the kind of depraved person that would rape a two-year-old, but it did happen, with sickening frequency. This was exactly why she stayed in crime. She couldn't write about James Bond movies or ballet or diabetes when degenerates out there were preying on the smallest, weakest and most vulnerable members of society. She wanted them found and put away and left to rot.

She felt a hand on her arm. She looked up into the eyes of Lindiwe Dlamini. They were warm and kind. She looked like someone who could still wake up in the morning and take a breath of fresh air and feel hope.

Lindiwe smiled. 'I think it's time we had a talk.'

16

Saturday, 4.30pm

Lindiwe led her into her office and shut the door. Orderly and bare, the room contained a desk, two chairs, an old computer, phone and filing cabinet. A burglar-barred window opened onto the front stoep where Balthasar had been shot five days before. They sat and she looked around. In comparison to the offices where she had just been, the walls were clear of posters. Instead, there were two portraits, one of Gandhi and another of Nelson Mandela. Lindiwe followed her glance.

'You know that both were arrested in Pietermaritzburg? Two of the greatest heroes of the twentieth century and our town's claim to fame is that we arrested them.' She smiled a sweet, ironic smile.

'Not much to be proud of, is it? When I was a teacher, back in the Eighties, I used to take my Matric history class on a day trip to Main Station to see where Gandhi was thrown out of that first-class carriage for not being white. It was our big day out; coming to town on the bus, going to the station, facing our apartheid heritage, getting chips afterwards. I think they mainly liked the chips.'

Her skin felt stretched and porous after the news of Grace's rape. She was relieved just to listen to Lindiwe talk while she grew her defences back.

'The headmaster at Edendale High was Mr Ndlovu. He was conservative, but he could just cope with me taking the class out of school for the day for Gandhi. When I suggested I should take the kids to Tweedie where Mandela was arrested, he put his foot down. In those days, you couldn't mention Mandela, except in a whisper. Now of course there's a memorial at Tweedie and bus-loads of kids file past to see it.'

She remembered when Mandela had given Gandhi a posthumous freedom of the city. The *Gazette* had covered it.

'Ndlovu was a Gandhi fan. He used to type epigrams and put them on the noticeboards to inspire the pupils and teachers. One of his favourites was 'It does not require money to be clean, neat and dignified'. You can imagine how well our teenagers responded to that.'

She nodded. She liked this intelligent woman.

'Oh and another one was, 'Victory attained by violence is tantamount to a defeat, for it is momentary.' That was also irrelevant to our kids. They weren't into passive resistance; they were on the streets protesting against the latest outrage of the Nationalist government. During most of the Eighties my classes were half-full. I understood why but I tried to persuade them that the best snub to a government that appeared to despise them was to study, get a Matric and a decent job.'

'I suppose they thought they had nothing to lose,' Maggie found her voice. It sounded foreign in her ears.

'Absolutely! They had nothing and could lose nothing, so they went onto the streets and fought with the police, got themselves arrested. Some of them never came back.' Lindiwe sipped a glass of water on her desk.

Maggie had also been at school in the Eighties, and her schooling couldn't have been more different. They were contained, laagered, and bullied into submission with the twin threats of God and the rod. They never came into contact with a black student and were even kept separate from the English-speaking teenagers, against whom they were occasionally allowed to play a bloody game of rugby or hockey. She said so.

Lindiwe raised her eyebrows. 'Divide and rule – the Nationalists' speciality.'

'When did you stop teaching?' Maggie asked.

'After my son died. I nursed him during his last year and afterwards I couldn't face going back. So I came to work here.'

She didn't ask what he had died of – in KwaZulu-Natal, when people of wage-earning age passed away, it was almost always clear what the cause was.

'You are not a parent, are you?'

'No, no kids.' She would never be a parent. That was a decision she had made many years ago.

'It is the worst thing in the world to watch your child die. You feel helpless. And angry.' Lindiwe leant her elbows on the desk and covered her cheeks and nose with her hands. Above the fence of fingers, her eyes welled. 'Days like today remind you.'

Maggie noticed that she spoke in the second person, as people often did when things were too personal or too painful to articulate.

Lindiwe flicked the tears away, dabbed her face with a tissue. 'It's why I carry on, you know, because I know that each person who dies is not just a number, but a beloved son, daughter, wife, husband, mother, father, aunt, uncle, grandchild or cousin. Every death is the end to scores of relationships. AIDS picks away at our communities, unravels them, and we end up with wrong and unnatural situations like the Sibanyoni kids living alone with no adult protection.'

'Mbali says you and Balthasar argued on the first day you visited them.'

Lindiwe regarded her with a keen eye. 'Oh, Balthasar and I often argued. He wasn't perfect, you know, and neither am I. He wanted to take the kids then and there, but I told him not to. I said they were better off in their community, being with the people they knew.'

'But if Balthasar had taken them that day, then Grace would not have been raped.'

'Raped? What you have to realise, Maggie, is that until six years ago, community was all we had. Community gave us power when we massed together, it gave us support when something terrible happened and it gave us joy when we needed to celebrate. We put the community first because without it we were nothing.'

She could tell what kind of a teacher Lindiwe had been. 'You mean Ubuntu.' The African belief that we are only people through other people.

'Exactly.'

She thought of her own family, living alone in their little box. They went to church for community, but it was a community of imperative, of duty, of being seen to do the right thing. There was no joy in it, certainly not for her or Christo.

A fly buzzed around the edges of Lindiwe's window. The City Hall clocked five. Outside Lindiwe's office there was still the sound of people talking, but she felt divorced from it.

'What happened to Grace was tragic, terrible,' Lindiwe said. 'It should never have happened. But it did, and Balthasar reacted by taking the Sibanyonis home.'

'The community having become too dangerous?'

'Fair point,' Lindiwe conceded. 'The community failed them, and this is what I mean when I say HIV/AIDS is unravelling society. A village that would have supported the Sibanyonis before the epidemic let them down.'

Maggie felt her temperature rise. 'You treated those kids like a social experiment! You should have let Balthasar take them right from the start.'

A shadow crossed the older woman's face. She put her elbows on her desk and rubbed her eyebrows and sighed. Then she looked Maggie in the eye. 'For me to get up and come here every day, I have to believe that community works. I've seen places where it does. If I don't believe it, then I might as well pack my bags and move to the South Coast and stare at the sea for the rest of my days.'

'So what's going to happen to the Sibanyonis?'

Lindiwe folded her arms. 'They have a roof over their heads and there is money. For now.'

'That doesn't sound very permanent.'

'It isn't. Balthasar's house will probably come under threat. He was in the process of adopting the Sibanyonis, but it wasn't complete. He didn't have the house recognised as an orphanage or a place of refuge. I don't even know if he even has a will. If not, the house will revert to his family.'

Maggie slumped in her chair. 'They could take the house and chuck the children out.'

'Exactly.'

'It's a mess.'

'A huge mess.' Lindiwe puffed out her cheeks. 'And then there's the matter of the threats.'

She thought of the white notes on her door the night before, the badly spelled hatred. 'What threats?'

'I don't know much. Balthasar phoned on Monday to say he had been getting threats to the orphans and himself. We planned to meet on Tuesday here at the Mission for him to tell me about it. I had to wait for a taxi, was ten minutes late and when I got here, well, you were here too. He was dying on the stoep.'

Lindiwe looked into the middle distance. 'I still can't believe it – that he's dead. I feel like he's going to waft in here any minute now, wearing those foolish white robes that he loved so much, being enthusiastic about everything and sweeping everyone off their feet.'

'Is that what he did?' Maggie murmured, half to herself. It was the first image she'd had of Balthasar from anyone that brought him to life, gave her an immediate image of the dead man. When she'd talked to Lourens Meiring about his son, all she'd learned about was Lourens Meiring and his retribution fantasies. When she talked to Sanet, she'd had a sepia image of a barely recognisable boy-man. His friends were dislocated from the adult Balthasar. From Mbali, she'd had the impression of a mantis-like saviour and from Nkosazana, a small precious boy who had taken refuge on her back. Everyone brought to their description of Balthasar a part of themselves, but that didn't help the puzzle she was trying to fit together. Lindiwe's words began to fix him for her. She told her that.

'I've only known him for a year and a half,' she said. 'But we've spent an inordinate amount of time together, driving all over the province. Cars are good places to get to know people.'

'Tell me more.' She felt hungry for details.

'He was liked by everyone and adored by the people we visited, but he had few friends. There was Mrs Chalik, a healer, and a man whose name I've forgotten. John? Jack?'

Spike Lyall. Her heart dive-bombed, landing in her stomach, but she kept her face blank. 'Why didn't you go to the funeral?'

'I phoned the Meirings on Wednesday to offer my condolences. Sanet Meiring told me to stay away. She didn't want to see anyone from Balthasar's new life there. That's why I arranged today's memorial – so that we could mourn the man we knew. And so that his children could see how loved he was.'

She remembered the notes. 'Lindiwe, I agree that the children could be in danger. I've also had threats. Someone doesn't want me having anything to do with them.'

Lindiwe gave her a look, one that Zacharius Patel would have described as shrewd. 'He never had the chance to tell me what his suspicions were.'

There was a knock on the door, and Mbali came in, bringing the noise of loud talking with her. She looked surprised and then relieved to see both women together.

'We're tired, Ma Dlamini. The boys are fighting and Grace wants to sleep.'

Lindiwe stood. 'I'll go and ask Sipho to run you home in the combi.'

Mbali hovered near Maggie's chair, and placed her hand on her arm. She glanced at her through her lashes.

'What is it Mbali?'

'Can you come home with us too?'

'I'll come,' she said.

'Will you spend the night?'

She thought of her fresh sheets, her immaculate, fuss-free flat. Then she thought of the two pieces of paper that had fluttered into her life yesterday.

'Yes.'

Within twenty minutes, Sipho had piled the four children and Nkosazana into the yellow AIDS Mission combi and was puttering towards Town Hill. She followed on the Chicken, trailing Sipho on autopilot and thinking about sleep. The storm earlier had cooled the air, but the humidity was back. Sweat gathered under her helmet and dribbled down her back. The atmosphere felt like a helium balloon that was either going to pop or take off into the sky.

As the combi and the Chicken came to rest at a traffic light at the bottom of Commercial Road, something in her rear-view mirror made the hot sweat on her back go cold. It was a black BMW.

17

Saturday, 6pm

Her head whipped around. She saw faces, sunglasses, but no distinct features. Were they after her or the children? Mbali waved to her from the back of the combi as she rifled through her options. It was fifty-fifty, but at least she'd know. When the traffic light turned green, she made her decision. Sipho trundled straight across the intersection, but she took a fierce left. Looking over her shoulder, she saw that the BMW was following her. That was good, but now she would have to lose them.

She opened the Chicken's throttle up Victoria Street. It was usually busy, full of offices and small businesses but on this early Saturday evening, it had emptied to a trickle of cars. A few pedestrians turned their heads at the sound of the Chicken's engine screaming. The BMW kept up easily, its silent progress along the street shark-like, unsleeping, tailing its prey.

In front of her was a red Opel Kadett with two grey heads in the front seats. They crawled along at a genteel pace. She had to get past them, to put some distance between herself and the BMW. She looked at the oncoming lane. There was a truck, thundering down towards Commercial Road and the highway turnoff. She dropped a gear, flashed past the Opel, earning a loud parp from the driver and an even louder bellow from the truck. She slid in front of the Opel just as the truck bore down on her. Now there was one car between her and her pursuers. The Opel's driver shook his fist at Maggie and conferred with his wife, who shook her head. They had no idea, she thought, that behind them was a team of thugs, possibly armed, who were after the ill-behaved motorcyclist in front.

She turned right just as the traffic light went red. The BMW driver ignored the traffic light, roared around the Opel and turned right behind her. Now the sedan was sniffing the Chicken's backside. Her breath caught in her throat.

She needed a plan, and fast.

Her apartment block was coming up on the right. They knew she was close to home and she knew that they knew. What would the BMW driver expect her to do? Buzz the security gate and let herself in, hoping it would clang shut before they could follow her?

That was too dangerous. If they got hold of her behind closed doors, who knew how much damage they could wreak before one of her neighbours woke up to the fact that she was in danger. Instead, she changed down another gear and headed into Taunton Road, scene of yesterday's run. The Chicken's gearbox screamed but she could feel the rear wheel torque clutch the road tighter. That was what she needed.

Her plan was to get to the top of the hill, across the traffic circle and down into Town Bush Road, where she could lose herself in the plantations. She went there nearly every weekend with her off-road club, and the Chicken was built for leaping dongas and skidding around tight corners.

Blood throbbing in her head, she urged the Chicken up the hill. What she would give to have Bond's Z8 right now, she thought, teeth gritted. The titanium plating and armour would be of assistance if these bastards started shooting at her. The missile pad would be good if she needed to shoot back.

Then up ahead, just before the road curved into the ravine, a driver in a battered estate car pulled into the road in front of her and her pursuers. Oblivious to the chase going on behind her, the driver cautiously hugged the road's curves. A black Doberman in the back of the estate lifted his chops and showed her his white fangs.

The BMW nosed her exhaust. They were trying to run Maggie off the road. Her heart flew out of her chest cavity and landed in her mouth. This was not the way she wanted to go. She would die in her sleep, maybe, or have a spectacular heart attack after a lifetime's indulgence, but she didn't want to be strawberry jam on a BMW's fender. The German car's engine roared in her ears. She could taste metal.

She overtook the estate. It was time to get lost. She wasn't going to make the plantations.

She looked at the gulley below. Its clogged bush would provide cover. Pulling the Chicken over to the side of the road, and leaving her flank-down on the ground, she dived into the ravine, feet meeting rocks, arms meeting thorny branches as she plunged into its leafy depths. From nowhere, a root snaked out and tripped her. She tumbled. She felt the ice of pain on her forehead before coming to rest against a tree trunk ten metres into the gulley. She heard her breath, ragged gasps, but it was drowned by mynah birds greeting the night with their noisy lullaby.

On the crest of the hill above her there was silence. Had her pursuers moved on? Headed off to nose the town's underbelly for other prey?

'Can't see the bitch,' came a voice from the top of the gulley. A Zulu voice, speaking English.

'Ja. Probably hit her head on a rock, hey?' The second voice had a strong Afrikaans accent.

Through her pain, she managed a wry smile. The thugs were too concerned about their designer suits to come sniffing around in the ravine for her. She heard their feet thump. She would give them a few minutes to leave before she clambered up the gulley.

Then she heard it: the sound of metal on metal. She put her fist in her mouth to stop herself from screaming. They were wasting the Chicken. It sounded like they were using mallets. She felt every crunch, every jolt, as they pulverized her bike. The carnage seemed to go on for hours. Then she heard doors slam and the BMW's growl as it took off.

She clambered up the embankment to have a look. Her poor bike, her baby, was history. She needed to get it to a garage. Pete Dickson, owner of Alpha Garage, was a member of her off-road club and the only person in town she'd trust with the Chicken.

She found her cell phone in her backpack. She called the AA and then she called Balthasar's house. Nkosazana answered.

'Maggie! Where are you?'

She told her she was stuck in the Taunton Road ravine with a broken bike. 'Could you ask Sipho to come and get me?'

There was a moment's talking on the other side and then Nkosazana said, 'He's on his way.'

'Nkosazana, some men in a BMW, they tried to run me off the road. Please don't tell the children. If they ask, just say my bike broke down.'

Nkosazana clicked her tongue and hung up.

She sat at the side of the road, counting her bruises as darkness fell. The mynah birds stopped their raucous song and crickets and frogs took up the chorus. She let their cheeps and burps fill her head. She didn't want to think about the thugs in the BMW who had tried to kill her, and then killed her bike instead, so she went empty, cold, a long-practised survival mechanism.

The trees in the ravine were looming black by the time Sipho arrived in the combi. He climbed out and took a look at the bike.

'Those guys were serious,' he said. Then he looked at her. 'Aish, sister, that looks nasty.'

'What?' she asked.

'I think you're going to have a black eye tomorrow.' He sat next to her. The warmth of his body was comforting next to hers. She was beginning to shake. Sipho quickly lifted his arm and put it around her.

'What about the cops?' Sipho asked. 'You going to report this?'

She had already chewed on this one. 'No.' A police report and any follow-ups would mean acknowledging to Patel that she had been at the memorial, that she was still sniffing around the Meiring case.

'What about insurance?'

'Don't have any.'

She didn't need to explain to Sipho that all her spare cash went into Christo's hospital care. After his years in state institutions – school, the army, jail – she now chose to pay the crippling fees of a private hospital. Insurance for the Chicken was a luxury she couldn't afford.

They sat in silence until the AA truck turned up.

Maggie could see him behind the steering wheel. It was a big fat Boer-boy, and even worse, a big fat Boer-boy she knew. Claasie Steenkamp. One of the bullies who'd taunted Lynn at school. *Hoer se kind. Hoer se kind.* Lynn's thin, underfed shoulders crumpled at the words. Her mother was too brassy, too blonde, too busty, too lipsticked to fit in with the other tannies. Maybe she was a prostitute, maybe she wasn't, but the point was she looked like one. And as far as the schoolchildren and the other parents were concerned, that was enough.

'Don't listen to them,' Maggie would tell her. 'They know bugger all.'

Pa would whip her for using swear words, but the situation called for them. Lynn gave her a small smile.

Claasie did a double-take when he saw her and Sipho sitting together on the railing, Sipho's arm draped over her shoulder.

'There was a call from a Miss Cloete,' he said, pulling his girth out of the truck's cab. He looked like he wanted to spit.

'That would be me, Claasie.' She stood up and stepped into the light of the truck's beam. 'Magdalena Cloete, from Hoërskool Andries Pretorius.'

'Ja, I remember.' He didn't look as if they were happy memories.

His nose, which he had broken more than once playing rugby, grew red as blood filled the veins.

'My bike's buggered.' She indicated the lifeless form against the tree. 'Can you take it to Alpha Garage?'

'What happened?' asked Claasie. 'You and your boyfriend have a fight?' He cast his eyes towards the combi, which, though battered, showed no signs of recent combat.

'No, some bastards in a BMW tried to run me off the road,' she said through clenched teeth.

'You realise it's Saturday night? Garage'll be closed.' Claasie informed her.

'The owner is a friend of mine. Just leave it there and I'll call him in the morning. No chance anyone's going to steal it in this state.'

Claasie sniffed his disapproval and glanced towards Sipho who was lighting a cigarette. She signed his forms as he lowered the back of the truck and winched the bike onto the truck-bed. Then he clambered in without saying goodbye.

'What an arse,' she said to his retreating back.

'You get arses everywhere,' said Sipho phlegmatically as they climbed into the combi, 'starting with the ones who tried to kill you.'

She shook. She was supposed to be the hardened one, fearless, the one who dodged bullets and chased baddies. But this time they had got to her, sent chills through her body. If she hadn't deflected them would they have gone for the children?

'How are the kids?'

'OK. Mbali is waiting up for you. She wants you to sleep in her room.'

At the house, Mbali rushed to grab her arm as she got out of the combi. Sipho waved them goodbye, and set off home. She realised she didn't know if he had a family or where he lived. A more conscientious journalist than she was right now would have asked.

Nkosazana greeted her with one of her extra-sweet cups of tea and a towel filled with ice. 'We've put a mattress into the girls' room for you,' she said.

They sat once more at the kitchen table, sipping their tea while Maggie pressed the towel to her eye. She told Nkosazana that Lourens Meiring had been to the memorial. 'Why didn't Sanet come?'

'She runs from everything.' Nkosazana answered. 'Even now that she knows the pain of losing a child, she's still running.'

It dawned on her that this woman in front of her had buried all her children. She felt full of words she couldn't say, so she just said, 'It must have been hard for you.'

Nkosazana smiled a gap-toothed smile, but it contained no joy. 'The biggest and hardest thing in my life.'

And now she'd lost another child. Balthasar. 'Lindiwe said Balthasar was getting threats. Do you know anything about them?'

'He told me.' Nkosazana sipped her tea. 'He said there were bad people who didn't like him looking after the AIDS orphans and doing his work. They wanted him to stop.'

Bad people who wanted her to stop too.

She needed to unwind before she slept. 'Do you mind if I watch a bit of TV first?' She wanted to plug into a news channel and be cast away on a different sea, away from threatening letters, murders, memorial services, gruesome rapes of tiny children. Bad news from someone else's country was always weirdly comforting.

Nkosazana led her to the sitting room, once elegant, now down-at-heel. An ancient TV nestled in its black-framed console in a corner of the room like a frog. She settled on a ragged green velvet sofa, watched the news and drifted. After half an hour, Mbali came in, dragging her duvet. She climbed onto the sofa next to her. The child's body was warm and Maggie felt herself beginning to relax.

She woke to the sound of the late news bulletin. Grace had joined them, managing to insinuate herself into the optimal cosy position between the two of them. Her eyes were open, watching the TV, and she had her thumb in her mouth. Maggie put her arm around her and felt the child nestle closer. She fitted like a puzzle piece.

'Hey baby,' Maggie said, stroking her cheek. Her eyes fluttered as if she were going back to sleep. Maggie's attention drifted to the TV again; a bomb in London, the US election, a plane down near the Dominican Republic, the president refusing to state his position on AIDS, a local ANC rally. There was footage of Pietermaritzburg and Dumisane Phiri, surrounded by his lackeys, glad-handing the crowds.

The noise nearly knocked her off the sofa. Grace had gone rigid. She was pointing at the screen, mouth wide open and screaming, a sound that grazed across her skin; incoherent, angry, terrified.

18

Saturday, 10pm

She picked Grace up. The child flailed in her arms, writhed as if she were having a fit. It took all her strength to carry her down the passage to her bedroom. She put her in bed, patted her back and stroked her forehead, but Grace didn't settle. After watching her attempts, Mbali said, 'She likes this', and climbed into bed with her sister. She arranged Grace's head on her chest and wrapped her arms around her. Grace's screams quietened and turned to sobs. The gaps between her sobs grew longer and she slept.

Mbali lay, her sister's head resting on her skinny chest, and looked at Maggie out of big, dark eyes. There was a crack of moonlight through the curtains.

'Does that happen often?' Maggie whispered.

'She screams when she has nightmares.'

'Has she ever screamed at the TV before?'

'Only once. Once when Balthasar was watching the news.'

'Was the same guy on? The one who was on tonight?'

Mbali sighed. The poor kid was exhausted. 'I don't know.' She disentangled her sister's hands from her pyjama top, laid her back on the pillow, pulled the duvet up around herself and closed her eyes.

'Goodnight, Maggie.'

'Goodnight.'

But it wasn't a good night. She lay awake, feeling her swollen left eye closing as she tried to piece things together. Grace had seen Dumisane Phiri and started screaming. Was he her rapist? The more her mind raced, the sleepier she felt, but the harder it was to switch off. She could hear Zacharius Patel's voice in her head, 'For God's sake, Cloete, where's your professional distance? You're not a psychologist or a nurse. Get out of there!'

She was torn. The kids needed help. They needed a champion, and their self-appointed hero, Maggie Cloete, had ridden in on her steel charger to sort things out. But someone hadn't wanted her sticking her nose in, so they had tried to get rid of her and her charger. The problem was that she hated bullies.

She went to the kitchen and rifled through the cupboards for something to drink. She was hoping to find alcohol, but there was nothing, not even an empty whisky bottle in which she could bury her nose in hope of some calming and restorative fumes. She resorted to Ma's remedy: hot milk and honey. She boiled the milk in a scarred saucepan, stirred in some honey and then sat at the kitchen table, still in the clothes she'd worn yesterday, sipping the drink.

It did not have the required effect. The milk only made her nauseous, and it dawned on her that she'd eaten nothing since her fry-up the previous day.

She wanted to get home. She wanted to get into her flat, lock the door, have a furious bath, wash her hair, put on some clean clothes, eat something and then hide there for the rest of the day. She wanted to shut out the world.

Since she had no transport, she would have to wait for daylight and walk. It was too risky to stroll around in the dark, even here in the suburbs. The lush suburban trees hid dark secrets. She knew from years on the crime beat that weird sinister stuff happened here, just as it happened in town, across town or in the townships outside town. As Lindiwe said, crime was a virus. And it could happen to anyone.

What kept her awake at night was when it happened to two-year-olds.

But here she was, sitting in Balthasar Meiring's kitchen at God knows what in the morning, when she really should be in her own bed sleeping and rejuvenating before another hard week of work. She needed to take a step back.

She couldn't do anything until it was light. She squinted with her one good eye at the clock on the ancient stove. Nearly five. Dawn would be starting and she could be on her way soon.

She washed her cup, and headed out of the kitchen. In the bedroom, she looked at the girls. Grace was balled up like a hedgehog, face to the wall. Mbali was splayed, arms and legs out of the duvet now. One of her arms lay across her sister's head. Maggie gently removed it and her eyes flickered open and then closed again. She lay down on her mattress.

The sound of a key in a lock woke her. Judging from the sunlight pouring through the crack in the curtains, it was now morning. Feet padded down the hallway towards whoever was letting themselves in and there was a whispered conversation. Then two sets of feet walked away in the direction of the sickroom.

She looked at Mbali. The child's eyes were open, staring.

'Who's that?' Maggie asked.

'The day-nurse,' she told her.

Balthasar's system, it turned out, was that either he or Nkosazana did the night shift with the sick children, sleeping on a spare bed in their room, while he paid for a day-nurse to free up their time and attention for Mbali and her siblings during the day. This Nkosazana told her as they ate toast and drank tea in the kitchen. Maggie was getting used to Nkosazana's sweet brew.

'How was your night?' she asked.

'Fine,' the old lady said. 'They all slept. Busi needed a nappy-change, but that was all.'

Nkosazana looked exhausted. In her seventies, she had a houseful of children to look after, three of whom were terribly ill. Maggie had no idea how she did the shopping or got the three healthy children to school. Did she have access to a bank account? Could she drive? She wondered at Balthasar's lack of back up plans.

'Did you hear Grace last night?'

'No.'

'She came to lie with me on the sofa and, during the news, she started screaming. I took her straight to bed and Mbali helped her go off to sleep.'

'She is a good child, Mbali.'

'Why did Grace scream at the TV, Nkosazana? Balthasar's friend was on, you know, Dumisane Phiri?'

Nkosazana drooped. It was as if the precious energy that she was holding onto in order to keep going was seeping out of her. 'It happened once before. Balthasar was very upset.'

'Did he do anything?'

She looked at Maggie over the rim of her mug. Her eyes were ringed with tiredness. 'I don't know.'

Nkosazana put her mug down on the table and folded her arms. Maggie had the feeling that she was closing down on her in order to protect her baby. Just a feeling, but sometimes that was all she had to go on.

Mondli and Lungi ran in and asked Maggie to come and watch them play soccer. She was desperate to go home, but said she'd watch for half an hour. They waited as she put her cup and plate in the dishwasher, and then danced up the hallway in front of her. Their limbs were spry and their bodies free of the virus that Grace was fighting off, the one that was slowly killing the three children in the sickroom.

The sitting room led onto a generous covered veranda, which was made of red brick like the house. There were two ancient non-matching sofas, which were torn and stained. She settled into one and it emitted foam discreetly. She watched the boys play while Mbali drew at a nearby table.

'Where's Grace?' Maggie asked.

'She's helping the nurse. She likes to be with the children,' Mbali replied.

'And you? Do you like it?'

She didn't raise her head. 'No I don't. I hate going in there.'

Mbali had cared for her brother Sbu in the months after her mother died. At the age of nine, she had had to be a grown-up, washing, cooking, cleaning and caring for her terminally ill brother. Sbu had died only two weeks after the Sibanyonis had moved in with Balthasar. The sickroom was scored with sadness. She could understand why Mbali avoided it.

The boys had set up their shoes as goal posts and were engaged in a competitive game. Lungi scored a goal and fell to his knees, arms upraised to the heavens, then did a lap of honour around the garden shouting 'Ladumaaaaa' just like the grown-up soccer fans. Mondli waited for the game to start again.

She sighed. It was so peaceful here. The house was set on a hill, with trees screening the view to town below. A magnolia rose above the house like a giant. She shut her eyes and felt a breeze waft through its branches.

'Auntie Claudie!' she heard Mbali shout and saw a tall woman with a sheet of dark hair bend over the child to hug her. Mondli and Lungi deserted their soccer pitch and ran up the three stairs onto the veranda to greet the newcomer. Maggie recognised her from the funeral. It was Claudine, Balthasar's sister and Christabel's twin. She had her mother's height and her father's dark colouring.

She turned to Maggie, one arm around each boy, with a puzzled smile on her face.

'Hello.'

She jumped up. 'Hi, I'm Maggie Cloete.'

'Maggie Cloete? Were you a friend of Balthasar's?' Claudine was trying to place her.

'No, not exactly.'

She took a step closer. 'I know you – you're that journalist who was at the funeral.'

'That's right.'

'What are you doing here? At my brother's house, on a Sunday morning?'

It was a fair question, she had to admit. What the hell was she doing there?

'Mbali called me on Friday, and asked me to meet her.'

'Friday? You've been here since Friday?' Her voice rose to a squeak of disbelief.

'No. I came briefly on Friday. After the memorial service yesterday,

Mbali asked me to come home with them. Then my bike broke down, and I got a lift here and spent the night.'

Claudine put her hands on her hips.

'Well, I'll ask to you to leave then. We are doing fine here without any help, thank you very much.' She flicked her hair over her shoulder, turned her back on Maggie and bent over Mbali and her drawing. The boys returned to their soccer match.

It was the ironic twist of her lips on the word 'help' that got to her. If Balthasar's sister hadn't done that, she would have left like a lamb, just got her backpack and walked out.

'Could I have a word please, in private?' she said to the elaborately turned back.

Claudine sighed and stalked into the sitting room. She followed and shut the French doors behind them.

'I realise this is a bad time for you –' she began.

'Bad time!' Claudine made no effort to suppress her anger. 'It's more than a bad time. My brother has just been murdered, and I come around on a Sunday to visit his family to find the local press has taken up camp in his house. And you're in quite a state too, I might add.' She indicated the black eye.

There was no more time to prevaricate. 'The only reason I am here is because Mbali was scared. I think she is frightened of something.'

'Of course she's scared. She's a child whose whole life has been turned upside down.'

'Grace is scared too.'

'Grace is the victim of an appalling crime. Balthasar was doing what he could to help her.'

'Yes,' she said, anger chilling her voice, 'and now he's gone. Are you going to come and live here and look after them? Because frankly, I don't think Nkosazana's got it in her. And your parents can't look beyond the confines of their religion.'

She had pushed Claudine Meiring too far. She pointed a finger at her. 'I don't need to listen to this. Get the hell out of my brother's house.'

She was crying. Maggie stepped forward, one arm outstretched.

'Just go!'

She walked out of the sitting room into the hallway. The skylight, now on her left, blazed a window of light onto the checked linoleum. She would have liked to have stepped right into that window and disappeared, but she had to keep walking, down the hall to the girls' room to fetch her backpack and helmet. A child's cry from the sickroom combined with the distant voices of the boys in the garden, a concert of voices telling her to go. She let herself out of the kitchen door, the disused scullery to her right. It smelled of dogs and regret.

'Wait!' She turned to see Mbali running after her. 'I've come to let you out,' she said, brandishing a key.

They crunched across the gravel. Mbali unlocked the gate and she walked out.

'I've got something for you.' The child fished in the pocket of her shorts and handed her a much-folded piece of paper. She tucked it into her jeans.

'Bye, Mbali,' she said.

'Bye.' She waved once, then went inside the gates and locked them. Through the iron fence posts, Maggie could see her running to be back inside with Balthasar's sister.

She walked home with concrete bricks on her feet, her skin thin to the world and Grace's scream still in her ears. The rhythm of her feet on the pavement, the sun at its apex in the sky and her sweat took her back to that day in Caluza. She heard the feet drumming on the hot February earth, the rhythms of the *toyi-toyi*, people protesting the Edendale attacks. Above her, she saw the stone arc against the impossibly blue sky. She heard silence as it followed its trajectory and then a crash as it met its target. The window of the police station shattered, the crowd roared and surged forward. In the rush of legs, she heard gunfire crackle. The police were shooting into the crowd.

She eased her head over the top of the car and Ed pulled her back down. 'For God's sake, Maggie! Do you want to die?'

'But they're shooting,' she said, bewildered.

'Of course they're shooting,' Ed replied, pushing the back of his head against the car's buckled door and pulling her into his side. 'This is war.'

She heard gunshots and screaming; wails of terror as people ran, screams of agony as they fell.

'Are they using live bullets?' she asked, face buried in Ed's armpit. She could smell his sweat; his body giving away his fear. The police had been known to use rubber bullets to disperse a crowd, but when they believed themselves to be under attack, they were permitted to use live ammunition.

'Sounds like it,' Ed replied, grim-faced.

Minutes stretched, grew elastic, as she and Ed waited for the bombardment to stop. Silence finally came, punctuated by the cries of the wounded.

'I'm going closer. To get some pics,' Ed muttered and before she could stop him, he was gone. She got onto her knees and watched as he ran, doubled over. He paused behind a house to take photographs of the scene in front of him. There were bodies, some moving, some not, runnels of blood leaking into the dry earth. Between herself and Ed she could see a small huddle of rags. The huddle twitched.

Horror rose in her throat. A child! She watched as the boy tried to raise himself onto his elbows, but sank back down. Putting her head down, she ran to him, body crouched like Ed's against any fresh fire.

She looked down into his eyes, widened with shock. 'Help me, miss.' He stretched an arm up to her. 'My leg.' She looked. Below the knee, his leg was shattered, bone and blood where there should be skin and muscle. Should she move him? Drag him to safety? Try to bandage it?

She ripped strips off her t-shirt and tried to contain the bleeding. Then she remembered.

'I'll be back.' She ran back to the burnt-out car, where she had left her backpack. Tucked inside it was her lightweight navy anorak. Grabbing it, she ran back to the boy and did her best to wrap it around his leg. Then she cradled him in her arms. He looked up at her, his eyes fearful.

She felt the shadow fall across them. She tried not to scream.

'Get up!' barked a voice, an Afrikaans voice.

She looked down at the bleeding boy in her arms. 'But he's injured.'

'He's arrested, that's what he is.' The cop leant down and scooped the boy into his arms. The child screamed silently, mouth open in agony.

'Careful!' She jumped to her feet. 'What are you doing? He's only a child.'

'If you care so much, *meisie*, you can come too. You are under arrest.'

The policeman threw the child in the back of a van, and pushed her in after him. He clanged the door shut. Inside was darkness, encumbered by heat and bodies. She scrabbled on the floor until she found the boy and she cradled him in her arms. His blood had soaked through the anorak she had tied around his leg and flowed freely onto the van floor. Her shorts were soaked.

The police van bounced over the township's dirt road. She predicted they were taking them to the central lock-up in town, which was larger and had more cells than the satellite station in the township.

The boy looked up her. 'Am I dying, Miss?' His voice was a whisper, a ghost's trail of sound.

'No,' she told him. 'You are going to be fine.'

His eyes rolled back in his head and he didn't speak again. She felt the tiniest pulse in his wrist. At the prison, his inert body was taken from her and she was put in a cell, where the apartheid state detained her without trial for eight days.

Foot sore, she pushed open the door to her apartment block and rode the lift up to the sixth floor. There were no grammar bombs on the door to welcome her home. She called Pete on his cell phone and told him that the Chicken was languishing outside Alpha Garage. Pete was amused by the story; he liked to imagine her combating criminals at every turn.

'You are off the map, Maggie,' he said, and promised to see to it as soon as he got into work the next day.

How was she going to pay him? This month was already looking tight, and she knew that Christo's hospital bills were due soon. Pete was a mate; she just had to hope he'd give her some leeway.

In the bathroom before her shower, she unwound Alicia's grubby bandage. The scar was a thin line through Lynn's name.

Hours later, after she had eaten enough pasta for a battalion and watched enough mind-numbing television to completely deaden her brain, she remembered the piece of paper Mbali had given her.

She located her jeans, dug through the pockets and found it. Standing in the bathroom, she opened the folds. It was a drawing. Mbali's style was childlike for a person of eleven, but then she had to remember that she had had sporadic schooling until Balthasar rescued her. To the right was a structure, and inside it, four people, one lying as if sick or dead on a bed. One of the standing people was tall and the other two were short. An arrow pointed at the structure, with the words 'my house.' On the left of the picture was another structure, also decorated with an arrow, saying 'naybor's house'. Inside that house, there were two people, one very tall and one very small. They were lying down, the big on top of the small one. And the big one had a large, unmistakably erect penis.

19

Monday, 8.30am

She walked to work, wearing sunglasses to hide her black eye. She was not looking forward to the questions in the newsroom. En route she stopped at a tearoom to buy a large bar of hazelnut milk chocolate. This was the way to get Alicia Labuschagne's attention. Not only was she ruler of the *Gazette*'s memory bank, but her blue rinse hid an impressive brain. Alicia might be just the person to answer her morning's questions. She took the stairs all the way up to Alicia's lair, steeling herself for stories of sleeplessness.

Alicia wore robes of the finest burnt sienna. She was drinking tea from a bone-china cup decorated with cherubs.

'What happened to your eye?' she asked.

'I went off-roading and fell off my bike,' she said, the lie sliding off her tongue. It was half-true anyway, so her Calvinist forefathers needn't roil too furiously in their graves. 'How did you sleep last night?'

While she listened to the woeful tale of lorries crashing their gears on the highway, she slid the chocolate out of her backpack and onto Alicia's desktop. Talking, elaborating, the archivist eased it into a pocket in her voluminous dress. Then she fixed her with an eagle eye. 'How can I help you today, chum?'

'What do you know about Dumisame Phiri?'

'Bag of tricks, there, bag of tricks.' Alicia tapped the side of her head. She was enjoying her power. 'Sly bastard, that's all I can say.'

'Come on Alicia, I know he's a lawyer turned ANC hotshot, but what else do we have on him?'

She sat and rubbed her chin. 'Now let me see. Precious first-born of a traditional chief and putative Edendale warlord, sent to Goodwill

College where he got an A Matric and played first team rugby, then law school at Wits. Returned to practise law in the oh-so-posh firm Scott, Cavendish and Orr, joined the ANC and now making a career in politics.'

She thought of Phiri sitting with Victor Ndlela at the steakhouse. 'Any crime links?'

Alicia looked at her sharply. 'There's no actual link between Phiri and any nefarious dealings.'

'Can I look at the files?'

'Phiri senior or junior?'

'Both.'

Alicia clacked off on a pair of preposterously high orange sandals into the archives. She rested her head on her arms. She didn't know where any of this was going. Let me find the answers, she asked the god of journalists, if not wrapped neatly in a pot of gold under a rainbow, then at least somewhere in Alicia's files.

'Here you go.' Alicia slapped down four files and she went to sit at a desk. 'What you have to remember is that Dumi Phiri doesn't have it easy. His father's the old guard and he's trying a new way of doing things – more open, more consultative. It's a tightrope, one which Phiri senior didn't have to bother about.'

Maggie struggled to find sympathy with Dumisane Phiri. He was a posh private school kid like the rest of Balthasar's friends. Granted, he'd had to span a big leap between the townships and Goodwill College, but that experience had stood him in good stead, had made him a politician. The sight of whom made Grace Sibanyoni scream.

She checked her watch. It was time to go.

'I'll be back,' she told Alicia. 'Would you mind doing some more research for me? I'm trying to establish a connection between the Phiris and Lucky Bean Msomi.' Alicia's eyebrows flirted with her blue hairline and she began paging through the files. That was good. The chocolate had done its trick. Alicia was on her side.

On the way to the newsroom, she stopped in the bathroom, where Sally-Anne stepped out of a cubicle. She had a large cold sore on her top lip.

'That looks nasty,' Maggie said.

'Thanks for your concern, Maggie.' There was no sugar substitute in the arts reporter's voice today. 'Although it looks like I should be more worried about you.'

She took stock in the well-lit bathroom mirror. Her right eye was nearly closed and surrounded by blue-black bruising.

'What happened?' Sally-Anne asked.

'Came off my bike,' she shrugged. 'It's nothing.'

By the time she followed Sally-Anne into the newsroom a couple of minutes later, the story had already spread. The subs cheered 'Fight! Fight!' as she passed their desks.

Zacharius Patel's eyes prickled her back. She turned and saw that he was not alone. Next to him stood a young man carrying a new and shiny leather briefcase. Next to the young man stood the editor, Jabulani Nzimande. He was a large person, both of girth and personality. Genial and friendly, he was popular as a speaker on the cocktail circuit. As a boss, he was hands-off, leaving Patel to conduct the daily business of running a paper. Nzimande preferred to hobnob with local celebrities, from actors to company directors to politicians, and spend languid hours in his office composing his daily editorial.

'Maggie, I want to –' the editor stopped as she neared. 'Hau, girl, what happened to your face?'

'Had an accident with my bike this weekend,' she said. 'Off-roading in the plantations.'

'Oho,' said Nzimande. She knew he was nonplussed by her hobby. Nzimande preferred females to enjoy womanly pursuits like having their nails done and drinking cappuccinos with their girlfriends at the mall. 'Well let me introduce you. This is Jabu Sibiya.' He clapped the young man on the shoulder. 'Our latest cub reporter. Jabu, this is Magdalena Cloete, the *Gazette*'s crime reporter.'

'Pleased to meet you.' The cub put his hand out and she shook it. He wore expensive-looking chinos and a crisp blue and white striped shirt. His shoes were shiny and he'd tucked a pair of tortoiseshell sunglasses into his shirt pocket. He looked as if he'd be more comfortable working at a lifestyle magazine than on a dusty provincial paper. Perhaps he saw the *Gazette* as a stepping-stone to better things.

'Jabu's going to be shadowing you, Maggie,' said the editor. 'I expect you to look after him and keep him out of trouble.'

'Excellent,' she said, thinking otherwise. Jabu's eyes were flickering nervously over her face. They rested on her black eye.

'My sister will kill you if you don't,' Nzimande laughed heartily. 'Now that I'm in *loco parentis* for her son.'

Great. Not only did she have a cub shadowing her every move, but he was the boss's nephew.

This was going to make following up on the Meiring story a lot more complicated. Patel looked wry; perhaps he thought the chances of Jabu Junior getting into trouble with Maggie around were fairly high.

Nzimande wandered back to his office to contemplate his editorial, while Patel and the reporters gathered for conference.

Her cell buzzed.

'It's Sven Schloegel.' The unfamiliar voice stopped her in her tracks. The AIDS cure doctor. She motioned for Jabu, who was taking the concept of shadowing seriously, to head into the room without her.

'Yes?'

'I need to talk to you, Miss Cloete. About Balthasar Meiring.'

'When do you want to meet?'

'World's View. 2pm. Come alone.'

'What about the trial?'

'It's postponed for the week. My lawyer's sick.'

She went into conference and offered Patel the tantalising news that she was meeting with the accused in the AIDS fraud case. She neglected to mention that he wanted to talk about Meiring.

'Are you going to take Jabu?'

The cub reporter straightened in his chair.

'No,' she said. 'I'll find him a nice case at the Mag Court and park him there.' Jabu slumped, but his shirt remained perfectly uncreased.

'Remember, Maggie, no reference to court evidence.' Patel steepled his hands and the avuncular gesture grated her. She knew that she could only discuss the case obliquely.

'Do you want any back-up?'

'No, the guy will only talk if I'm on my own.'

'Take your cell phone. Have the police on speed-dial. Don't get into his car.'

'Thanks, Zacharius,' she said, rolling her eyes. Aslan caught her expression across the table and grinned. After conference he came to shake his floppy fringe in her direction. 'I'm a bit worried, Maggie. World's View is a lonely spot.'

He was right. Pietermaritzburg town centre was set at the bottom of a bowl of hills like a fruit salad. World's View was the north-western lip of the bowl. However, there was no way she was going to jeopardise her chance to talk to Schloegel by taking someone with her.

'It's not that lonely. Lots of people out with their dogs,' she reassured Aslan, 'and all those suburban ladies speed-walking.'

She ran some weekends with a running club, and they'd come across large gangs of fifty-something women hitting the road. Joggers didn't chat; at least not after they'd run up the vertiginous side of the bowl, and they could always hear the walkers coming. If talking burned calories, they'd be thin.

'Sounds like a set-up to me,' Aslan muttered.

'If it is, I'll cope,' she told him.

At court she found Jabu a juicy armed robbery case to cover.

'Bow to the judge as you go into court, sit at the front and write everything down. Afterwards introduce yourself to the prosecutor, tell her you're from the *Gazette* and ask to see the case sheet,' Maggie told him. 'Use it to check spellings and the exact charge. I'll be back in a few hours.'

Jabu nodded and got his notebook out ready to write. She headed out of the courts and walked through Freedom Square, where street vendors sold fake designer trainers, cheap clothes and wooden statues. Christmas beetles zithered in the jacaranda trees. As summer reached its height, their calls became increasingly desperate. It was not a harmonious sound. A Rasta band with artful dreads played Bob Marley to a small crowd, some of whom dutifully bopped. The tang of dagga sweetened the air, fighting with the smell of curry floating from the open door of a cafe.

She went in and bought a bunny chow – a hollowed-out half-loaf filled with chicken curry – and ate it as she walked. When she got to East Street, she decided to walk past the AIDS Mission, but before she got there, she spotted a spaza shop with a hand-painted sign that she recognised: 'Godfrey's Trading'.

She walked into the shop. It was dark after the blinding sunshine outside and her eyes took a couple of seconds to adjust. She heard East Coast Radio blaring from a set on the window-sill and then a familiar voice said, 'Can I help you, Miss?' Godfrey Mhkize rested his hands palm-down on the counter of his shop.

'Hi Godfrey,' she said approaching him. 'It's me, Maggie Cloete.'

'*Ehe.*' Yes. 'The one from the *Gazette*. I remember you.'

'Can I get a cooldrink?' She thought it would be polite to buy something before pressing the guy for information. He swung around to a fridge behind him and passed her a cold can. She paid, opened the can and swigged.

'Any word on the HIV House murder?' she asked.

He pursed his lips. 'Not really, Miss.'

'Call me Maggie.'

'Sure, Maggie.' He leant his elbows back on the counter. 'This is a poor area. Lots of people with nothing. You could understand a thief robbing someone, getting scared and then getting stupid with a gun.'

No new insights there. Disappointed, she handed Mhkize a business card. 'If you hear anything else, give me a call.' He agreed and she passed him the empty can, which he tossed in a bin. On her way out of the shop a flapping notice caught her eye and she put her hand out to it.

'*If you or a family member have taken Schloegel's Herbals as an AIDS cure, a class action lawsuit may affect your rights. This notice has been authorised by the High Court of South Africa. This is not a solicitation by a lawyer.*'

The notice waffled on about whose rights could be affected and why. She turned back to Godfrey. 'Who brought this in?'

He waved his hand. 'Some court person, I think.'

'When?'

''Bout two weeks ago.'

'Do you know anyone who takes these vitamins?' She imbued the last word with as much scorn as she could muster.

'Sure I do. There are a lot of sick people out there. They all want to be well again.'

'It's fake medicine, Godfrey,' she said. 'It doesn't cure anything. Someone's making a lot of money out of this.'

He shrugged. 'We're all trying to make our way.'

'By taking these, people waste money they could spend on real drugs. Ones that work.'

He gave a placatory grin. 'Okay, Maggie, okay.' Maybe she was being a little shrill.

'Tell everyone who comes in here not to take them.'

'Sharp, Maggie,' Godfrey reached out a hand and turned up the radio. He didn't want to hear her lecture any more.

She took Aslan out for lunch at the Mooi Boy, where she picked the seeds off her salad roll and took a few half-hearted bites. Aslan demolished a baked potato.

'How's the newbie?'

'Seems fine.' Jabu had indicated that the case would continue into the afternoon and that he was happy to sit it out alone. Independence. That was a quality she liked in a rookie. She was not the world's best hand-holder.

After lunch, they strolled through the lanes back towards the *Gazette*. They passed The Lock and Key and she waved to the proprietor, Dennis Mukerjee, but he didn't see her. Before landing her gig as maestro photocopier at the *Gazette*, she had worked for Dennis. Trade had been slow and Dennis had used the quiet hours to teach her some of the tricks of his trade. Judging by all the people in the shop, business had picked up since then.

Down Theatre Lane they spied Spike Lyall, juggling balls flying through the air. Did the man have nothing else to do but lie in wait for innocent reporters on their way back to the office?

She pulled Aslan down a side street. He looked at her curiously and she smiled back, trying to look inscrutable.

'Don't think your Nefertiti look works on me, Magdalena Cloete.'

She didn't respond, but Aslan continued. 'An engaged woman is always more agreeable than a disengaged. You and your temper might bear that in mind.'

She punched his arm, and he rubbed the sore spot, making a moue of pain. As they walked into the *Gazette*'s office, he said, 'Seriously, Maggie, you should think about that Lyall boy. He looks like a keeper.'

That was rich coming from Pietermaritzburg's most outrageous flirt. She chose to ignore it.

20

Monday, 13.40pm

She let Patel know she was leaving and went downstairs to requisition a car. On the stairs, she passed Ed and Sally-Anne whispering and it didn't look like pillow talk. Her cold sore had grown bigger. Ed's arms were folded across his body and he looked broody.

Ernie hooked a key onto his long baby fingernail and flicked it in her direction. He returned to salivating over his magazine as she signed her name, the time and the car's registration in the logbook.

'Don't damage this one, Cloete,' he called as she walked across the lot, and cackled as she showed him the finger. She had a reputation at the *Gazette* for abusing cars. In December she'd given chase to two bank robbers and driven the green Toyota into a ditch. That was what she called commitment, and what Patel called an entanglement. The kind she was supposed to avoid.

With ten minutes to spare, she decided to drive through town rather than take the highway. The city was alive with shoppers and informal traders and she had to keep her wits about her for pedestrians launching themselves onto the road with little respect for the colour of the traffic lights. She weaved around a taxi with the phrase 'Burning Spear' emblazoned on its side in lurid red and orange. The Spear had stopped to disgorge its passengers in front of a supermarket instead of at the taxi rank one hundred metres down the road.

The traffic lights at the bottom of Commercial Road were free of BMW-shaped sharks. She touched her eye and then regretted it. It stung.

She headed up Old Howick Road, wishing the Toyota had the same pull as the Chicken, but the car clung to the slow lane, coughing as she changed down. She drove up the hill in second and finally changed to third gear as the road flattened out near Wylie Park. This was where she had met with Mbali on Friday night and Maggie wondered how she was. She hoped Claudine was doing her duty by Balthasar's kids. She was now taking a step back with regard to their personal welfare. She had flunked the basic journalist's test this weekend – keep your distance – and from now on she was going to make sure that she stuck to the rules.

Except when it came to the animal who raped Grace. There were no rules for the likes of him.

She wove up the side of the fruit bowl. The suburbs here were not leafy, they were plush. Every piece of manicured grass was a uniform green and no plants dared to grow where they weren't wanted. She rolled down her window and smelled roses and high-powered lawnmowers.

This was where the judges lived, the surgeons and the wealthy businessmen who pulled the strings in town. Their driveways were so long, you couldn't see the houses from the road, but the elaborate gates signalled the kind of wealth that lived within. The road flattened slightly and she pointed the Toyota left towards World's View.

The car park was empty when she arrived. Her watch said it was five minutes to two.

She parked and walked to the paved open area that formed World's View. She pressed her stomach against the railing and looked out across the city. With all the summer rainfall, it was a profusion of green all the way out to the horizon, where she could see emKhambathini, KwaZulu-Natal's very own Table Mountain. It was flat, like the one in Cape Town, but since it only overlooked the Valley of a Thousand Hills, rural villages and goatherds, instead of Africa's hippest city, it didn't get the same attention. It was a modest mountain, not a show-off.

She turned, and saw that a car had arrived.

She watched Schloegel climb out of his silver Golf and walk towards her. He was in casual instead of court clothes – long shorts that came below his knee and a short-sleeved shirt, stiffly ironed. On his feet he wore sandals with camel-coloured socks that reached mid-calf.

They shook hands and sat on the broad stone semicircle of the monument. A giant aloe behind them shook its fleshy leaves, but the brief breeze wasn't cooling, and there was no shade from the early afternoon sun. Schloegel's pate glistened. She examined his face as he lit a cigarette. The skin around his eyes was pouchy and he had the beginnings of a double chin. She guessed he was in his early fifties.

Schloegel exhaled a puff of smoke that floated out over town.

'Why are you here?' His German accent was strong.

She frowned. 'You asked me to meet you.'

'It's because I mentioned Meiring, isn't it? If I'd said I wanted to talk about the weather or the court case, you wouldn't have come.'

'I don't cover the weather. But I cover crime and Meiring was killed last week. Anything that sheds light on the case is of interest.'

He ground the cigarette out on the stones between them, then removed a chamois from his pocket, took off his angular spectacles and proceeded to polish them. 'What if I told you that Meiring was bankrolling the case against me? That he had an interest in seeing my business go under? Would you still think he was a bleeding-heart liberal then?'

'There's no such thing as bankrolling a class action suit. If there wasn't clear evidence against you, they wouldn't be prosecuting.'

'Who brought those five families together? They're rural, uneducated people. How would they know about a class action suit, unless some stinking AIDS activists told them?'

'Sorry, Mr Schloegel –'

'Doktor Schloegel, in actual fact.'

She ignored this. He could shove his fancy title.

'Balthasar Meiring helped people with AIDS and their families. If he'd helped arrange the case, it would have been part of the gamut of his duties at HIV House. Nothing unusual there.'

She felt the prickle of puzzle pieces slotting together, but she kept her poker face, the one Claasie Steenkamp and the other school bullies had taught her to use.

'It might have a bearing on his death.' Schloegel looked into the middle distance and waited for that to have an effect on her. 'Nice up here, isn't it? Never been here before. *Sehr schön.*'

'So you know why I'm here. Why are you here?' Fair question, she thought. Why would a class action accused want to have private chats with a court reporter?

'You think Balthasar Meiring behaved ethically? Let me tell you, he didn't. He confronted my salespeople and publicly bad-mouthed my product.' Schloegel's chest swelled with the injustice.

'Maybe he believed that you misled people with your claims about an AIDS cure.'

'No, it wasn't that. Not at all. *Nein.*' He was getting excited. 'It's because he wanted to put his own product on the market, his lotion.' Schloegel pronounced the word with distaste.

'Why would his lotion compete with your cure? They were two different products.'

'I have a whole range of products!' Schloegel stood up, waved his arms for the benefit of the aloe. 'I have creams too. Scientifically designed ones that I have brought all the way from Germany.' The more excited he became, the stronger his accent grew.

The afternoon sun was shining off his spectacles. Something made her look up, journalist's instinct perhaps, and in the car park there it was. A sleek, black BMW, hovering next to her *Gazette* rust bucket and Schloegel's Golf as if it were about to guzzle them both. She felt sweat prickle her scalp.

Schloegel looked up, as two men got out of the car and leant against its bodywork. One had scars slashed down his cheeks. The other, a white guy, was huge. It was the brick shithouse.

'It's Msomi's people,' she told him.

If Schloegel had been sweating before, he was a waterfall now. He glanced at the side of the fruit bowl as if envisaging plunging off the edge.

'Look,' she said. 'I'm a journalist. I'm immune. They can't do anything to harm me. We're just going to walk to our cars, get in and drive away.'

From recent experience she knew the opposite was true, but she picked up her backpack and began the walk. Schloegel tailed her. As they walked, she rifled around for her cell phone, cursing herself for not keeping it glued in her hand. Schloegel was walking so slowly that she felt as if she were towing him. With each step, her legs grew heavier. Where was that bloody phone?

With a sudden shriek Schloegel bolted left across a patch of open grass that led towards the forest. Brick Shithouse ran after him and felled him with a rugby tackle. Tribal Scars pointed something at Maggie. A small but very nasty-looking pistol.

'Get your hand out of your bag.' He walked the last few paces between them and grabbed her arm. She twisted her body away from him. Towering over the German, Brick Shithouse dragged him back towards the car.

'In,' said Scars, pointing the gun at her head. 'I mean it.'

She had no doubt. He ripped the backpack from her and threw it towards a stand of casarina trees, then he pushed her into the car, tied her hands and forced her down into the foot well between the seats. She could hear bumping that she presumed was Schloegel being put into the boot. Both front doors slammed and the car took off. Neither of the goons had bothered to put on their seat-belts.

Her heart pounded. Her blood sounded a tattoo in her ears. If these were the same thugs as the ones who'd followed her on Saturday and totalled the Chicken, then she knew that they were serious. Deadly serious. She wrestled the rope around her wrists, but it did not give. She could hear banging and shouts from the boot. The louder the shouts grew, the more her blood thumped. Her breath came in short bursts. She was dizzy, suffocating.

'Shit!' said the driver, and the car suddenly swung right and began to skid. The brakes squealed and she could feel the driver bearing down on the steering wheel as if trying to get it under control again. She was flung about like a rag doll and her head hit the car door.

Then everything went blank.

She came to and found herself lying on a prickly surface. Maybe grass? A spherical object blocked out the sun and something tickled her face. There was a new throbbing in there, one to accompany the pain in her eye.

'Bloody hell, Maggie, you're in a state,' Ed said.

21

Monday, 2.49pm

'Where are they?' she said, trying to sit up. The sky looked fuzzy so she lay down again.

'Keep still, Maggie man,' said Ed, who to her puzzlement was topless. Putting her hand up to her head, she felt ragged strips of fabric. He'd ripped up his t-shirt and bandaged her head.

'I need to get to Schloegel,' she muttered. Ed put one hand on her chest to stop her from getting up. It was like being held down by a bear. 'He's in the boot of that car.'

'Schloegel's gone,' he said, 'you've got a head-wound and were knocked unconscious. You're bloody well going to lie still until the ambulance comes.'

'I don't need a fucking ambulance,' she said, scrabbling at the bear-paw. 'I need to call the cops.'

He sighed. 'If you promise to lie still and wait for the ambulance, I'll let you use my cell phone.'

Ed was bigger than her and stronger. There was no fighting him, so she lay back. He lifted his paw and she began to breathe more easily.

'What the hell are you doing here?' The time for social niceties had gone.

'Patel told me to follow you and take photographs. As back-up, you know, in case things got nasty. I was parked here when I saw the Beemer drive past towards World's View. I started pulling out when I heard the screaming.'

She didn't remember any screaming. Had she screamed?

'I pulled out into the road and blocked their path. They swerved to avoid me and hit that road barrier.'

She managed to pull herself up to one elbow and look across the road. There were skid marks across the grass and the road barrier was dented. As she lay back down, she looked to her right. Staring at her through the poles of a green metal fence were a woman in a powder blue maid's uniform, a small boy and a dog. All three looked equally surprised to see a woman with a bandaged head lying on the verge outside their house talking to a topless man. Maggie waved and the little boy waved back.

'I went over. The passenger looked as if he'd had a bad knock and the driver was stunned, so I opened the door and got you out. I carried you across the road and bandaged your head. While I was doing that, the driver must have come to, because he drove off.'

'Registration number?'

'KZN 36-something.'

She rolled her eyes.

'Sorry, Maggie, but I was worried about you. I didn't have time to take down a reg number.' She couldn't blame Ed; she'd also not managed to note down a registration number when the BMW had chased her on Saturday. It was not something you did when you were running for your life.

'Give me the phone,' she said.

Officer Mathonsi's number was burned into her brain. She answered promptly and listened while Maggie briefed her.

'You know I can't do anything unless you come in and lay charges?'

She considered this. She could lay charges. But even if they caught the guys, they would deny their connection with Lucky Bean Msomi. Lackeys were loyal that way. She was worried about Sven Schloegel. He'd been rugby-tackled by a human tank, thrown into the boot of a car, chucked around inside and was now on his way to being beaten, tortured or killed.

'If we get a missing person with Schloegel's description, I'll come back to you,' Mathonsi promised.

She could hear the ambulance making its way up Old Howick Road. She remembered her backpack and asked Ed to fetch it. He jogged off.

Her head was pounding and her body felt weak, but a new energy was coursing through her. It was her old friend, anger, icing her body so that her teeth chattered. She had been Sven Schloegel's protection. With her there, the Msomi goons might not have threatened his life. Ed's foolhardy rescue attempt might be the death of him.

The ambulance guys arrived and despite her protestations, piled her in. 'Listen, Miss, you were knocked out and you've got a bad head wound there. We've got to get you in for observation.'

She muttered imprecations, but there was nothing she could do. Ed handed her the backpack and gave her a cheerful wave as they closed the doors. He thought he'd done her a favour, but he'd actually ripped a story right out of her hands. She'd had the chance to get to grips with Msomi's relationship with Schloegel, and any connection to Balthasar, and Ed had erased that by acting the hero. Bloody idiot.

The hospital processed her with surprising speed and put her to rest in a general ward. She didn't fight the sleep that came.

She woke a few hours later to find Zacharius Patel sitting at her bedside. He leaned forward in his chair so that both elbows were resting on the bed, so close she could smell his spearmint chewing gum.

'That was some attention-seeking behaviour, Cloete,' he said through his teeth. 'Kidnapped, in a car accident and knocked out all in the space of a minute. That's possibly the zenith of your achievements so far.'

She stared at him. A little compassion would have been nice. 'All thanks to Ed Bromfield's heroics.'

'Ed Bromfield saved your life,' said Patel, sitting up straight and crossing his arms.

'No. Bromfield caused an accident that could have killed me. And who knows what it did to Sven Schloegel who was in the boot of that car.' She only realised that she was shouting when other visitors sitting around other beds turned their heads to stare.

'The police will do their best to retrieve Schloegel,' said Patel.

'It's probably too late,' she muttered. The tide of anger washed away, replaced by a fresh wave of exhaustion. She didn't have the story and she had compromised Schloegel's life. She didn't particularly like the slimy doctor, but she didn't want his death on her hands.

'Here's the deal, Cloete,' said Patel, standing up. 'When they release you from hospital tomorrow, you are taking an enforced week's sick leave. You are going to stay at home, take a rest, and when you come back, we'll review things.'

He put up his hand as she started to protest. 'I don't want to see you back in the office till Monday.'

With a blithe wave, he left. She stewed for a while and then slept.

The doctors released her next morning and, like a ministering angel, Aslan came to drive her home. He folded her into his car as if she were a delicate piece of china. At the flat, he tucked her into bed and then unpacked a range of ready-meals.

'I have the most perfect refreshments from Woolworths,' he called from the kitchen. 'And some of Ma's lamb curry.'

She had refused the flabby chicken, cold cauliflower cheese and toothpaste-coloured jelly that had constituted hospital supper the night before and had only had a yogurt from her breakfast tray. Her stomach groaned.

Without asking, Aslan popped one of his mother's Tupperwares into the microwave and when the machine pinged, served her the meal on a tray.

'Nice place you have here,' he said, perching on the end of her bed as she forked her way through the curry. 'I had no idea you were such a neat freak.'

She kept her home pristine and empty. The last person who'd been here was Ed. She remembered lying safe and warm in those bear-arms. Then she erased the fantasy because Ed was the idiot who'd stuffed up her story.

'Big talk about you in the office today,' said Aslan. 'Some people are saying you're suspended.'

She chewed and shook her head. 'Bullshit. Patel's just given me some sick leave.'

'And you are actually going to take it?'

She raised her eyebrows and Aslan laughed. 'Don't get out of bed yet, honey,' he patted her shoulder. 'I'll keep the fort while you're gone. And I'll keep an eye on little Jabu for you.'

He winked and left. She knew Jabu would be very happy in Aslan's capable hands. He'd probably be writing front-page stories by the end of the week.

Dammit! She needed to be in the office. There was so much to do. She rummaged through her backpack for her phone and dialled Alicia's extension. If she had to have enforced bed rest the least she could do was some research.

The hazelnut chocolate was still top of mind, and after muttering some concerns about Maggie's health, Alicia agreed to lend her the Phiri files. Within the hour, a *Gazette* messenger buzzed her doorbell from downstairs and delivered them. She creaked to the door, took them and settled down on the sofa to read.

A knock woke her. It was her neighbour, Grant, with a bouquet of hideous flowers – orange roses and baby's breath. She loathed cut flowers. They reminded her of her mother, who'd liked nothing more than a big florist's bundle of orange, red and yellow blooms.

Grant frowned, but there was a twinkle of amusement in his eyes. 'How are you? Been fighting with the bad boys again?'

'How did you know?' she asked, trying to look grateful for the ugly flowers.

'You're headlines,' he said, waving that morning's *Gazette*. Emblazoned across the front page was the strap '*Gazette* reporter kidnapped, rescued'. Underneath, like a barehanded slap, was Jabu's by-line and a blurry photograph taken from the back of two figures sitting on the World's View flagstone steps. She had made the front page. The difference was that this time she was the news.

'Can I borrow this?' she waved the *Gazette*.

'Sure,' he said. 'Let me know if you need anything, darling.'

She dumped the flowers on the coffee table and read the article standing up. Damn the lot of them for turning her into fodder.

She'd been fodder once before and she hadn't liked it.

Bert Townsend had warned her. 'Maggie, you have the potential to be a bloody good journalist. But if you want to keep this job, you must remain neutral. You are there to report the story, not become it.'

He slapped that day's *Gazette* down on the conference table.

She picked it up. The front page shouted 'Journalist released from detention'.

'I've risked a lot getting you this position,' Bert peered at her. He was no good without his glasses, which he was always mislaying. 'You have no training and no relative experience, apart from making photocopies in HR. Until recently you struggled to write a sentence without a grammatical error in it. One false step, my girl, and the boss will have you out.'

Later Michael de Vries, the *Gazette*'s terrifyingly chilly Oxford-educated editor, called her into his office. He sat in the large leather chair behind the desk, but did not invite her to sit. Then he underscored Bert's threat with one of his own.

'That was your last mistake on this paper, Miss Cloete. I will not have the *Gazette*'s reputation as a fair organ of record sullied by rookies who can't stop their bleeding hearts from leaking out onto the pavements of this city. I expect nothing less than professional behaviour from you. One more step out of line, and I will have to ask you to leave.'

Her throbbing head kept her awake and in the very early morning she got up to slug a painkiller. In the bright light of the bathroom, she realised it was a week since Balthasar had been killed. Since then she'd had her bike smashed up, received two threatening letters, been thrown out of Balthasar's house, been kidnapped at gunpoint and shafted by her closest work colleagues. Michael de Vries would have looked down his imperious nose at the chaos of her life.

Her present bosses wanted to control which stories she wrote and they didn't want her straying from their agenda. However, they were more than happy to make her the news.

She wasn't going to let them control her. She would wrest control back. To do so, she'd go back to where it all began.

22

Tuesday

Gazette *reporter kidnapped, rescued*
  By Jabu Sibiye, Junior Crime Reporter, and Aslan Chetty
  In a hostage drama that unfolded in the quiet World's View suburb yesterday, two unidentified armed men kidnapped Gazette *crime reporter Magdalena Cloete and a man she was interviewing. Both were tied up*

and thrown into a car. Cloete had a lucky escape when Gazette chief photographer Ed Bromfield, charged with recording the encounter, managed to stop the kidnappers and rescue her.

'I heard screaming and a car taking off,' said Bromfield after the dramatic incident. 'I pulled out into the road to block their path and they swerved to avoid me and crashed against the road barrier. Both men were briefly stunned and I took the chance to rescue Maggie.'

Bromfield, 34, who has worked at the Gazette for 14 years and received a national award for his coverage of the KwaZulu-Natal civil war in the late Eighties, said he was not able to rescue the second hostage.

'I carried Maggie across the road. She was unconscious and bleeding heavily from the head. While I was trying to stem the blood, the kidnappers must have come to, because I heard the car taking off.'

Bromfield said he did not see the other hostage in the back of the car where Cloete was lying. 'I presume he was in the boot.'

After reviving Cloete, Bromfield called an ambulance, which took the injured reporter to Shepstone's Hospital. Hospital spokesperson Cheryl Manuel said yesterday that Cloete's head-wound had been superficial and that she was spending a night in hospital under observation.

Eyewitness Khonzile Zondi said she 'heard noises' at the neighbouring World's View site at about 2.30pm while she was inside the house, looking after her employer's young son. 'I went out to see what was going on, and I saw a black car driving off the road into the bush on the other side. Then I saw a man run across the road and drag a woman out of the car. A bit later the black car drove off.'

Zondi said the woman was bleeding and that she had been frightened that she was dead.

Gazette news editor Zacharius Patel said that the entire staff was grateful to Bromfield for his courage in the line of duty. 'We salute his bravery. Without his actions, the outcome could have been far worse. We wish Miss Cloete a speedy recovery.'

Patel said that while he knew the identity of the kidnapped man, the Gazette reserved its right to protect the identity of its sources. 'We are sure that the police will act speedily to resolve this.'

Senior police liaison officer Officer Thandi Mathonsi confirmed that police had received a report of the incident but that no charges had been laid. Police had a description of the kidnapped man and would match it with any missing persons reports they received. They were also looking for the two kidnappers matching Bromfield's description.

The journalist bitch had got a big slap. Maybe now she'd stop hanging around the house, now that someone had showed her her place. Give him a chance to do what he was here to do.

The new South Africa had created these new women, who thought they were so clever. Respect. That's what had gone. The respect of a woman for her man, the respect of a child for its father, the respect of the youth for the adult.

That man had not respected his right to preserve what was his. He'd not listened.

He didn't like it when people didn't listen.

The little girl hadn't listened. She played his games wrong, not played the way he wanted to. Or she wanted to play her baby games, which were so boring. One day he told her she was stupid and after that she didn't play with him anymore. She went back to the other children, and he went back to trailing behind them after school, feet kicking up dust.

He watched the children come back from school and let themselves in at the gate.

For a while he slept. A noise at the gate woke him and he felt his shirt sticky against the car seat. It was the oldest child. He did not know how old she was, maybe ten or eleven, but she was growing into a woman.

He watched her unlock the gate with a key she wore on a cord around her neck, opened it, stepped through and then shut it. Without looking over her shoulder, she locked the gate and walked down the road. She picked a dandelion growing amongst the weeds outside the house and blew the seeds off as she walked.

A piece of paper from the nurse curled in his hand. A life sentence, no better than death at the stake or stoning. The nurse looked at him from behind glasses, her eyes tired from the many, many deaths. She told him he had it. It was his duty to tell his wife. It burnt his soul, this responsibility to tell his wife. It was admitting failure, a weakness. The crack in the dam.

He walked toward his house, dry earth beneath his feet. In winter the world became yellow, dusty, so dry that one cigarette butt could light up a hillside. They burnt fire breaks across the land, black scars to stop the fires leaping.

Inside, his wife was preparing supper. He got a beer, looked at her, shoved the piece of paper into his pocket. Her mouth opened and shut, but he did not reply.

Now, he felt his heart swell and fill with ice. He couldn't switch off the pictures in his head. It was a house full of women. He'd gone there the first time when his wife was away and had sex with a woman with a flabby lip. When he pushed into her, he looked at her fat mouth, bruised and swollen. The next time she wasn't there, so he chose another one. Sex with each of them, one by one, fast and dry. If he knew now which one of them had given him the disease, he would put a knife in her.

He put his hand on the key, ready to start the car.

23

Wednesday, 8am

She removed the bandage from her head and examined her wound. It was negligible. That little scrape had pulled her off the job. Her black eye looked far worse. It was purple now with green around the edges. She had a scorching shower and, rejecting Aslan's chicken korma as traitor's food, ate a handful of stale Romany Creams instead. They tasted of dust.

She stepped out of the block and hailed a passing taxi, one called 'Warrior'. She told the driver where she was going, and clambered in. The passengers made space for her in the middle row, and in a fog of Zulu breakfast radio, she allowed herself to be transported to HIV House. It was going to be another scorcher of a day, but the breezes blowing in through the taxi window held only the promise of humidity.

Lindiwe let her in. After ushering Maggie to her office, she went off to boil the kettle and make them each a cup of coffee. She sat there, in the august presence of Nelson and Gandhi, and wondered how she was going to make sense of the mess. She had nothing to go on but her instinct. Could she trust it? One thing was for sure, she couldn't trust anyone at the *Gazette*.

Handing her a mug of coffee, Lindiwe sat behind her desk. She regarded Maggie with her calm eyes and said she'd read about her in the *Gazette*. Reining in temptation to rage against her colleagues, Maggie gave her a run-down of what had happened.

'What's the background to this court case?' she asked. 'Sounds like you and Balthasar were pretty involved.'

Lindiwe explained that she and Balthasar kept encountering be-reaved families whose loved ones had taken Schloegel's Herbals and then died. Balthasar consulted a lawyer to see if there was scope for a class action suit to stop the doctor. 'He thought there was scope, so we started to find families who were prepared to testify.'

'Not many,' she guessed.

'No. When it comes to AIDS, people are shy about putting themselves on the line. It's such a deep shame that people feel, one we are working to counteract.'

She thought of Balthasar's family who wanted nothing to do with him and his orphans. She remembered her humiliating ejection from Balthasar's house.

'He clearly trusted one member of his family,' she said. 'Claudine.'

'Yes,' said Lindiwe, 'but Claudine lives in Durban and has a full-time job. Not much use on day-to-day basis.'

'Mbali gave me this.' She handed Lindiwe the drawing.

The older woman glanced at it and sucked air in through her teeth. 'I'm going out to Shongweni this morning to do some home visits. You could come with me, see the Sibanyoni's house and maybe ask some questions. Do you drive?'

Lindiwe had to rely on HIV House staff like Sipho, and Balthasar before he'd been killed, to get her to and from the outlying villages. She didn't drive and sometimes had to take taxis but they were expensive for long journeys and not always reliable. They drank their coffee and, leaving a message for Sipho with a staff member who had just turned up for work, they left the office.

The older woman handed her the keys to the yellow combi and climbed into the passenger seat. As she turned the keys in the ignition, Lindiwe said, 'We'll be making a stop in Northdale first.'

'Visiting someone?'

'No,' she said, looking over her right shoulder as they reversed into the busy Loop Street traffic. 'Collecting something.'

When they arrived at the turquoise house with the Buddha in the garden, it became clear what they were collecting: Balthasar's ointment. To be delivered to the sick and ailing.

Mrs Chalik opened the door. She gestured for them to hurry into the house and looked into the street as if expecting to see someone behind them. She was not her serene self. A storm had disturbed her tranquil waters. There were two suitcases in the hallway.

'This is Maggie Cloete,' Lindiwe began.

'I know Miss Cloete,' Mrs Chalik interrupted. 'We need to be quick, please. My husband is about to drive me to my sister's in Stanger.'

'Going on holiday?' she asked. Mrs Chalik gave her a steely look. Her aura was all scratchy.

'I'm leaving. Just for a while,' she said, leading them down the hall-way to the dining room where there was a pile of cardboard boxes on the table. Filled with the lotion, she presumed. She ran her finger along the dust-free surface of the table.

'What's wrong, Mrs Chalik?' Lindiwe looked concerned.

'I've had visitors.' She sat in one of her dining-room chairs. 'Un-pleasant ones.'

'Tell me,' Maggie said, dropping into a chair opposite Mrs Chalik. Her neck prickled; she knew all about unpleasant visitors.

Mrs Chalik pulled a well-used tissue out of her sari's undershirt and patted her eyes. 'It was late yesterday afternoon. Ravesh had just got home from work and we were having a cup of mint tea. There was a knock on the door and two men were there. They asked to come in. I didn't want to let them in the house, but they were so neat, so well-dressed. Ravesh thought it would be okay.'

She buried her head in her hands, gave a loud sniff.

'They said I had to stop making the cream. That there were powerful people who didn't want me to make my cream anymore.'

Maggie felt the ice of anger in her veins.

'Then Ravesh told them they had no right to say so, so they, they –'

She gave in to a flurry of crying. Maggie looked at Lindiwe, who stood behind a chair, both hands clamped on its back. Her knuckles shone.

'They punched him. In the stomach. My poor Ravesh.' Fresh sobs. When she had recovered, she said, 'And they took my herbs. All my special herbs that I use to make the lotion. To stop me, they said.'

'Mrs Chalik,' Maggie said gently. 'Could you describe the men?'

'Both in suits. One white one, very large. A black man, smaller,' Mrs Chalik said.

'Did the black guy have tribal scars?'

The healer looked at her, eyes veiled with tears, and nodded. Then she whispered, 'They called me a witch. They told me I knew what happened to witches and if I reported them to the police, they'd come for me.'

Maggie also knew what happened to witches. There had been a spate of witch burnings north of Johannesburg that had made headlines across the country. She understood why the healer wanted to flee.

'I've made up as much lotion as I can,' Mrs Chalik told Lindiwe. 'While we're away Ravesh will do the numbers. I don't know if I'll be able to carry on with it, though.'

Lindiwe told her she understood. The three women carried the boxes of Balthasar's cream to the combi.

'Before I go,' the healer turned to Maggie, 'I have a message for you. It's from Balthasar.'

Her inner sceptic wriggled, but she restrained it. 'What?'

'He thanks you for keeping the children safe. He says the path you are on is the right one.'

Experience had taught her that losing her objectivity didn't pay. Just one week ago she was a neutral observer, but now she'd voluntarily become a participant in the drama of Balthasar's life. To top it all, he was now sending her messages from beyond the veil. Zacharius Patel would raise one very cynical eyebrow if he heard.

Pushing away her own mixed feelings about Mrs Chalik's pronouncement, she climbed into the driver's seat. The healer held Lindiwe's hand through the passenger window. 'I'll come in for a meeting when I'm back. Let you know what my decision is.'

'So tell me about this lotion,' Maggie said as she and Lindiwe swung onto the N3 heading east to Shongweni. The highway was thick with lorries but she kept an eye on the rearview mirror in case a black BMW popped up behind them.

Lindiwe explained that while in London, Balthasar had experimented with combinations of herbs to soothe his ailing lover's Kaposi's. He'd brought his secret recipe home and had Mrs Chalik make it up.

'Is it expensive?'

'She makes it for us at cost,' Lindiwe replied. 'As a favour to Balthasar.'

'And now he's gone, could the price go up?'

'No, there's a contract and she's agreed to continue supplying us at this rate. Of course, we are going to have to find a way to fund it, now that Balthasar's not here to pay for it anymore.'

'Would you just stop? Your money could be better spent elsewhere.'

Lindiwe folded her hands in her lap. She blew out her cheeks and exhaled.

'The people we work with are dying, Maggie. Until we have universal availability of antiretrovirals, they will keep dying. We help their families to provide palliative care and a big part of the care is Balthasar's balm. It brings relief. These are people who are frantic with discomfort.'

'How does it differ from what Schloegel offered?' Mrs Chalik had already answered this question, but she wanted to see how Lindiwe would handle it.

The woman hugged her giant handbag. 'There is a vast difference between offering people release from their discomfort and fraudulently claiming to cure their disease. We are talking about villagers, Maggie, people who can't read a newspaper, let alone the small print on a bottle of vitamins. Schloegel was exploiting their ignorance and Balthasar wanted to stop that.'

She tightened her hands around the steering wheel. 'A world of difference,' Mrs Chalik had said. But had Balthasar's attempt to stop Schloegel through legal channels brought about his death? She lost herself in the scenery. As the hills rolled down towards the sea, everything became lush. The peppermint green of sugar-cane fields joined with banana plants and palm trees in a verdant, prolific mix. In the distance she caught a glimpse of the sea, innocently blue.

Like the blue of Youvashnee Chalik's sari. 'What did Mrs Chalik say about numbers?' Lindiwe didn't flinch. She was used to her questions.

'The Chaliks and I are thinking of putting the lotion on the market to pay production costs. We would keep supplying it free to the needy, but we'd like to sell it to pharmacies for general use and then feed the profits back into our AIDS work.'

Now she could see why Sven Schloegel was getting hot under the collar. Not only did Balthasar initiate legal action against him, but his balm would compete with his products on an open market. Would that be enough to make him send Msomi's Rottweilers after Youvashnee Chalik?

She made a mental note to call Thandi Mathonsi later to ask if Schloegel had turned up. She would also call Errol Mdunge's office to see if they had anything to report about their client.

Soon the highway split and, after consultation with Lindiwe, she took the old Durban road. Most of the traffic flowed away from them onto the new highway and towards the sea. They took an exit, and drove for ten minutes past stables where expensive horses shook their tails and their indulged, glossy rear-ends and chomped on opulent swaths of green grass. This was some of the most expensive real estate in the province, and it took armies of workers to tame the land and complex irrigation networks to keep these fields so green. Just so that people like Sally-Anne Shepherd and Balthasar's other so-called friends could spend their weekends pottering around on horseback or playing golf.

She caught a last whiff of horse manure before pointing the combi left and down the steep sides of a valley, the one made of a thousand hills. The pockmarked tarmac road snaked down the hill and she kept her foot firmly on the brake pedal. The road was not only used by cars, but it was a thoroughfare for people and animals too, and she didn't need to run over anyone or anything. A woman carrying a bundle of sticks on her head waved to them from the side of the road and they waved back.

Lindiwe sighed. 'They say it's a thousand people a day.'

'Who are infected?'

'No, a thousand a day who die. One person per day for each of these beautiful hills. It's a valley of death.' No wonder the cemeteries were full and gangsters like Lucky Bean Msomi were making bucketsful of cash.

'Are you angry?' Maggie asked.

'Sometimes angry,' she said, turning to gaze out of the window 'Sometimes desperately sad. Sometimes both.'

They bounced along a rutted road that led them downhill towards a small river, a tributary of the Umsinduzi that wound its way through the province. Before the river, the tarmac petered out and turned to dirt. The combi crossed the river on a low stone bridge before climbing up towards the Sibanyoni's village. Aloes greeted them with their burnished red flowers and a skinny dog trotted along the road next to them, ears lifted hopefully. Fat white clouds bounced in the blue sky, roofs glistened on the nearby hills while the distant ones faded to violet. It was a perfect day. Maggie sighed.

The village was a mixture of traditional thatched rondavels and small square brick houses with tin roofs. In between the houses were bare patches of red earth worn to dust by the feet of people and animals, and cultivated areas where mealies and other vegetables grew. These were surrounded by wire to protect them from marauding goats that wandered free like pickpockets in a crowd.

Lindiwe told her to park near a modern house painted white with a horizontal black stripe at knee-level. A woman walked out of the house to greet them. It was Brenda Tshabalala, who she'd met on Saturday at Balthasar's memorial.

Her personal jury was still out on Brenda. Mbali didn't like her. Why had she not managed to protect the Sibanyoni children from the predators in their village or badger the police to follow up on Grace's rape?

The two women greeted each other formally and then Brenda set about telling Lindiwe something in great detail, rubbing her shoulders as she did so. Lindiwe nodded in sympathy.

Brenda finished her litany of woes and, now speaking English, offered the women tea. Maggie was about to refuse, when Lindiwe said she would love a cup. Maggie reminded herself that she was on leave and had no deadline pressure. She could afford to sit in the sun on this beautiful day, have a cup of tea and listen to the women talk. Brenda brought three white plastic chairs out of her house and settled Lindiwe and her in them before bringing them hot, sweet tea in blue enamel mugs.

Her head throbbed, but it was pleasant sitting there in the morning sunshine. She watched a goat stick its head through the barbed wire fence around Brenda's mealie patch, garotting itself as it tried to eat a plant. Brenda shouted, and it looked at her in mild surprise and wandered off to try its luck somewhere else.

'Brenda and I are going to start our visits,' said Lindiwe, gathering their cups and handing them to Brenda. 'Do you want to come with us? On the way we can show you the Sibanyoni's house.'

Brenda put the mugs inside and came out wearing a big sunhat. 'So hot today,' she said. Maggie agreed that it was getting very hot.

They picked their way between the houses, where washing hung on fences and small children played with homemade toys. This had been the Sibanyoni's gentle, rural life – until their father contracted the disease and their lives changed forever. As they walked, curious heads popped round doors and peered out of windows. Lindiwe was a familiar face in the village, but Maggie was a stranger and her presence had been noted.

Their first stop was at *Gogo* Chamane's. Lindiwe told her that when *Gogo*'s daughter Buselaphi discovered she was HIV positive, she'd accused her husband of giving her the disease. Denying it, he had beaten her up, thrown her out of their home and refused her access to their three children. She was now living with her mother, who, in her old age, had become her daughter's carer.

Gogo came to the door of her house, and greeted the three women in the traditional Zulu manner – forearms crossed and both palms to the sky, revealing no hidden weapons or desire to betray them. She was very old and wrinkled like a walnut and when she smiled there were gaps where teeth had once been.

Inside they found Buselaphi lying on a mattress on the floor. The inside of the one-room house was hot because *Gogo* cooked all their meals on a fire in the centre of the room.

Brenda bustled around, giving *Gogo* instructions. Maggie didn't like the way she didn't modulate her voice in deference to the sick woman. While *Gogo* listened to Brenda, Maggie watched Lindiwe. Now there was a bedside manner. She went to sit with Buselaphi, greeted her and sat next to her, reaching across the brown tartan blanket to take her tiny hand. They murmured to each other. Lindiwe delved into her handbag and retrieved a jar of Balthasar's lotion, which she opened and gently rubbed into Buselaphi's hands and arms.

When they left, Lindiwe said, 'It is terrible. She is going down fast. She can't eat anymore.'

'Is she on ARVs?' she asked.

'No, Maggie,' Lindiwe said. 'There's no money for them.'

She felt a wash of shame. Of course not.

Brenda, not wasting time on sentimentality, looked at her list. 'The next house is here,' she said, pointing up the hill.

She didn't want to watch another thick-skinned performance from Brenda, so she asked for directions to the Sibanyoni house.

'Over there,' Brenda pointed. 'The one with the blue roof.'

Roof was an optimistic description of what she found at the Sibanyoni's. What had once been a two-room brick house like Brenda's was now a shell. All the windows had been removed, there were no doors left and there were only about twenty tiles left. She walked through the gaping doorway and staggered right out again. Someone had been using the house as a public toilet and it reeked of faeces.

Breathing through her mouth and keeping her eyes peeled, she went back in. There were rectangular marks on the dusty, shit-strewn floor that indicated where the furniture had once stood, but every piece of furniture, every amenity had been removed. The house had been taken apart.

She walked round the outside and peered through the window of the back room. This would have been the bedroom. There were curtain runners, but no curtains and the rest of the room was empty, except for a few tattered pictures from magazines still clinging to the brick walls. She squinted and saw that the pictures were mostly of soccer stars, and thought of the two little soccer fans now living in Balthasar's house. She remembered Mondli's patient waiting while Lungi completed his victory laps round the garden. Had the twosome been playing ball when Grace was raped?

Behind the house was a tangle of weeds that could have once been a vegetable patch. She could see there had been a fence, but that had also been stolen. On the other side of it was a house. She pulled out Mbali's picture, and checked that this was the house where Mbali indicated that Grace had been raped. There were no signs of life from the house, so she sat in the shade of the Sibanyoni's walls to watch and wait.

She sat on her haunches with her back against the wall and watched the sky through her one good eye. Across the valley, from where she and Lindiwe had driven that morning, thunderclouds were building. They were still pale grey, but Maggie and Lindiwe would have to leave before the rain came: getting across a rushing river in the battered HIV House combi would be a challenge.

Geckos chased each other up and down the walls. A small barefoot child walked down to the river with a load of washing on her head. Three chickens stopped near her for a brief peck.

After about forty minutes, a woman came out of the house opposite and stared at her. Maggie waved, but the woman ignored the gesture. Not very neighbourly. She threw a bucket of water into her mealie patch and, with a final stare over her shoulder, went back inside. She did not look welcoming, but then Maggie was a journalist and used to bluffing her way into people's houses.

She knocked on the door and the woman answered swiftly.

'*Sawubona*,' she said in her rudimentary Zulu. '*Wena unjani?*'

'*Ngiyaphila, wena unjani?*' The woman followed the rituals of politeness, but there was no warmth in her voice. Her eyes slid sideways to the Sibanyoni house.

'I am a visitor here. Can I have a drink of water? It is so hot.' Her Zulu ran out and she fanned herself to make her message clear.

The woman looked at her for a long time. Then she clicked her tongue and went inside.

Maggie waited, noticing that from the neighbour's house she could see directly into the Sibanyoni's bedroom. The woman came out and handed her some water in a mug. She watched as Maggie drank and Maggie watched her back. She had young arms but a lined, bitter face.

'What happened to that house there?' She pointed at the Sibanyoni's place.

'They left,' she said. 'The parents died, then the children went away.'

'What happened to their stuff?'

The woman turned the corners of her mouth further down. 'People are poor.'

'Are you alone?'

She nodded, took the mug and closed herself inside her house. Maggie took that as an indication that their conversation was over.

24

Wednesday, 1pm

She walked back to Brenda Tshabalala's house. The two women were not back from their visits, so she found some shade behind the house and went to sit in it, propped against the wall. The thunderclouds across the valley were building into towers above the thousand hills and the air puddled around her in stagnant pools. Her head wound pulsed and she rubbed it.

How here, in this village where everybody watched everybody and where people all knew each other's business, could a two-year-old disappear into someone's house, be raped and then left for dead at the side of the river, without anybody noticing? She found it hard to understand.

In the sky, a falcon spiralled high on the thermals, at one with its surroundings. She felt alone, a speck in the eye of a giant. It was all too big for her, too much. She should forget it all; go home, rest, return to work next week and cover crime. Just report it, as Patel would say. This attempt to go beyond, to investigate, to be compassionate, had brought her nothing. She was not one step closer to finding out who'd killed Balthasar and who'd raped Grace.

She heard voices approaching; Lindiwe's deep voice and Brenda's shriller one. As they neared the house, she got up and walked around to see them, her head light and her legs weak.

'I need a cooldrink, preferably one with bubbles and a lot of sugar,' she said. 'Is there a spaza shop here?'

'There is,' said Brenda. 'My husband drinks there at night. It's up the hill.' She pointed to a ragged path leading behind the village.

'Can I buy everyone some lunch?' Maggie asked.

The two women agreed and moved on to their next visit. She began the uphill hike to the shop. The air was heavy. It was so damn hot. She hoped there would be a slight breeze higher up the hill, but there wasn't. The plastic packets that attached themselves to the fences around people's vegetable patches did not flap. Neither did the washing hung out to dry.

The spaza shop was a long, low building. She climbed three concrete steps and stood in the shade of the veranda to catch her breath. She was a runner and fit, but the combination of the heat and the hill had made her pant. She walked into the darkness of the shop. It was cooler there. When her eyes adjusted, she saw that it was lined with almost-empty shelves. It was a shop with no merchandise. Empty. Just the way she felt.

'*Sawubona*,' came a voice. In the dark recess of the shop, an old man sitting in one of those ubiquitous white plastic chairs cracked his knees to stand and serve her.

'*Sawubona baba*,' she said, using the greeting of respect.

'How are you?' he asked. It was the Zulu tradition to engage in niceties before getting down to business.

'I am fine, how are you?'

He nodded his head and leant his elbows on the counter. Then he said in English, 'I am bad. My bones, they are sore.'

'That is not good.'

He shook his head in agreement. 'What is your business in the village?'

'I am with Lindiwe Dlamini. From the AIDS Mission.'

'She is a good woman. She is helping the sick, and there are too, too many of them.'

He was right. There were far too many of them.

Looking around the empty shop, she tried to locate something that might make a lunch. She decided on a loaf of bread, a tin of pilchards, a packet of salt and vinegar chips and three cool-drinks. In a murky corner, she saw a box of marshmallow fish. Her favourites. She asked him for ten.

He creaked around the shelves, gathering her purchases and put them tenderly into a plastic packet.

She paid and he passed her the change. 'The young people are all dead. The only ones left are the children and the old people. What will happen to this village?'

'I don't know,' she told him.

'The government, they have forgotten us,' he said, heading back to his plastic chair in the corner.

As she walked towards the door, he called, 'Big rain today. Don't cross the river.'

To the right of the door, pinned with two blue tacks, hung another class action notice. She pointed to it. 'Who put this here?'

'The AIDS man,' he told her. 'The tall white one.'

As she stepped onto the veranda, the first drop of rain nailed the ground. The thunderclouds had burst hours earlier than they should, turning the sky purple and black. Trees lashed each other and torrents of brown water ran down the hill as she hurtled back to Brenda's house, bent double against the rain. A dog ran across her path, its tail tucked between its legs. Goats huddled under trees and women rushed out of their houses to pull in their washing.

She and Lindiwe had to get across the bridge and out of the valley before it became impassable. Sodden, she opened the door to Brenda's house, where the two women sat waiting for her. 'Are we leaving?'

Lindiwe smiled. 'Not right now. Let's wait it out.'

Brenda fetched a towel and Maggie did her best to dry herself off. The rain hammered on the tin roof as the women ate their lunch. Maggie chewed on a stale marshmallow fish. 'If this doesn't stop soon, we aren't going to make it out of the valley.'

Then she remembered her earlier encounter, the heavily-lined face and unfriendly manner.

'Brenda, who's the woman who lives next door to the Sibanyoni house?'

'That is Mrs Ndlela,' Brenda said, her face closed.

Seven different chills went down her spine, but she kept her face blank. 'Has she always lived alone?'

'No, she has a husband. He used to be there.'

'Why did he leave?'

'Don't know. They say he is a cousin of Dumisane Phiri's. He went to work for him.'

'When was that?'

'I don't know.' Brenda wasn't enjoying the line of questioning. She got up and threw their cans in the bin.

'Was it around the time the Sibanyoni children left?'

Brenda put her hands on her big hips. 'I am feeling very tired. This rain is making me sleepy. I will lie down for a bit.'

She disappeared into the other room.

'Lindiwe, I know who raped Grace,' she leant forward, blood throbbing in her ears.

'When she had that screaming fit at Balthasar's house, Dumisane Phiri was on TV. Vincent Ndlela was standing behind him. I thought Grace was screaming at Phiri, but it was Ndlela she was seeing. And now I find out he was her neighbour.'

Lindiwe's honest eyes were sad. 'The community here has closed ranks. They don't want trouble.'

In her job, Maggie had seen the worst that people do, but Vincent Ndlela was the lowest, the most despicable.

'I want to have Ndlela put away.'

Lindiwe clicked her tongue and stared out of the window at the rain. It thrashed the ground, making streams and rivers that flowed downhill to join the brown waters that were now coursing across the bridge. She spoke in a dreamy voice.

'In my village, a neighbour's child was once washed away by a flash flood. My granny said she was taken in a wave of brown water and washed into the sea. At night, I would lie awake and think of that poor child. The boys said that when it flooded, the sharks would swim up the river. I always avoided the river until long after the floods were over. I didn't want to meet any of those big fish.'

Maggie asked her where she was from.

'A village on the South Coast. If I climbed the highest hill near my grandparents' home, I could see the sea.' She looked at Maggie. 'But I never went to the beach.'

Maggie's family hadn't gone in for holidays. Ma didn't like being away from her kitchen, and Pa didn't like being away from his workshop, where he tooled leather Bible covers. Her hobby was cooking and eating her output and his was cutting animal skin with sharp knives. She and Christo spent hot summers playing on the street, watching the tarmac melt and poking it with sticks.

'I spent my time near the river,' Lindiwe continued. 'Our grannies would give us a pile of clothes and some washing powder and send us down to the river to wash. It was hard work, but then we would arrange the clothes on the rocks to dry, find a rock for ourselves and lie in the sun like lizards.'

'Where was your mother?'

Lindiwe shook her head. Her eyes were sharp.

'Sorry, Lindiwe. I get it.' Lindiwe's mother, like most young black women, would have lived away from her parents and children, working in a white family's home.

'So you lived with your grandparents?'

'*Ehe.*' Yes. Lindiwe folded her arms around her body, as if folding a memory into herself. 'My mother went to work in Pietermaritzburg, so I had to stay with them. I only saw her twice a year.'

Maggie breathed out. 'That must have been hard.'

'Yes. I missed her. All the other mothers worked in Durban, or Port Shepstone, so they could come home more often. The boys in the village told me that my mother stayed away because the tokoloshe had turned her into an evil spirit that would come to curse her ancestral home.'

'So you never lived with her?'

'No, she always had live-in jobs. When I was twelve she brought me to Pietermaritzburg. I lived with a woman called Auntie and my mother paid her rent so that I could live there. Then I saw her more often – she was allowed Sundays off and when she wasn't with her boyfriend, then she would come and see me.'

'That was better for you.'

'Yes, it was.' Lindiwe gave a half-smile.

'Now the children are still being raised by the grandparents,' Maggie said, 'Except it's because their parents have died.'

'The orphan generation.'

She thought of the seven orphans at Balthasar's house. 'It makes me so angry.'

'I'm angry too.'

'What about your son, Lindiwe? What happened with him?'

Lindiwe's hand covered her heart, an automatic gesture. 'Peter. Such a beautiful boy. So stubborn. Wouldn't test, refused. Just got weaker and weaker.' She looked at Maggie through a curtain of tears. 'I still find it hard to talk about it.'

Her pulse quickened. She grabbed the older woman's hand. 'Lindiwe, we still have a chance to do something about Grace Sibanyoni. Help me. We know something happened in the Ndlela house. We know he's working with Phiri. Together we can find out more.'

She needed Lindiwe's help. She wanted to get onto her knees. If she was going to break all the rules of journalistic objectivity and neutrality, then she needed help, someone from within the community who could help her break through the wall of silence.

'Please, Lindiwe.'

Before they could talk any more, Brenda came out of the bedroom looking ruffled. She looked out of the window at the rain. 'It's not stopping. You will be spending the night in the village tonight.'

25

Thursday, 6am

She woke dislocated. Not only was she not in her bed, there was someone sleeping next to her and, for the first time in many hours, she couldn't hear the sound of rain. At home she was woken each morning by the lawyers in her block revving their sports-cars up the drive to the road in their urgency to get to their offices and start billing their clients. The hooting of taxis backed them up. Here, in the valley, she could hear a chorus of birdsong, a thousand different voices singing different tunes.

She heard doves murmur and the call of the Piet-my-vrou, the red-chested cuckoo. Towards the end of summer, having laid their single eggs in other birds' nests, these migrants flew back to central Africa, job done, leaving someone else to raise their hatchlings. A case of lazy parenting.

The body on the bed next to her was Lindiwe. Brenda had given them a supper of pap and beans. Brenda's husband hoovered up his meal and said little, discomforted by the visitors. Afterwards, he stomped out into the rain to the spaza shop and Brenda went to bed. Lindiwe and Maggie cleared up and climbed onto the mattresses Brenda had put out for them, still in their clothes.

'Please Maggie, I don't want to talk about the Sibanyonis or Balthasar tonight,' Lindiwe told her, staring up at the ceiling of Brenda's house as they lay side by side with the rain drumming tattoos on the tin above them.

'Okay,' she said.

'But I do want to tell you about Peter. He was my beautiful boy, my first-born. When he was little he would grab my cheeks and stare into my eyes. Then he'd wriggle till I put him down and go off to play.

'He was such a naughty boy,' Lindiwe laughed softly to herself. 'So naughty! He never listened to me. He would play soccer with his friends until long after dark and come back sweaty and smiling. I should have disciplined him but I couldn't. He'd tell a joke to make me laugh or put his arms around me and I'd forget to give him the discipline he needed.'

She sighed. 'It was easy when he was a little boy, but when he grew bigger he was harder to manage. His father was gone, you know, to Joburg, and I was all alone with the three children.'

'Where did his father go?'

'To the mines.'

'Did he come back?'

'Once.' Lindiwe's voice was throaty and quiet in the dark. 'Then we got the message that there'd been an explosion. Forty-four miners died that day.'

She sucked in her breath and let it out slowly. 'I'm sorry, Lindiwe.'

'It was hard for me and the children,' the older woman said, 'but hardest for Peter. He needed a man. He was too slippery for me, too quick and clever.

'On the day that Mandela was released, the headmaster, Mr Ndlovu, hired a TV for us all to watch. We were floating, we couldn't believe it was happening. The schoolchildren and the teachers all filled up the hall, jostling to get close to the TV screen. My two youngest sat like good children on the floor, but Peter, he came in with his friends. He was wearing an ANC t-shirt. I didn't know where he got it from. They all stood against the back wall of the hall, arms folded. He didn't come to me or look at me. I realised, in the happiness of that day, that my son was leaving me.'

Maggie turned on her side to face Lindiwe, who remained on her back facing the ceiling.

'There was a huge party in Edendale that night. It went on till midnight, in some places longer. I had to drag my two youngest home.'

She remembered the sullen silence in her home on that February day; the morose predictions of terror and blood and white people being driven into the sea. Ma made an emergency visit to Checkers to stockpile tinned food and other non-perishables.

'The party went on much longer for Peter. He came home five days later. I knew then that my son was not a boy anymore. He was a man and I could no longer tell him what to do.'

Lindiwe let out a long breath. 'He stopped going to school. He would stay at home for a while, and then he would go away again, for weeks. I worried about him all the time, I wished I had the power to keep him at home, to control him. But I knew I couldn't.

'Then he started coming home with money. Wearing good clothes and giving me money for things. The routes had opened up into Africa and he started working as a truck-driver. He was proud of his job and we were so proud of him. His little brother and sister would ask him questions about Africa and he would sit late into the night, telling us stories.'

Lindiwe sighed. Maggie shifted position. Her body wanted sleep, but she was caught in the web of Lindiwe's tale.

'Once he was gone for six months. When he came back, he was thin, so thin. He still had the good clothes and the money, but he didn't look well. It was so strange, because he had always been such a healthy child. He kept getting sick. Every time someone else had a cold, Peter would get it and so much worse than anyone else. He kept getting thinner. I begged him to go to the doctor, but he refused.'

Her head throbbed and she could feel the pap and beans swirling in her stomach. Her heart pulsed. She recognised the story.

'I had heard about AIDS and I started to read more. I went to the library in town and tried to find books about it, but there was no information. I found a few things in the magazines and I read about the symptoms – the lowered immune system, the way the body weakens and feeds upon itself. I realised that Peter had AIDS.

'My beautiful boy had a death sentence. He refused to test and even if he had, the drugs were so expensive then, I couldn't afford them on my teacher's salary. He just got weaker and weaker. He needed constant nursing, so I stopped working. My other son left school and got a job to support us. We had very little at that time.

'He was 45 kilograms when he died. Like a leaf, he was so thin. I would try to feed him, but in the end everything just came up.'

'I'm sorry, Lindiwe.' Maggie reached out to touch her hand.

Lindiwe let her take it for a minute. Then she pulled her hand away.

'I blame myself. If I had been tougher on him when he was young maybe he would have learnt to control himself. I can forgive him everything, but I can't forgive myself.'

There was silence, a heaviness in the air.

'I will help you, Maggie,' Lindiwe said. 'And I'll do it because of Peter.'

'Thank you,' she whispered in the dark. From a nearby house, she heard the three-part harmony of a hymn. A church meeting. The sound was comforting in the dark. Then she turned over and went to sleep.

Now the rain had stopped. She got up and looked out of the window. Puddles glistened in the morning light: everything looked clean, even the goats. She put on her shoes and stepped outside to check the river. She could see where the flash flood had covered the grass – it was flattened and littered with branches. The water itself flowed ankle-deep across the bridge. Refusing Brenda's offer of tea, they left.

'Please would you stop in Edendale on the way back,' Lindiwe asked. 'I need to freshen up.'

The township was morning quiet. She had been here many times before, covering protest marches against the old government and joyous rallies when the new government swept in. Now the scene was peaceful, domestic; a couple of old men sat in a front-yard smoking in the sun, women clattered in kitchens and hung out their washing. Young men clustered around the entrance to a spaza shop, listening to Arthur Mafokate on the radio.

Lindiwe invited her to come inside, but she chose to sit and brood in the car instead. She rolled down the window, put her arm on the door and watched two guys, one with dreads and the other wearing a China Sam's t-shirt, kick a soccer ball to each other. To bring in Ndlela she needed evidence of a crime. She needed evidence that Balthasar's death was somehow linked to Schloegel's Herbals and Lucky Bean Msomi. How was she going to produce this? It was all such a bloody mess.

'Yes, it is a bloody mess,' said Lindiwe, climbing into the combi. Maggie hadn't realised she'd been talking aloud. 'And I suggest we start with Dumisane Phiri.'

'Oh, he's just going to fob us off with smooth answers,' she said, refusing to be comforted.

'Perhaps. But we don't only learn from what people say, we learn from what they don't say.'

She felt very slightly calmed by the older woman's wisdom. 'Okay, how do you propose we approach him?'

'He loves to talk to the Press, doesn't he? Set up a joint interview with him and me, to talk about AIDS, and let's see where it takes us.'

26

Thursday, 11am

She dropped Lindiwe and the combi off at HIV House, and took a taxi home, desperate for a bath, a meal and a rest. As she buzzed the gate to her apartment block open, a slickly-dressed man with a hard face stepped in front of her. Vincent Ndlela. Now that she had Lindiwe Dlamini on her side, the god of journalists was playing into her hands.

Before she had time to ask him any of the myriad questions buzzing in her mind, Ndlela had grabbed her right arm and pulled her through the gate, which began to close behind them. He twisted her arm behind her back and pushed her face against the wall, her right cheek grazed by the rough, red bricks.

'You don't listen, do you?' He spoke through his teeth, his face close to hers. She couldn't focus on him, because her left eye was still slightly swollen, but she could smell his last cigarette and the undertow of something else, a chemical tang.

'Get off me,' she struggled, but he pushed her arm further up her back. She grunted in pain.

'You think you're so clever. Miss clever-clever journalist. But you don't listen.'

'To what?'

'I have sent you messages to keep away from the children. Just like I sent Meiring messages. Just like him, you don't listen to me.'

The pain spread from her arm into her shoulder. 'Did you kill him?'

Ndlela leaned in closer, his body resting against hers. He panted, his breath coming in ragged bursts, and Maggie felt that he was battling to maintain his strength. 'Stay away from the AIDS children, Magdalena Cloete. You're wasting your time.'

He pulled away, shoving her so that she stumbled and fell. He grabbed her keys out of her hand and buzzed the gate. In the seconds as it trundled open, she saw the oozing patch on his arm. He stepped through, throwing the keys onto the ground next to her.

'I know what you did, Vincent Ndlela!' she shouted after his retreating back. 'I'm after you.'

She dragged herself up, touched her stinging cheek and winced. 'Bastard.'

Letting herself into the block, she stopped to open her post box. One letter caused her heart to drop into her stomach. It was from Kitchener Clinic. Standing there, in the vestibule of her flats, her cheek stinging and her shoulders aching, she ripped the letter open.

It was a final request for Christo's December bill, a sum of R4500. That was more than she had in her bank account now, far more.

She limped to the lift and let herself into the flat. Her refuge. Except that today it felt violated.

Biting back anxiety, she called the hospital.

'It's Maggie Cloete,' she told the receptionist. 'Accounts please.'

Tom Hurst of the Accounts Department at Kitchener Clinic was one of Maggie's running-club friends. They'd crossed the line together at the Midmar half-marathon only four weeks before.

'Hey, Maggie,' he said. 'How are you?'

'I can't pay my bill, Tom.' She'd been in this position before and he'd helped her out. 'Can you wait until the end of the month?'

'I don't think so, Maggie.' His voice was kind. She could see him fiddling with his glasses and looking out of the window. 'I want to make it easy for you, but I'm under pressure here. The bosses want me to crack down on unpaid bills.'

'It's going to be hard for me to pay right now, Tom. I've got another big bill coming.' She thought of the Chicken. 'Just give me two weeks to come up with the money.'

His voice softened. 'Have you thought about Broadlands?'

Broadlands was the state mental institution. People who went in there only came out feet first. At least at Kitchener Clinic Christo had a chance of rehabilitation. His doctors kept telling her that. The last thing she wanted to do was put her baby brother in the hands of the state. Not again. But if she couldn't pay his bill, she might just have to.

'A week, Maggie, a week,' Tom Hurst said. 'I can't give you any longer than that.'

To take her mind off Christo, she paged through the Phiri files. Dumisane was new to politics; but somehow, by being in the right place at the right time, he'd won a place in the provincial legislature and not only that, he'd strolled onto the Exco and been handed the health portfolio. Judging by the articles she'd read he'd been treading carefully, toeing the party line.

Dumi's father, Shayabantu Phiri, an Inkatha chief who had a reputation as a warlord in the Eighties and early Nineties, remained a staunch Inkatha traditionalist. She wondered how the political divide had gone down *chez* Phiri. It must have made for some awkward dinner table conversations.

She flicked through Chief Shayabantu's files. He'd chosen to remain a traditional leader rather than upset his dignity by campaigning for office. That would preclude any direct competition with Dumisane. She wondered how he was making his money now that he wasn't getting shipments of weapons from the police and illegally seizing people's land from them. Then she found it. An advertorial. She had to commend Alicia for being thorough.

Chief Shayabantu stood in front of a table piled high with the green and white products that she had learned about in the Magistrate's Court last week – Schloegel's Herbals. In the background, amongst the interested crowd, who were all wearing green and white baseball caps, were none other than the Herr Doktor himself and the Chief Shark, Lucky Bean Msomi. She looked closer. On inspection he looked more like a toad.

Her hair stood on end. In one lousy ad, she'd connected Msomi to the Phiri family and to Sven Schloegel. Now that she thought about it, it was pretty neat: as a crime-lord you fed AIDS victims a cure that potentially hastened their deaths, or at the very least did nothing to obviate it, then you lent the grieving families thousands of rands to hold a funeral. When they couldn't pay you back, you turned them into Schloegel's Herbals salespeople. And the money just kept on rolling in.

She called Alicia. 'I need another favour.'

'Mmm-hmm.' The archivist took notes.

Next she dialled Dumisane Phiri's office and explained to his eager assistant that she was writing a piece on AIDS in the province and would like to interview him along with the prominent AIDS campaigner, Lindiwe Dlamini. They made an appointment for the next day.

Then she called Officer Mathonsi to find out if Sven Schloegel had turned up. She said that he hadn't but also that no one of his description had been reported missing.

'He's either dead, or back to business as usual,' she said.

Her next call was to Sven Schloegel's lawyer, Errol Mdunge. His secretary put her through.

'Mdunge.'

'Maggie Cloete, here, from the *Gazette*.'

'Hi, Maggie!' Errol was a member of the same cocktail circuit as Jabulani Nzimande and Dumisane Phiri. He loved a high-profile case that got his name into the papers, so his tone with journalists was always friendly.

'I heard you were sick,' she said.

'Oh just a stomach bug. I'm back at the grindstone already.'

'When's the Schloegel case going back into court?'

'Monday. You'll be there?'

'Yes,' she said. 'Listen, Errol, is Dr Schloegel okay?' She didn't want to tell his lawyer that the last time she saw Sven Schloegel he was being rugby-tackled by a human tank and thrown into the boot of a car. That was the doctor's job.

'Yes, Maggie, he's good. We had lunch yesterday to discuss the case.'

So Schloegel was back in the land of the living. Mulling this over, she turned back to the Phiri files. She needed to get this web sorted into neat, solvable strands because at the moment it was one big tangle. Balthasar, friends with Dumisane Phiri, got shot – apparently by mistake – not long after receiving a series of threats about his orphan charges. When she'd visited the orphans, she had also received threats. One of the orphans had been raped by an animal who was associated with Phiri. And Phiri's family had some connection with Schloegel's Herbals and, by extension, Lucky Bean Msomi.

Sven Schloegel wanted to get rid of Balthasar, who he claimed had initiated the class action suit and who was stirring up his customer base. Lucky Bean Msomi had some interest in the Schloegel case and had sent his thugs to kidnap her when she met with Schloegel. Balthasar and Mrs Chalik had wanted to bring out a rival set of products and Msomi had sent his thugs around to threaten the healer too.

Msomi's style was basic and brutal: bulldoze anyone who got in his way. By following up on the class action suit, she'd got herself in his way. All he had to do was persuade Schloegel to pick a lonely meeting-point and lure her there with promises of more details about Balthasar. They knew she wouldn't resist.

She'd half-suspected it was a set-up, but she'd gone through with it in order to learn more. Thanks to Ed, she was still here, alive and ready to aggravate Schloegel and Msomi with more questions.

She scrolled through the numbers on her phone for Schloegel's cell number and put a call through. When she got his voice-mail, she said, 'Glad to hear you're out of the BMW's boot, Herr Doktor Schloegel. When you have a moment, please feel free to call me and tell me what you were trying to prove with that ridiculous kidnap exercise.'

She was about to call Lindiwe, when her phone rang again. It was Pete Dickson from Alpha Garage.

'Howzit Maggie?'

'Hi Pete,' she said. 'How's my baby?'

'She's ready, man. I'm going to send her round with one of my guys right now, along with a nice fat bill for you, Maggie.'

Her gut churned. She wasn't ready to tell Pete she wouldn't be able to pay him yet. 'She's fixed up then?'

'Fixed and ready to thunder, Maggie.'

She thanked Pete and sighed. While she waited for the delivery, she called Lindiwe to tell her that their assignation with Phiri was set up for Friday. They agreed to meet outside Phiri's City Hall office ten minutes before the meeting. She made a cup of coffee and stared at the wall, willing an answer to emerge. Who killed Balthasar Meiring and why?

Someone buzzed her from downstairs, announcing the delivery. Instead of taking the lift, she flew down the stairs, ready to be reunited with her baby. She opened the door and was met by a pair of dazzling green eyes. Spike Lyall.

27

Thursday, 1pm

'What the hell –?'

'Just bringing your bike back, Ms Cloete,' Spike said with a grin, as he and the Alpha Garage guy began getting the Chicken off the back of the truck. 'She's all better.' He scrunched up his face. 'But you look a little rough.'

She waved her hand to dismiss his comment. 'Since when do you work for Pete Dickson?'

'Juggling doesn't pay.'

'Don't you have some university job?'

'Ja, I teach, but it's not enough to have two jobs nowadays.'

She noted that while the other guy was neatly dressed in red Alpha Garage fatigues, Spike was in his standard surfer's uniform.

'Oh please,' she said, ignoring him and going over to stroke the Chicken. Her bodywork was all shiny and there was no sign of the ordeal she had gone through. Pete Dickson had done a fine job.

'Look,' said Spike, handing her an envelope from Pete. 'Dickson's my mate and I happened to be in his office when he called you. He let Bongi here bring me along for the ride.'

This was one of the downsides of living in a small town. There was no such thing as six degrees of separation; it was no more than two. Helpful when you wanted to get information from someone, less helpful if you needed to hide or investigate a murder that your bosses had decided was yesterday's news.

Bongi was already back in the truck, revving the engine.

'Aren't you going to get back in?' she asked. 'He wants to leave.'

'I was hoping to stay a little longer.' The green eyes glinted. 'Or do you have one of your many boyfriends closeted upstairs?'

Exhaust fumes perfumed the air. They turned her head. She waved to Bongi and he set the truck in motion.

'Wait here,' she told Spike. She ran upstairs, grabbed her two bike helmets and flew down again, taking the stairs two at a time. She liked Spike Lyall, really liked him, but before she let him get any closer, she was going to test his mettle.

She handed him a helmet. 'Put this on.'

She kick-started the Chicken, let it idle for a bit and signalled for Spike to get on. The XT 350 was not made for two adults, and he had to squash up right behind her. She could feel the hard lines of his chest against her back.

The Chicken's rear sagged a bit, but that was okay. She'd had Pete strip all the street gear off her for off-road duty and tweak the shocks so that she was sleek and mean. Spike Lyall was about to find out just how mean.

She opened the throttle.

'Whoa!' He grabbed her tighter round the waist as they roared up the driveway. She indicated right and headed uphill towards the leafy suburbs. She passed the site of the Chicken's beating and the clogged undergrowth of the ravine that had saved her from the thugs.

She took Spike Lyall to her off-road playground; the plantations above Chase Valley on the opposite side of the fruit bowl to World's View. Trees flashed past them. The Chicken cornered tightly on the wide, rutted dirt roads, and she felt rather than heard Lyall draw in his breath. She was scaring him. Good. The Chicken was a nimble off-roader, manouevering well round corners and over potholes, but he didn't know that. Between them, both she and the Chicken bounced Spike Lyall and threw him around a bit.

The sun was high in the sky when she decided Lyall had had enough.

She stopped. He got off the bike with trembling legs and sat on the grass verge.

'I thought you Goodwill College boys were made of tougher stuff,' Maggie said, swinging her helmet in one hand.

He got his breath back and said, 'I could do that again.'

'First talk to me about Balthasar.' She sat next to him on the verge. 'Why did everyone reject him?'

'Maggie, Balthasar rejected us. He came back from London after Steve died and he was angry. He refused to see his family, apart from Claudine. We, his friends, we felt like he judged us.'

'For what?'

'For not being activists, like himself. He couldn't understand how people could live here and not take part in the fight against AIDS.'

Balthasar had a point. 'Why don't you?'

Spike looked out across the Pietermaritzburg bowl. She followed his gaze. Below them lay suburban gardens, paeans to English flowers and trees; a golf course now studded with the tiny figures of golfers and their carts. Beyond lay the city centre, where the *Gazette*'s offices snuggled up to the City Hall and the courts complex. From here all she could hear was bird-song and the distant roar of trucks on the highway, but she knew that it would it be thick with the noise of taxis and pedestrians and vendors, all the sounds of city life. Beyond the city were the townships, some closer, like Edendale and more urban, and others out on the hills near Table Mountain were rural. Instead of the oaks and cedars of suburbia, there grew African trees; flat-topped acacias and erythrinas.

And out there was Balthasar's constituency, the hundreds and thousands of people with AIDS and no recourse to life-saving drugs.

'Where do you start?' he said. 'Do you help one person or ten? Do you give to a charity or take in a family? It seems insurmountable.'

'It's compassion fatigue,' she told him. 'It hurts too much to care, so you just stop caring. And until you're personally affected, like Balthasar was, you don't do anything.'

'I'm personally affected now.' Spike turned to her, his green eyes dark. 'Now that my friend has been killed.'

It was the first genuine sign of grief she'd seen and she liked him for it. But she wasn't letting him off the hook that easily.

'There was a memorial service, you know, at the AIDS Mission –'

'I know,' said Lyall. 'I was there.'

'I didn't see you.'

'I left during the thunderstorm.'

She gave him a sideways look. Spike Lyall was going up in her estimation.

'How's that war wound?' He grabbed her hand, uncurled her fingers with his own and looked at her palm. The scar was just a thin line. 'Who's Lynn?'

'She was my best friend.' Her throat filled up.

'Was?'

'She died. She was murdered.'

'What happened?'

She told him how Lynn's mother was killed by one of her regular day-time customers. There was an argument and he'd battered her to death. Lynn, home from school and hiding in a cupboard, saw everything. In her terror, she'd fallen out of the cupboard and the man had scooped her up and thrown her tiny eleven-year-old frame into the boot of his car. Two weeks had gone by before her body was found in the veld near Oribi Airport. She'd been strangled.

'So now I carry her with me. Everywhere I go.'

'I am sorry Maggie.' Spike's lovely eyes sought hers, but she couldn't look into them. She shook her head, wordless.

'Did they ever catch the guy?'

'Yes,' she said. 'It was one of the *dominees* from church. In the end, he got the death penalty.'

But that had been no comfort to her. Lynn's death left her alone – at school and in her family. She turned her back on church, refused to return. She became a renegade.

'And now you're a crime reporter, crusading for the rights of the victims.' Spike looked out across the valley. 'Just like Balthasar.'

She stared down at her hand.

'Come on, it's getting hot.' Spike leapt up. 'There's a crappy pub down the road from here that sells ice-cold beer. I'll buy you one.'

Sitting on a deck shaded by an umbrella and some elephant's ear plants, with Spike's grin and the beer taking its effect on her veins, Maggie began to relax. Being on sick leave wasn't so bad after all.

'I read about the kidnap,' Spike said. 'Is that what happened to your eye?'

Something about the properties of ice-cold beer on a sunny afternoon combined with the intensity of Spike's gaze made her disclose her research. She missed working with Aslan and it was a relief to share the details with someone. Spike listened, sipping his beer. His face was calm, until she told him about Balthasar's children. He put the glass down.

'I didn't know,' he said.

'How could you not?' she asked. 'You were his friend.'

He rested both elbows on the table, put his head in his hands and shook it slowly. Under the tan, his skin was pale with shock. 'He didn't trust anyone. Not even me.'

'I think he trusted the people at work,' she said. 'They knew.'

Spike covered his face. 'But not me. He chose not to share that part of his life with me. I let him down.'

She put out a hand to touch his arm. 'I let him down too.'

'How?' Spike looked up. There was a wash of tears in his eyes.

She told him how she'd brushed Balthasar off a week before he died. 'But he told Mbali to call me if anything happened to him. And it did.' She took Spike's hand and he looked down at their interlocked fingers as if they were the petals of a flower newly unfurled. 'So here I am, trying to help him.'

'I'll help too,' Spike said. 'Let's start by going to see this Schloegel jerk.'

'I don't know where to find him.'

'I do,' Spike said. He drained his drink.

Across town lay the university, surrounded by houses rented out by students or used for businesses. Spike directed her to one whose pitched roof sported a large green and white sign: Schloegel's Herbals.

'I see this eyesore every day from my office,' Spike told her.

Carrying their helmets, Maggie and Spike let themselves into the front garden through a waist-high gate. The house was brick, like most of Maritzburg's architecture, and was surrounded by a veranda. They walked up three stairs to the front door and she knocked. They listened for feet, but no one came to answer the door. She tried the handle. Locked.

She and Spike walked around the veranda, noticing open windows, to the back of the house. The back door swung open. Either someone had just arrived or just left.

'Not much security here,' muttered Spike.

'When you have Msomi's protection, maybe you don't need it,' she replied. 'Come on, I'm going in.'

'I'll check out the garden, and that shed,' Spike told her. 'Catch you in a minute.'

She walked into what had once been a sitting room, but which was now a storage facility for Schloegel's products. Piles of brown cardboard boxes lay everywhere. Schloegel had clearly invested in his products and had confidence they would sell. She opened a door that lead her into a corridor with rooms on either side. First she found a kitchen, then a bathroom. Nothing there.

She heard a scuffle. Her hand tightened on her bike helmet. Someone was in the house.

She pushed open a door. Her first impression was of a room full of books. Her second impression was of Sven Schloegel sitting at a desk in front of the open window. He was holding a gun, which he had trained on her.

'Get out of my office,' he hissed. 'You're trespassing.'

'Just came to see if you're doing alright, Herr Doktor. Last time I saw you, you were being thrown into the boot of a BMW.'

'Thanks to that idiot of a photographer of yours, I had a concussion.'

'Sorry to hear that,' she said. 'Me too. But if you play around with fake kidnappings, these things can happen.'

'We weren't going to hurt you,' Schloegel said. 'Just give you a bit of a fright.'

'Run me off a story?' She couldn't keep the contempt out of her voice.

'Ja. *Oder etwas.*'

'Your case is in the public record, Herr Doktor. If you'd scared me off, my paper would have put someone else onto it.'

'It's not that!' Schloegel banged his spare hand on the desk in front of him. 'It's that I'm tired of do-gooders. First Meiring nosing around and stuffing up my business, and then you.'

'So you'd like to be left alone to cheat and rob and assault people. Is that it?' She knew she was goading him. She couldn't help it. 'Is that why you had Balthasar taken out?'

'We didn't kill him,' a smile played over the doctor's fleshy features, 'but we were very happy when someone else did.'

She took a step closer. 'Who did then?'

His smile grew wider, even more self-satisfied. 'Wish I knew. I'd shake his hand.'

She heard a creak. Schloegel heard it too. 'Who's there?' he shouted, getting up from his desk. 'Don't come in here, or I'll shoot the reporter.'

Then with a crack, he crumpled to the floor.

Spike leant in through the window. 'Handy, this,' he said, waving Maggie's spare bike helmet. 'Let's go.'

'I don't think he was going to shoot me,' she said as they walked back to the Chicken.

Spike stopped and looked down at her. His green eyes were dark. He lifted a hand to brush a stray hair out of her eyes. 'I wasn't going to take the chance.'

She wasn't used to tenderness. It made her nervous, but his hand stroked the back of her head and drew her in towards his chest. She relaxed into his hug. She felt the arms around her of a man whose presence made the world seem more manageable, less crazy. A man whose hands were stroking her back.

'I want you to come home with me,' Spike said into the nape of her neck.

28

Thursday, 6pm

She stretched her limbs and looked at Spike lying next to her. He was asleep, sprawled on his back, one hand resting on his very flat stomach. She traced a finger from his hand over the beaded bracelet he wore around his wrist, to his forearm, threaded with veins, and up to the biceps she had admired from afar. On close inspection, his biceps had proved more than satisfactory, as had other parts of him. All-in-all, Spike Lyall was a very attractive proposition.

There was a familiar jangling noise from her backpack, which was buried under a pile of clothes, hers and Spike's.

'Don't answer it,' muttered Spike.

'I'm a journalist; I answer my phone,' she said. She swung her legs off the bed, onto the floor and strode across the room, narrowly avoiding an empty condom packet that they had discarded an hour before.

'Nice view,' he said, lifting himself up on one elbow.

She flashed him the finger and answered the phone. 'Cloete.'

'Ms Cloete, it's Claudine Meiring.' Balthasar's sister sounded panicky. 'I need your help. Mbali has gone missing.'

'Since when?' She climbed back onto the bed and covered herself with the duvet. She was cold and she didn't want to be naked anymore.

'She skipped a class at school today. When the others all walked home, she wasn't with them. Nkosazana waited a while but when she didn't arrive she called me. I'm on my way up from Durban now.'

'Have you called the police?'

'Yes, they've been there, taken an identification, but Nkosazana's frantic. Can you get to her?'

'Why me?' She wanted to help Mbali, but she needed justification from Claudine. The last time she'd seen the woman, Claudine had been red-faced and yelling.

'Nkosazana trusts you. You get things done.'

'Okay, I'm on my way.'

'Mbali is missing,' she told Spike, throwing on her clothes. 'They need us at the house.'

The Chicken flew across town, dodging lorries on the highway, and up the hill to Balthasar's house. She pulled up at the gate and buzzed to be let in.

Nkosazana came trotting out of the house towards them. Her hair, usually tucked under a doek, was coming awry and there were salty tracks of dried tears on her cheeks.

'Maggie, thank you for coming,' she panted as she heaved the gate open. 'We are so worried about Mbali. The police are searching for her, but we haven't heard anything.'

'How are the children?' she asked.

'Upset. Very upset. Grace won't talk and the boys are crying. You'd better come in and see them.'

Nkosazana didn't offer tea, but led them to the sitting room where the two boys and Grace were sitting in a silent row on the sofa. Spike went over, and knelt down next to them.

'What happened?' she asked.

'She went to school with the others, but she didn't come home with them. I called the school but no one answered. Then I called Claudine and the police. They came and picked up a photo of Mbali and promised to look for her, but I don't know, I just don't know how hard they'll try.'

Nkosazana's reaction was not unusual. People found it hard to trust a police force that was over-worked, underpaid and often corrupt. There were good, solid career cops who made it their business to put the bad guys away, but there were also slackers who didn't appear to care.

'Do you want me to go and see if I can find her?' she asked. She looked over at Spike, who was busy pulling a fifty-cent coin out of Lungi's ear and getting a wan smile for his efforts.

'Yes, please, Maggie,' the old woman said. She sat down on the green velvet sofa as if her legs weren't doing their job anymore.

She left Spike behind. He seemed to be doing fine keeping Mbali's family entertained. She decided to look in Wylie Park first – it was right next to Mbali's school and where they had met. She parked outside the gates and ran in, hoping to find Mbali on the bench. She wasn't there.

The sun was setting and it was a diamond evening – a cool breeze, a chalky pink sky, birds roosting in trees – but she had no time to luxuriate. She walked down to the stream that ran through the park and followed it for a while, calling Mbali's name. There was no way she could cover the whole park, by herself, but she kept going for another half an hour, calling and peering into bushes.

Back at the Chicken, she wondered where she should go next. She drove the short distance to Mbali's school and wandered around the empty buildings and onto the playground, lonely in the gathering twilight. If the child didn't want to be found, she could quite easily be hiding anywhere here, but Maggie had to assume that she would respond to her. Any other thought was too depressing to contemplate.

She took a slow drive through the suburbs, the lush ones she and Spike had seen from the hillside, keeping her eyes peeled for a girl in a brown and white school uniform. No Mbali. Stopping outside the flats where she thought Mbali might have turned up to see her, she called Officer Mathonsi for the second time that day. She didn't sound thrilled to hear from her again.

'A missing child?'

'Yes.'

'Has it been reported?'

'Yes.'

'Well then, Maggie, I am sorry about the child, but we are going to have to assume that the police are following the correct procedures.'

'Thandi, I've been out looking for her. I didn't see any police search parties –'

'Maggie,' she interrupted. 'Believe me, the police are doing their best. I promise I'll look into it.'

She had to accept that. Mbali was an orphan, already tossed aside by society. If she were one of Zacharius Patel's kids, or Jabulani Nzimande's, or one of Sally-Anne Shepherd's fragrant little nieces or nephews, then the police would be running all over town trying to find her. But Mbali was nobody. And nobody goes to find nobody.

Except Maggie. She needed to find Mbali and tell her how special she was, before something happened to her.

So she drove the streets, dicing with taxis and pedestrians, slowing down whenever she saw a brown and white uniform. She combed town, up and down the grid, increasingly frantic that Mbali was somewhere, but not where she was looking.

The blanket of night had fallen. Other children were tucked in their beds, sleeping safely, but Mbali was still out there.

Other children. *Other children.* She'd been so frantic, she hadn't thought to ask the kids in Mbali's class. Somebody may have noticed something. She roared back up the hill through the velvet darkness to Balthasar's house.

'No luck,' she said as Claudine let her in the gate with a hopeful look. 'Listen, have you talked to anyone at school?'

'I spoke to her teacher,' Claudine said. 'She said Mbali asked to be excused to go the toilet and she never came back.'

'Anyone in her class?'

'Yes,' said Claudine. 'Nkosazana and I went through the class list. We didn't reach everyone.'

'Let's call the ones you missed. In fact, let's call them all, in case someone's remembered something.' She strode ahead into the house. As they let themselves in the front door, Claudine turned to her.

'Listen, Maggie, I just want to apologise for Sunday. I over-reacted, and –'

'Please,' she said, holding up her hands. 'It was a natural reaction. I've forgotten about it.'

Inside, Spike was drawing pictures with Mbali's siblings, while Nkosazana paced and cried. Maggie and Claudine divided up the class list and sat at the kitchen to make their calls. They became more despondent as each call led to nothing.

Then one of the mothers called back.

'Hi it's Sam Edwards.' Her posh tones made Maggie's skin crawl. She was of Sally-Anne's ilk – the private school crowd whose sense of entitlement ballooned around them like very special oxygen.

'Stupid me,' she said, and Maggie could almost hear her perfectly highlighted tresses swishing as she talked. 'When you asked if Catherine had noticed anything today, I forgot that I have other kids in the school. After I put the phone down I asked Cameron, but he's only in grade one and you know how unobservant they are at that age.'

She giggled. Maggie was supposed to agree, but she was not in the mood for agreeing or giggling.

'Well, our domestic worker is Princess. She and her kids are living with us now because she's well, you know. Sick.' The euphemism again. 'Anyway, I've got all four kids in school together because I think it's the right thing to do.'

She was fishing for praise but all Maggie wanted was to know about Mbali.

'I asked Thuli and Bheki if they had seen anything. Bheki said no, but Thuli, you know she is in the same standard as Mbali and Catherine, but in a different class. We didn't think it was appropriate to put the two girls together, because of the potential strain on their friendship.'

She gritted her teeth and hoped the woman was nearing her point.

'Anyway, Thuli said she saw Mbali standing outside school. She said she saw her getting into a big white bakkie. The car was still for a while and then it drove away.'

'Why didn't she tell anyone?' she asked, relieved that they had a lead, but enraged that it had taken so long to find one.

'No one asked her,' said Sam. 'Till now. My fault, probably.'

She didn't assuage Sam Edward's guilt, but she thanked her and hung up. Claudine looked at her with a question mark written across her face. As Maggie briefed her, she rubbed her hands up and down her cheeks.

'White bakkie,' Balthasar's sister whispered. 'There are hundreds of white bakkies, thousands.'

'Do we know anyone who drives one?' She remembered her meeting with Lourens Meiring. He'd been propped up against a bakkie. 'How about your father?'

Claudine frowned. 'But how would he know about –?' Maggie could tell she didn't want to acknowledge the fissure in her family, the deep misunderstanding that had driven them apart.

'Claudine, I told him.'

'Oh.' She sat on the nearest chair and looked up at her. 'Why would you do that?'

'I thought he and Sanet needed to know. Take responsibility for Balthasar's children.'

'And it was your job to tell them?' Claudine ran a hand through her hair. 'When Balthasar had chosen not to? You are spectacularly interfering, did you know that?'

'Let's not debate my role right now, Claudine. We have a child to find.' Her neck prickled. 'Why don't you go out to the farm?'

'On the minute possibility that my father has Mbali? It would be easier to just phone him.'

'No, you'll go and I'll come with you. While you talk to your parents,'

I'll look in the garages and those outbuildings for Mbali. If we don't find her, I'll call the police.'

'What do you mean the police?' Claudine said, standing up. She was about to get haughty again.

'In case Mbali is in danger,' Maggie said.

'At my father's hands?'

'It's a possibility we can't afford to ignore, Claudine. There is a connection between Mbali and your father, however tenuous you find it.'

'Yes,' said Claudine, getting up. 'There is a connection, now. Thanks to you.'

29

Thursday, 8pm

Claudine began clattering around and throwing things into her handbag. Spike came out of the boys' room.

'I need you to stay with Nkosazana and the children,' Maggie said.

'Fine.' Spike put his hand on her shoulder. 'Be careful. And let me know if you need me.'

Claudine's face was stony as she drove out of town. 'I read that article of yours. What gives you the right to judge people? What my father did was ancient history and yet you dragged it out into the open again.'

'You can't deny that your father murdered Pontius Ncube.'

'It was self-defence.'

'That's what he says.'

'As did the law!'

She stared out of the window at the dark hills outside, now just shadows against the sky. Tiny lights twinkled where curtains had not yet been closed against the night. This investigation – into Balthasar's death and Mbali's disappearance – could just as easily be snuffed out. She was the last person still asking questions, a lone light in the dark.

She looked back at Claudine whose profile was chiselled grey in the murk.

'Your father thinks that the Ncubes killed Balthasar,' she said. 'In revenge. Do you think that's possible?'

Claudine shook her head. 'You don't stop, do you? You never stop.'

'That's my job,' Maggie said. 'Plus a kid's missing and I want her safe before she turns up dead like your brother.'

Pain flickered over the woman's face and she exhaled a long drawn-out breath.

'I guess there's no harm in you knowing. We grew up with Pontius Ncube. He was four or five years older than Balthasar, but they were good friends. As soon as Pa was out on the farm and Ma busy in the garden, Balthasar would go and find Pontius. If we were lucky, he'd take us with him.'

'What did you do?'

'Wander around the farm, catch lizards, go swimming in the river. Kids' stuff.'

'Did the friendship last?'

'Until Pa got wind of it. Then he shipped us all off to boarding-school in a rage. We went to an all-girls' school in town and Balthasar went to Goodwill.'

'How did you find it?'

'Oh God, we were misfits. At least Christa and I had each other.'

Maggie remembered Sally-Anne's mockery of the twins and felt a twinge of pity for them. 'And Balthasar?'

'He made friends, settled down. But then he was always good at that.'

She rolled that idea around: Balthasar as the social chameleon. That was a new one to add to the pantheon of animal metaphors people had used to describe the dead man. 'How about Pontius?'

'He stopped going to school after standard seven, went to work for Pa and after that he seemed too grown-up for us and our kids' preoccupations. He distanced himself from us, Balthasar especially.'

'That must have hurt.'

'We girls didn't really notice, but I think Balthasar felt snubbed. Then one year, Balthasar must have been about fourteen, we came back from school and Pontius was gone.'

'Where to?'

'No-one knew. He came back, about a year later, and we had the feeling he was no longer a boy. He was scary then, hard-faced, angry. Balthasar always said he'd gone out of the country for military training.'

'What gave him that idea?'

Claudine shrugged. 'Pontius was nineteen, boastful. He told Balthasar he had a stash of weapons buried on the farm, and that he was required to defend them with his life.'

'Do you think your father found them? Maybe that's what their argument was about?' ANC cadres were trained outside the country and sent back in to carry out covert operations. If Lourens Meiring had found such a stash, she could see him acting in rage.

'Possibly, but it never came up in the trial.'

'And how was it on the farm after the murder?'

'Pa pulled Christabel and me out of school, tried to shelter us from the worst of it. Balthasar refused to leave his school. After that he hardly ever came home. He'd arrange to spend holidays with his friends – Francois Bezuidenhout mostly, or the Lyalls.'

Her blood pulsed faster at the name. Spike Lyall had got under her skin. She deflected the thoughts of that afternoon by focussing on the job. 'Could I talk to any of the Ncubes? Are they still in Greytown?'

'His sister, Cora.' She remembered Cora, tall, cold. She'd served them water on the veranda, and she'd watched them leave. What Maggie couldn't understand is why she'd still be working for the man who'd killed her brother, whether in self-defence or not.

Claudine sensed the question brewing and answered, 'Pa took her on as part of the reparations. Pontius had been the family's main breadwinner, and without him had nothing.'

Well, that put paid to the Ncube theory. If anyone were going to kill Balthasar Meiring or any member of his family, it would have been Cora. And she would have done it by now. But would she know about a secret stash of guns?

The click-click of the indicator told Maggie they were turning off the main road. Claudine's car bounced over the potholes in the dirt road to the farm. Her thoughts turned back to Mbali. Could she be here, tied and gagged in one of the many outbuildings?

Claudine buzzed the gate. '*Ma, ek's hier.*'

Maggie opened her car door, got out and followed Claudine's vehicle through the gates, which swung shut behind her. As she skirted right into the bank of azalea bushes that fringed the property, she saw Sanet come out to greet her daughter, arms wide. The alsatian was on her heels and the beast sniffed the air and barked.

'Don't be silly, *meisie*,' Sanet yanked on the dog's collar. 'It's just Claudie.'

The two women walked inside, leaving her caged in the bushes.

Keeping the azaleas between her and the house, she skirted round until she was behind the garage. Meiring's white bakkie and Sanet's small silver Opel were parked there for the night. She checked the insides of both vehicles. Empty. She walked around to the boot of the

Opel and knocked on it. It sounded hollow and no knock answered her from inside.

At the back of the garage were two rooms – an empty bedroom (Cora evidently slept out) with a steel bedstead, a bare, stained mattress and a tiny bathroom. This was probably where Nkosazana had slept when she had worked for the family, where Balthasar had visited her to cuddle and listen to stories. The bed was on bricks against the tokoloshe and there was a faint smell of years of cooking. The friendly smells of food and life were long gone. The room was a shell.

She looked under the bed. Nothing but dust. Then she saw a glint. She reached for it, her cheek resting on the grimy floor and pulled a small steel box towards her. It was clean, not dusty, as if someone had recently used it. She opened the lid and fingered the small strips, some of which had been punctured, others that were still full of fat tablets.

Norvir. D4T. 3TC.

Anti-retrovirals. Someone in the house had AIDS and didn't want anyone else to know about it. Could it be Cora?

She put the drugs back and pushed the box under the bed. She checked the rest of the room and the bathroom, but there were no trap-doors, no locked cupboards, no places where someone could hide something, or someone. The room left no messages.

Next to the garage lay a second outbuilding. This contained a laundry room and a workroom full of tools and garden equipment. She searched them both. Empty.

She crept behind the hedge again and skirted the apex of the house, heading down the other side of the garden. She came to a third outbuilding. The door was closed and, after a short struggle with the latch, she let herself in.

It felt like a church – quiet, dusty and reverential. There was a long worktable, splashed with paint, and a number of objects leaning against the wall shrouded in a dust-cloth. She pulled the cloth off, coughing with the dust, and saw that the objects were canvasses. She flicked through them. Mostly flower paintings, the kind her mother would love, and landscapes of the mountains. The last painting, the one closest to the wall, was not a floral tribute but a portrait. She shifted the others to one side and propped it upright so that she could get a better look.

It was of a man, a young man. Balthasar. She recognised him partly from the school photo they'd published in the *Gazette* and from the strong nose he'd inherited from his mother. The picture was done in grey and beige oils, layered on top of one another. He was glancing back over his shoulder, with a slight smile on his lips. The look in his eyes was regretful, as if he were looking at someone whose love had let him down.

Someone who'd buried him in a graveyard of forgotten paintings.

'Maggie!'

It was Claudine, shouting her name into the night.

30

Thursday, 10pm

What was the woman doing?

'Maggie!' The shout came again.

She looked around the art studio. It was dark, but she couldn't see any cupboards or places where a person, even a small one, could be hidden. She sighed and pushed open the studio door. What was Claudine playing at?

'Pa says come in for a drink.' Claudine stood in a pool of light that spilled out of the house – the dining room, as far as she could remember from her previous visit. She waved, a smile glazed on her face, as Maggie walked across the lawn towards her.

'Did you ask about Mbali?'

'Yes. He says he's never met her.'

'That doesn't mean he doesn't have her locked up somewhere.'

Claudine put her arm through hers. 'Pa says it's time to stop working. Come and relax; have a drink.'

She didn't feel relaxed. She'd been combing the Meirings' outbuildings for a missing child – with their knowledge, thanks to Claudine – and now she was expected to unwind with them over a beer.

They stepped through the French doors and into the dining room, the Meiring ancestors still trapped in their gloomy frames. Claudine led her out of the room and into the corridor. They stopped outside a room where she could hear the blast of a TV. Claudine widened her eyes and raised her hand to knock. Maggie saw the grey pallor under her skin. Was it fear?

'Come in, come in,' Lourens Meiring rose from his armchair. He shook her hand, his free one dwarfing a half-empty brandy glass. Judging from the fumes of his breath, she doubted it was the first drink of the evening.

'Sit,' he said. She sat on the edge of the brown corduroy sofa. Claudine perched next to her and took up a glass of wine, which she twirled between her fingertips. 'What would you like to drink?'

She glanced around the room. She didn't want to drink from any bottle that she couldn't see and the only bottle in the room was the brandy. 'Same as you.'

'Good!' Meiring nodded and began sloshing brandy into a glass. He passed her what looked like a double in a heavy crystal glass. She clutched it to her chest like a weapon.

'My wife sends you her apologies,' he told her, sitting back in his armchair. The chair was centrally placed in the room so that from it he'd have vantage of the TV and whoever passed by in the corridor or garden. The commander's seat. 'She has to be up early for Bible study tomorrow.'

'No problem,' she said, sipping the brandy. There was no ice there, just pure fire. It burnt a track of flame all the way into her gullet.

'Claudine says one of the children is missing.' His tone was bland but a tiny grimace, the long-lost cousin of a smile, flickered in one corner of his mouth.

'Yes,' she began.

'She insisted on coming here, Pa!' Claudine said from behind her wineglass. Gone was the Durban sophisticate. In the presence of her father, the woman was reduced to a simpering teenager, a teenager desperate to get herself off the hook. Maggie felt her neck prickle. This was an old family dynamic, an underground stream of coercion and power and fear. Had this dynamic chased Balthasar away?

'She said she'd call the police if we didn't come.'

Lourens Meiring ignored his daughter, who took refuge in her glass again. Maggie wished she could offer her some comfort.

'I admire your work,' he told Maggie, who remembered that Balthasar had said something similar the day she'd spoken to him. Back then, Balthasar was just a caller out of the blue. Now he was dead and here was his father mouthing his words back at her.

She sipped her fiery drink. 'Balthasar told Mbali to contact me if anything happened to him and now she's missing. It makes me think that his death and her disappearance could be linked.'

'Could be.'

'And she said he was arguing on the phone in the weeks before his death. Who could he have been arguing with?'

Meiring shrugged. He picked up a control and aimed it at the TV, switching off the news pundits. 'He chose his associates, Miss Coetzee, and kept apart from his family. If he'd let us in maybe we'd have been able to help him.'

Claudine was nodding, making mouse-like noises of assent into her wine glass.

'Did you also feel distanced from Balthasar?' Maggie asked her. 'I thought you saw him.'

'I saw him, but he never let me get close.' The woman's lips pouted; a tear trembled on her lower lid and then coursed over the edge. A second followed. She made no attempt to wipe them.

'If he stayed away from Pontius Ncube all along, this would never have happened,' Meiring told Maggie, leaning towards her with his drink inclining precariously to one side. 'The man influenced him, taught him things he would never have learnt in this house. Politics. The ANC. So much rubbish!' He fixed her with a furious eye, and then keeping her in sight, allowed his head to rest against the back of his commander's chair. He drained his brandy, eyes never moving from her face.

'If only we had never met him,' Claudine began.

'Shut up!' Meiring turned on his daughter. 'I'm sick of your snivelling! Just like your mother.' Claudine crumpled, her body folding in on itself. It looked like instinct, a habit she had formed out of self-preservation.

'Take her home, please,' he said to Maggie, his tone pleasant again. 'She's drunk and pathetic.'

His eyes flickered closed, indicating that cocktail hour was over.

'Let's go.' She shook Claudine, who staggered to her feet. The woman shook, whether from fear or too much booze she wasn't sure.

'Give me your keys,' she said. 'I'm driving.'

31

Friday, 10am

She woke with a clang in her heart. Mbali. She showered and, grabbing an elderly apple from the fruit-bowl, flung her backpack over her shoulder and headed downstairs to the Chicken. She drove up the hill to Balthasar's house. If she couldn't be with Mbali, at least she could be with her siblings until it was time for her meeting with Phiri.

Nkosazana let her in. Her face was lined with exhaustion and worry.

'The boys have left for school,' she said. 'The day-nurse is here, but Busi cried all night and I am just so tired.'

'I'll look after Grace for you. You go and rest,' she said. 'Just one thing, though, combination therapy drugs – how much do they cost a month?'

'Over R4000.' The old lady turned and headed for her bedroom.

She found Grace playing in the room she shared with Mbali. She didn't look up, but when Maggie sat on the floor next to her, she handed her a toy. It was a small bear. Grace herself had a baby doll. Both were shabby from frequent playing.

Grace mothered her doll, dressing and undressing her, and talking to her in a low monotonous voice. Maggie thought of the packets of drugs she'd found at the farm yesterday. They were beyond the reach of a person earning a domestic worker's salary. Unless someone with more ready money was buying Cora's drugs in exchange for something – her silence, perhaps – they would have to belong to one of the two people who lived inside the main house.

Could Lourens or Sanet Meiring have HIV?

Grace's voice grew angrier and she returned her attention to the small child, who was throwing the doll around, her voice now strident.

Dolly was in trouble. Grace wagged her finger in the doll's face, telling her off. Maggie recognised a few phrases: 'You're naughty', 'I'll hit you'. Then she grabbed the bear from Maggie, and using his body as the weapon, ground Dolly into the floor.

It was a rape scene.

She watched, horrified, her senses singing. Teddy was punishing Dolly for being a bad girl. When he had finished, he aimed a kick at her. Then he swaggered off. Dolly lay there for a while, crying. Grace forgave Dolly, picked her up and hugged her again, patting her back and making soothing noises.

Grace made eye contact with Maggie for the first time. 'Zana?' she asked.

'Nkosazana is resting,' she told the little girl. 'I'll play with you.'

Oppressed by the tiny room and what she had just witnessed, she said, 'Let's go outside.'

To her relief, Grace abandoned both toys and followed her. Grace wanted to play soccer – a version of her brothers' game in which Maggie was goalie and she was triumphant scorer. She spent much of the game doing laps of honour while Maggie stood in goal waiting for her next attempt.

A hadeda landed near them and squawked, distracting Grace from soccer. She became a 'ha-ha-hadeda' and was vastly amused by Maggie's attempt to be a dove. Then she took Maggie's hand in hers and led her on a tour of the garden. She squatted under an erythrina tree and held up between her fingers one of their jewel-like red seeds. A lucky bean.

Grace and Maggie made piles of lucky beans. First they collected all the beans they could find on the ground under the tree, then she showed Maggie how to split open the skinny black pods with her fingernail, revealing the treasures within. When Maggie tired of foraging, she sat with her back against the tree, watching the child play with the beans they'd found.

Her face was sweetly round, with a little dent under each eye. They were not dimples, which turned up when she smiled, but permanent dents of sweetness on both cheeks. Her gorge rose. Some animal had used her for his own ends, oblivious to her suffering and pain. She fought the horror down, swearing to herself that no matter what, she would find him and make sure he got put away for life.

She knew that Dumisane Phiri was the key.

32

Friday, 1.50pm

She arrived early for her meeting and parked the Chicken under a tree. She strolled towards the City Hall, and found Lindiwe waiting for her, dressed in black and hefting her weighty handbag. Maggie told her that Mbali had vanished and that she'd followed her diminishing trail as far as the Meiring farm.

'Do you suspect Meiring?' Lindiwe searched her face.

'I don't trust him. But I don't discount Ndlela. He also has a motive for getting rid of the Sibanyonis.' She remembered his chemical breath and his vicious threats.

After consulting a receptionist, they proceeded to Phiri's office. Phiri's assistant showed them to a meeting room.

'He has a meeting with the Mayor,' she told them, wide-eyed, 'but he will be here soon.'

Phiri breezed in, fifteen minutes late, suited and tied but with his jacket off and shirt sleeves rolled up. He glad-handed both women, and fell into a chair, yanking his tie to one side as he did so.

Glinting his teeth at Maggie, he said, 'My assistant told me, but I have forgotten, so remind me why we are here.'

'Well,' she said. 'Mrs Dlamini, as you know, runs the AIDS Mission, a church-funded organisation to bring services and education to people with HIV and AIDS and their families. With the Durban International AIDS conference looming, I thought it would make an interesting article to bring her and you, as MEP for Health and Social Equity, together to talk about the progress we are making both on the ground and at policy level.'

'Excellent, excellent,' he said, grinning. This was a different grin from the one he'd given Maggie at the funeral. This was a politician's smile, one judged to make its audience feel warm and fuzzy. 'Just one question – aren't you the crime reporter? Is AIDS your area?'

She knew he was going to ask that, and she had her reply. 'Aslan Chetty is out of town and he asked me to run this story. Also, AIDS is a personal interest of mine. We are all affected by it, one way or another.'

It sounded glib, but he seemed to swallow it.

Both Lindiwe and Phiri agreed to have her tape recorder on.

'Mrs Dlamini, if I can start with you. The first international AIDS conference to be held in South Africa will take place in Durban next month. What do you think are the main issues the conference should be addressing and how do these affect us at local level?'

'Well, Maggie, the issue of access is number one. Pregnant mothers are transferring HIV to their unborn babies, literally giving them a death sentence, and this could be stopped if the government would make antiretrovirals accessible to all. The drugs have been proven to hinder the development of full-blown AIDS in adult patients and to prevent mother to child transfer. We have already lost a generation of people who have developed AIDS through lack of education, and we desperately need to prevent losing another generation.'

It was the answer she expected from her. Lindiwe settled back in her chair, waiting for the politician's response. His was more unexpected.

'From where I stand,' he smiled, 'we need to go much further back than that. The questions that are being asked in government – do ARVs stem the development of full-blown AIDS? Does HIV even cause AIDS? If not, then what does? These are the questions that I am thinking about right now.'

Lindiwe opened her mouth to speak, but he leaned forward, putting both elbows on the desk.

'I mean, this drug, this AZT, it is not proven. What if it is poisoning people and is not making them better? Activists, like yourself –' he gestured to Lindiwe '–are asking the government to put millions of rands into giving untested drugs to people when in fact they could potentially be killers.'

'The drugs are tested,' Lindiwe said with conviction. 'People with AIDS in the USA have been taking and living with AZT and drugs of its kind for decades. They work.'

'I don't know about that,' Phiri smiled. 'Some scientists are claiming that antiretrovirals cause AIDS.'

This was the president's new line and Phiri had swallowed it. She could see a vein ticking on Lindiwe's forehead. She stepped in. 'Let's recap, Mr Phiri. You think the 2000 Aids Conference should address whether HIV causes AIDS, and if antiretrovirals are an effective antidote?'

'My message is that further research is needed before the government can get behind an antiretroviral campaign. We need to know what we are dealing with and not blindly accept what the first world says works. The situation here in Africa is different – there is poverty, poor sanitation, lack of services. There are other diseases, like malaria, TB and cholera. We have a different model here. We need to work out what works for us.'

'People are dying,' Lindiwe said. 'We don't have time to work out a new model.'

'Mrs Dlamini,' she said. 'Perhaps you could talk about the tenets of an effective AIDS campaign?'

Lindiwe shook herself. 'Education, first and foremost, on condom usage and safe sex. We need community outreach, an army of lay practitioners who can educate people in the furthest communities. We need nurses and clinic staff who are prepared to tell people how to change their behaviours. And we need the drugs.'

She leaned forward and looked at Phiri who had folded his hands on his non-existent belly. 'The drugs that we already know work.' He held her glare.

'Mr Phiri, what is your stance on safe sex?' Maggie asked.

'I am absolutely behind it,' he said. 'Condom usage is vital in preventing the spread of HIV.'

'There is so much misinformation out there, myths that, for example, sex with a virgin will cure HIV. Mr Phiri how do you recommend that we counteract these?'

'Campaigns, education.' He waved his hands. Non-committal.

'Do you mean the kinds of campaigns that Mrs Dlamini and other activists are already running? Or do you mean government campaigns?'

'I think the only way we will change behaviour is through sustained campaigns at government and NGO level.'

'Is it surprising to you that the myth that raping a virgin still persists?' she asked.

'Miss Cloete, we are dealing with people who were victims of a systematic campaign of chronic under-education. We can thank apartheid for that.'

'So apartheid is the reason men rape?' She couldn't keep the disbelief out of her voice.

Phiri sat up straight. 'I don't know where you are coming from. I thought we were talking about AIDS campaigns.' He was starting to squirm.

'Mr Phiri,' Lindiwe gave a conciliatory smile. 'We know that rape is a tool of war. When this province was torn apart by a Nationalist-sanctioned civil war, women were raped. Now that the province is facing the largest AIDS epidemic the world has ever seen, women are being raped. Rape of both women and children is part and parcel of the spreading of HIV. I'd like to know what the government is going to do about it.'

'People must report rape and the police will investigate,' he said, pulling his tie back into place.

'And what if the victim is a two-year-old child?' Maggie asked. Her stomach roiled, but she kept her voice level. 'A child who can barely speak, let alone give evidence in court. What then?'

'I don't know why you are asking me this.' Phiri began unrolling his shirtsleeves.

'How do you, as a leader, plan to protect women and children from the scourge of rape?' asked Lindiwe.

'It's not my job to protect,' he said, buttoning a cuff.

'But it is your job to prevent,' Maggie replied.

'I don't know what this is all about,' Phiri stood up. 'I've got better things to do with my time than be attacked by a cabal of feminists.'

Blood pulsed in her head. She stood too. 'I'll tell you what it's about. It's about a man who raped a baby girl and who now has your protection. I want to know what you are going to do about it.'

'Switch that thing off,' he pointed to the tape recorder. She did.

'Miss Cloete,' he said. 'You are right out of order. If you continue making these wild accusations, I will report you to your editor.'

'You can't report me,' said Lindiwe flatly. 'I know for a fact that your cousin, Vincent Ndlela, formerly of Simunye village, raped Grace Sibanyoni there last year. Afterwards you took him in and he is now working as a member of your household.'

'Wild allegations,' he said, running his fingers through his hair.

Lindiwe stood. She was the epitome of calm. 'Hand him over to the police. He must confess and be taken to trial and face his punishment. Rape cannot be condoned.'

Phiri laughed. It was not a pleasant sound. 'He must confess. On what grounds? The word of a three-year-old and a couple of speculating women? You know as well as I do that anyone in that village could have raped the child. It could have been one of her own brothers, for that matter.'

Lindiwe drew herself up. Maggie watched in admiration as she went for the throat.

'If your cousin denies raping Grace Sibanyoni, then why were you paying money to Balthasar Meiring?'

Phiri looked at her, dumbfounded. Maggie kept her face blank but she was equally astonished.

'I have documentation here,' she said, pulling a file out of her outsize handbag, 'which shows that you were buying Balthasar's silence.'

She began to read, 'November 18. Visited Phiri. Laid accusation against Vincent Ndlela. Phiri denied. I threatened to go to press with the story. November 21. Call from Phiri, asking me to keep information to myself. Politically inexpedient to have scandal. Prepared to pay towards Grace's drugs. November 30. First tranche of money in my bank account. R5000 to be paid on the 30th of every month.'

Lindiwe shook the envelope and more paperwork scattered out. 'Here I have bank statements. You paid R5000 into Balthasar Meiring's account on the 30th of November, December and January. Will you be paying the money this month? Now that he's conveniently dead?'

Phiri sat down again. He put his head into his hands. When he looked up, the whites of his eyes were yellow. He began talking quietly, all bluster gone.

'Vincent came to me in August last year. He said the police had been asking questions in the village and he needed a place to lay low. He said there had been an incident with a child, but he didn't go into details and I didn't want to know. I gave him a job as a bodyguard. He's very good, very tough. Then in November Balthasar came to see me. He told me that he suspected Vincent Ndlela of raping the child. He wanted me to hand him over to the police, but I begged him not to. I was in the middle of campaigning and didn't need a scandal. Then I offered him money towards the child's care. I pay for her drugs, the ones that keep her alive.'

'Then, when you were elected, you had Balthasar killed,' Maggie said coldly. 'Killing two birds with one stone.'

'No!' he said, turning to her, 'Balthasar Meiring was my friend! I had nothing to do with his murder. It was appalling, terrible.'

Phiri was either a very convincing actor, or he was telling the truth. She wasn't sure which.

'Listen, Phiri,' she said. 'It's no longer about you. It's about Vincent Ndlela. I need to know how to find him and fast. Grace's sister Mbali has disappeared and I think he's got her.'

'He's not at home now,' the lawyer said.

'Where is he then?'

'He has another job.'

'Mr Phiri, Lindiwe is leaving this room to go straight to the police to report Vincent Ndlela for the rape of Grace Sibanyoni. And if you don't cooperate with us, she will report you for obstruction.'

The lawyer spoke in a low voice.

'He works for Lucky Bean Msomi.'

33

Friday

He had the child. She was small and quiet, which was good, except when she cried. She cried for the old lady, and for the other children, and for that man, forgetting that he was dead.

It was the sweeties that had done it. Like a little lamb she'd come for the sweeties. Then he'd given her mango juice, and she'd started to yawn almost right away. It was nearly too easy.

Right now she was somewhere safe, in a place where nobody would look. It was too full of memories, too full of good times long gone. A dark and dusty place that everyone avoided. She was safe there for now. Until he decided what he was going to do with her.

Now that he was taking the pills, his vision was getting better, he had fewer pains, even the sores were starting to clear up. He was a man of action again, taking steps. Decisions would come, as simply as a striking a match.

34

Friday, 3pm

'Balthasar knew?' she accosted Lindiwe outside the City Hall. Her hands were shaking. If she smoked, she would have lit up just for the calming hit of nicotine.

'Rape is hard to prove,' Lindiwe gave her the benefit of a wise look, 'especially when the victim is a two-year-old child. He probably weighed up the impact of a trial on Grace, a trial that they wouldn't necessarily win, against a peaceful, safe life with Phiri paying for her antiretrovirals.'

Maggie gritted her teeth. 'I don't get it, I just don't. Why take Phiri's dirty money? Why not have Ndlela put away?' Her vision of Balthasar as the conquering hero was tainted. She wanted him perfect and shining, a highly evolved being as Mrs Chalik had intimated. She didn't want him full of motley morals like everyone else.

'He didn't trust the system. Do you blame him?'

She knew only too well how badly the police were struggling with their caseloads. And law courts were fickle places; a court had given Balthasar's father a suspended sentence for murder.

'When did he give you the documents?'

'He didn't. Sipho found them when he cleared out Balthasar's desk this morning.'

'And Balthasar was on his way to tell you about them and the threats when he was killed.'

She sat on the low wall surrounding the City Hall parking lot. Her neck prickled and she cast around in the sea of words she and Lindiwe were making. What had she just said? *A two-year-old child*. She thought of Mbali's picture of Ndlela raping a child. How could she have known? Grace was two at the time; she wouldn't have been able to articulate an erect penis, a rape. She would have told her family about a bad man, but she would not have been able to say what he did. Mbali must have witnessed something else and that was what she had depicted in her picture.

She stood up and grabbed Lindiwe's arm. 'There was more than one rape! Ndlela is a serial rapist. And I think Mbali witnessed something and he's snatched her.'

'Not Lourens Meiring?'

'We found no sign of her at the farm.' She paced up and down on the pavement. 'No, it's Ndlela and he's taken her because she was a witness. I've got to find him, Lindiwe.'

Lindiwe put Maggie's theory into her giant handbag along with Balthasar's paperwork and marched off to the police station to report Ndlela for Grace's rape and Mbali's abduction. She would also tell them he was implicated in the murder of Balthasar Meiring.

Maggie climbed onto the Chicken. Despite the shade she'd found, the bike was boiling and the seething bodywork seared her legs. The sooner she got moving, the quicker the metal would cool down.

First she had a call to make. 'Any luck, Alicia?'

'Oh yes,' the older woman said. 'We've struck gold.'

The address that Alicia gave her was in Edendale. Lucky Bean Msomi had clearly decided to stay in the community that he robbed and exploited instead of moving across town to the plush suburbs that had once been closed to him. The house was easy to find – it was twice the size of any of its neighbours and had a fleet of black BMWs in the drive, parked safely behind a two-metre fence topped with coils of razor wire.

She drove past the house and turned left into the next street, where she parked. She put her phone onto vibrate and slid it into her pocket. She needed to be able to watch the house, but she didn't need to alert his thugs. Then she walked back into Msomi's street. She found a vantage point behind a car parked opposite the mansion. It afforded her a tiny patch of shade, but she sweltered as the sun lowered itself. Four o'clock on a February afternoon was not a pleasant time to be sitting outside. She picked up a stick and poked the tarmac at the side of the road. It was soft to the touch. One trail of sweat trickled down her spine, followed by another.

She could do nothing but wait and watch. Msomi's house had three

Palladian columns to signify his status and every window was shut and burglar-barred. The only sign that anyone was home was the line of cars in the drive. She poked the tarmac some more. She was trained to wait, but it hurt to do nothing when Mbali's life was on the line.

Could she be inside Msomi's palace, locked and bound, fearing for her life? Or worse, already dead?

The front door swung open. Lucky Bean Msomi walked out and stood on the front step, framed by his columns. His belly strained over his well-pressed cream linen pants and his crocodile-skin brogues glinted in the sunlight. Two men followed him out of the house: the brick shithouse who'd wrestled Sven Schloegel to the grass up at World's View and a man she'd seen yesterday as he breathed his noxious threats at her. Vincent Ndlela.

She stilled her breathing and watched as Ndlela and the henchman talked with Msomi, their heads close together. There was something about the white guy that rang alarm bells, something about the way he stood, his arms hanging down and his little head inclined towards Msomi's as if he were concentrating very hard on his instructions. Then he glanced up and she saw that rugby-ruined nose. Just like his brother's. It was Yskas Steenkamp, Claasie's older brother, who had earned his nickname at Hoërskool Andries Pretorius because he was just as big and as clever as a fridge.

Yskas and Ndlela climbed into a car together, the former at the wheel. The gate slid open and the car reversed onto the road, pulling away from her. Msomi did not stop to watch them; he turned on his brogues and went back into his house.

She had a second to decide: did she follow the car or did she stay to case Msomi's house?

She took one look at the barred windows and ran to the Chicken. The last time she'd tailed a car she'd been shot at for her trouble. She was going to have to keep the BMW in sight, without the two men knowing that she was following them.

Keeping four cars between them, she followed the sedan out of Edendale towards Camp's Drift. Before it reached the river, the car swung right towards The Grange. Her stomach clenched. This was where she had once lived, part of the happy family that was Ma, Pa, Christo and Maggie. After Christo was jailed, her parents sold their small suburban house, funding their next purchase down the coast and leaving her to find somewhere else to live. That had been her final conversation with her parents.

The black car swam on through the heat of the late afternoon. She followed it towards Mkondeni, the town's main industrial area, home to a municipal market, various businesses and the traffic department, where queues of teenagers lined up every day, sweaty-palmed, to do their driver's licence tests.

Msomi's BMW slowed to a halt outside the traffic department. The driver did not signal to turn in, but pulled over and parked. She slid in a few metres behind the car, putting a four-wheel drive truck and an old yellow Escort between herself and Msomi's thugs.

What were they doing here? What business did Msomi have at the traffic department?

She turned to look at the buildings inside the fence. There was the main building, squat and ugly, and in front of it lay the practice-ground, complete with road markings in white and yellow where a blue Golf was laboriously trying to parallel park in a bay. A man stood watching with a clipboard in his hand. He was shaking his head. A kid dressed head to toe in black and sporting a coif of green hair climbed out of the Golf, shoulders slumped.

Behind the main building there were a series of identical grey units. Probably warehouses for spare vehicles and road-repair equipment.

She remembered her deep-throat, the guy that had disappeared. Could this be the facility he had talked about?

A car door slammed. Ndlela trotted across the road to a petrol station. He came back a couple of minutes later with two cooldrinks. He and his accomplice clearly had time on their hands. Waiting for darkness to fall.

She called Spike.

'Why there?' he asked when she told him where she was.

'I think Ndlela may have Mbali locked away somewhere here. I'm going to need back-up. Can you come?'

'Sure.'

She told him her plan. 'And I'm going to need a camera. Electrical wire or rope. And a lock-pick.'

'Anything else?'

'No, those will do fine, thanks.'

She sat and watched as the traffic department shut up shop. The civil servants filed out of the building to their cars, or walked across the practice-ground to get into taxis waiting on the forecourt of the petrol station. The last person to leave closed the gates and padlocked them. When the files of cars and people had disappeared for the night, she saw the brake lights of the BMW flash. They were going in.

Ndlela climbed out of the car again and unlocked the gate, leaving it open as the BMW drove through. The sedan motored across the practice-ground, ignoring the painted lines on the tarmac and Ndlela trotted after it. She watched as they made their way to one of the units furthest from the main building.

Glancing around, Maggie got off the Chicken. After sitting for an hour, her legs were stiff. She grabbed one foot after another, pointing her knee to the ground and stretching her thigh muscles.

An ancient Mercedes pulled in at the petrol station and the driver waved. Her back-up had arrived.

'Got your stuff,' Spike held up a backpack.

Lampposts on the perimeter of the ground threw swathes of light onto the pretend roads. She pointed to the main building. 'We need to get into those shadows.'

They sprinted across the practice ground and fell into the dark, breathing hard.

'I want to see what's in these units,' she said. She could feel her own pulse throbbing and hear Spike's breathing behind her as she got out the lock-pick and the torsion wrench.

Her fingers grew sweaty as she slid the wrench into the keyhole. She turned it first one way and then the other. There it was! The torque. Dennis Mukerjee had taught her how to be gentle. 'Picking is not for the ham-fisted,' he'd told her. 'Be sensitive.' Keeping the wrench firmly in place, she slid the pick into the top of the keyhole. She counted the pins and found five. Starting at the back she set each pin, listening for each successful click. She pushed the wrench further to turn the cylinder and felt the door give.

'Hey! We're in,' she whispered to Spike. The door creaked open; the warehouse was packed full of front-loaders, bulldozers and cement mixers. She closed the door. 'Does what it says on the can. Let's try the next one.'

It was full of road-mending equipment. The next one was the same, and the next. Her hands were slippery now. Dennis always said you had to keep your cool, but her chest had grown tight.

'Just one more,' she said. 'Before I go and see what Ndlela and Yskas are doing.' She could hear clanging from one of the warehouses nearby, as if the two men were lifting heavy objects.

'Yskas?' asked Spike with a half-grin.

'Built like a fridge.' She bent over the lock.

'How do you know –?' he began, but his question remained unfinished. His words were arrested by the sight that greeted them in the shed.

Coffins.

Piles of wood and steel coffins, stacked one on top of each other to the ceiling.

35

Friday, 7pm

She walked towards the nearest bank of rectangles and traced her hand along the side of a wooden coffin. It was smoothly planed and varnished.

'I can't believe it,' said Spike.

'I can,' she said, teeth set. 'Pass me the camera.' He dug in the backpack and gave it to her.

She heard the single lens reflex whirring as her finger pushed the button. This was the evidence she'd been after for months; evidence that Lucky Bean Msomi was a fraudster, manipulating funeral expenses to bankrupt the grieving. She found a logo on the coffin; a subtle plate on one of the short sides of the rectangle. *LB Msomi and Co.*

When she was satisfied that she had enough pictures of the logo and of Msomi's stockpile, she turned to Spike.

'It's time.'

Taking the backpack and her helmet, he walked down the length of the warehouse to the end. She heard muffled sounds as he followed her instructions.

'Ready when you are.' Spike's voice was soft.

Maggie walked out of the warehouse, camera bouncing. This was the part of the plan that could not go awry. She felt acid drip into her stomach.

She walked towards the storage unit where Msomi's two men, one a serial rapist, the other a serial thug, were working. Craning her head around the doorway, she saw them at the opposite end of the unit, each on either side of a blackwood coffin. She drew a breath and stepped into the doorway, camera raised.

'Yskas Steenkamp! Vincent Ndlela!'

Their two faces turned towards her and the camera purred. With a whomp, she heard them drop the coffin. She ran out into the night, pausing in the doorway of the warehouse where Spike waited before flying through it as she saw Yskas exit the doorway first. She ran down the rows of coffins. He was large but nimble and she could feel his breath on her back. He reached for the camera bouncing on her back, his fingers grazing her t-shirt. Dry-mouthed, she wrenched away. She could hear him panting – it was the same sound her heart was making inside her chest, a thrumming beat of terror.

At the end of the row she leapt, right leg drawn up in front of her, left leg flying out behind.

Yskas did not see the rope and crashed to the floor. She heard the crack as Spike thunked him on the head with the helmet. The giant was out. Spike got a second length of rope and set about binding his hands and feet.

She rounded the corner. Where was Ndlela? He had followed her out of the warehouse, but where was he now?

He'd been clever enough not to follow her into Spike's trap.

Part of her wanted to run. To flee. This was the man who'd lured two-year-old Grace Sibanyoni into his house and raped her. Other girls too. When Balthasar had discovered his crime, he'd told Ndlela's employer, who'd paid for his silence. But Ndlela had not been able to keep away. He'd threatened Balthasar. He'd threatened her. And now he had Mbali.

She ducked between the rows, head down, looking both ways to see if she could see him. The lights from outside threw shadows into the warehouse, areas of grey where he could hide.

She stopped. Better to be still and listen.

She heard it. Ragged breath. He was in there, somewhere.

'Ndlela,' she called. 'Where are you?' She was giving away her position, she knew that.

'Ndlela, I know that you raped Grace Sibanyoni. By now the cops know too. It's over, Ndlela.'

Silence. He was listening.

'Where's Mbali? What have you done with her?'

A scrabbling sound. Feet getting purchase and knees scraping. He was climbing a wall of coffins.

'Stop!' he shouted. 'I have a gun!'

That meant he didn't want to use it. Someone who was trigger-happy would have pumped shots at her already.

'I don't believe you, Ndlela.'

Silence again.

'You're tired of it. Tired of being hunted. First Balthasar, then me. You're sick, aren't you? You'd like to go back to the village, to your wife, and let her look after you. Tell me where Mbali is. Tell me where to find her. Tell me that she's still alive.'

She waited and listened, head tilted upwards. She could hear breathing.

'Tell me how I can stop it before it's too late, Vincent.'

A flash at ground level caught her eye. Spike. Climbing up the wall of coffins, one foot gaining purchase after the other. He nodded at her. *Carry on.*

'You don't want any more deaths on your hands, Vincent. You're tired. Sick and tired.'

Spike was on top of the coffins now, pulling himself along on hands and knees.

'You want it all to end, don't you?'

A grunt told her that Spike had reached Ndlela. She hadn't seen him take the helmet up with him. Acid ate away at her stomach lining. The two men grappled on top of the stack of coffins. Something had to give.

She heard a crack and a whine and dust flew from the ceiling. Ndlela did have a gun, and he was trying to use it on Spike. The pants and grunts of the two men above her were too much. She turned to the bank of coffins and began to climb.

Her first foothold felt secure. But the second one did not. The pile of coffins swayed. She grabbed the handle of the coffin above and pulled. The stack swayed again and, instincts blaring, she jumped aside as the edifice came down. The floor shook as one coffin after another hit the ground. Dust flew. She heard two thuds. Softer than wood or steel. Human thuds.

Spike pulled himself up to a sitting position.

'The bloody pile fell down.' He rubbed one shoulder and winced. 'You mad woman.'

She cast around for Ndlela. He lay prone on the tiled floor of the warehouse, one leg trapped under a stainless steel coffin. He tried to lift himself up on one elbow when he saw her, but sank back onto the floor.

She knelt next to him. 'Where's Mbali?' she said through her teeth. 'You bastard, where is she?'

Vincent Ndlela opened one eye. He lifted his lips and showed his teeth. He was in pain.

'I don't know.'

She stood up, fighting the urge to kick him in the stomach. Lying next to one of the opened coffins, she saw his gun. She bent over and picked it up.

Then she pointed it at Ndlela.

'Tell me where Mbali Sibanyoni is. Or I'll kill you.'

This time he opened both eyes. 'I don't know where she is.'

'Liar! You've snatched her and hidden her somewhere. Or you've already raped and killed her. Just like you raped her sister and left her for dead.'

She felt the heft of the gun in her hand. Anger iced her veins and her finger hovered on the trigger.

'Maggie, no!' said Spike. 'He says he doesn't know. Look at him, Maggie.'

Ndlela had his arms over his face. She saw now that he was sweating. Grace's rapist feared for his life and she had the power to end it.

'Maggie –' his voice caught in his throat. 'I don't know where the child is. I promise you. I only wanted to you to stay away from them, to stop asking questions.'

'What about your threats to Balthasar?'

'He said he'd go to the police. I wanted to stop him.'

The man looked up at her. She felt a vestige of pity for him, then wiped it away. He was scum. She still trained the gun on him, but slowly she took her finger off the trigger. 'Where are the herbs?'

'The herbs?' He was prevaricating, she knew that. She aimed a swift kick at his trapped leg and he groaned in pain.

'Mrs Chalik's herbs! You work for Msomi, where does he have them?'

With his free arm, Ndlela pointed to a storage box in the corner of the warehouse.

She passed the gun to Spike. 'Keep this on him.'

She jogged over to the box Ndlela had indicated and opened it. Msomi was so over-confident he hadn't bothered to lock it. Inside were a number of small hessian sacks. She pulled one open and dug her fingers in. She expected to feel leaves, but instead she found small resinous nuggets. She grabbed a handful and took it over to Spike.

'Don't tell me Msomi's running drugs too?'

'No, Maggie,' Spike said. 'That's not hash.'

'What is it?'

Spike ran a finger over the brown lumps on her palm.

'It's myrrh.'

36

Saturday, 9am

'Cloete!' Patel barked. 'I want to see you in the office. This minute.'

'But it's Saturday,' she said, holding one hand over her eyes. She didn't need Patel on her case. She had been up beyond midnight answering the police's questions. Thanks to Lindiwe Dlamini, Vincent Ndlela was behind bars as a rape suspect. Thanks to herself and Spike, the cops were looking into Lucky Bean Msomi's mysterious stockpile of coffins. But nobody had found Mbali.

Her news editor was unsympathetic. 'Get here now.'

She parked in her usual spot behind Ernie's shed and headed upstairs. She opened the door to the newsroom. The usual weekend skeleton staff was there. There was no Sunday edition, but a reporter came in to cover the wires for Monday's paper. Today it was Aslan. He waved to her, but she ignored him. She still hadn't forgiven him for turning her into news fodder. As she walked to Patel's desk she felt his eyes follow her across the room.

'Reporting for duty,' she said to Patel, who didn't crack a smile.

'Come,' he said and got up without catching her eye. She followed him. It was clear where they were going – to Mr Nzimande's office. Her blood ran cold.

Patel knocked. 'Patel and Cloete.'

'Come in.'

Jabulani Nzimande's mouth did not curve into its usual benevolent smile when she walked in. It set itself in a firm line and he got straight to the point.

'Magdalena, I've had a complaint. Dumisane Phiri called yesterday to tell me you've been threatening him.'

'I can explain –' she began.

'Oh you don't need to.' He sat square behind his vast expanse of desk, his large shoulders echoing the spread of mahogany in front of him. 'Zacharius and I have pieced it together. You were called off the Balthasar Meiring story last week, but according to Phiri and Sally-Anne Shepherd, you turned up at the funeral. Now, despite being on sick leave, you fabricated a reason to get into Phiri's office where you accused him of harbouring a rapist.'

'But it's true, he is and I have proof,' she exclaimed, looking from one man to the other. She saw stony faces. 'Lindiwe Dlamini laid a charge against him yesterday. Ask Thandi.'

'That may be so, Maggie,' said Patel. 'But the point is, you don't wander into people's offices under the guise of writing a story. You had no authorisation from me to do so.'

'Not to mention last night's shenanigans at the traffic department,' said Nzimande. 'I heard about those this morning.'

'I helped to catch a rapist. A serial rapist.' Both faces were still blank.

'You have gone too far this time, Magdalena,' said Nzimande, arms folded squarely across his belly. 'You are suspended until further notice.'

'I don't believe this!' she said, turning to Patel. 'Zacharius you know me! You know I always bring in a story.'

'Maggie, it's not your ability we're questioning, it's your methods.' To do him justice, Patel looked embarrassed. He hated it when politics invaded the newsroom.

'Here's the deal, Magdalena,' said Nzimande. When he called her that it reminded her of her father. He arranged his forearms on his desk like a patriarch and meted out his justice. 'You are suspended for two weeks. After that time, you will return for a hearing in which you can present your side of the story. If we find that you have acted irresponsibly, we will have to let you go.'

Let you go. Those three words reverberated in her head as Patel led her out of Nzimande's office. This job was her life, it was everything. She had grown from a nothing to a respected, well-known, efficient journalist with a reputation for getting the story. She had a by-line, a name in this town. Without that she would be nothing again.

Without a job she would not be able to keep Christo at Kitchener Clinic. He would have to go to Broadlands, an institution like the other institutions that had helped him lose his mind. She had over-stepped the mark, the big line in the sand, and now the one thing that she cared about, her brother, was at risk. She felt disgust. This time with herself.

Patel led her to the door of the newsroom. He patted her shoulder. For once he looked kind and he lowered his voice so that the twitching ears couldn't hear him. 'Go home, Maggie. Take a break. You've really let this Meiring story get to you. Go see a doctor, get a diagnosis of stress and we'll see what we can do for you in two weeks' time.'

She heard a river of talk and saw her life being swept downstream. The rushing sensation increased as she walked downstairs to the

Chicken. She had worked for the *Gazette* for eleven years, years in which she'd risked her life, all in the name of making headlines and selling papers. And now they wanted to jettison her.

She sat on the curb, her head in her hands. She heard passers-by click their tongues in concern.

She thought of her first story. She'd been working at the *Gazette* in HR for a year. One of the journalists, an old soak called Reinhard van der Merwe, took a shine to her. He'd take her out for lunch and give her tips on how to become a journalist. After lunch, she'd pour him back into his chair to write his stories.

One night, soon after Christo was released from jail, there was a fire down the road from their home. Grabbing some paper and a pen, forgetting to put on shoes, she ran. The burning house belonged to a young family – the husband had got home from a late shift to find firemen trying to rescue his wife and two kids from the inferno. They didn't succeed. She got an eyewitness account, burnt feet and an interview with the frantic man.

She stayed up all night, writing and rewriting her story. The next morning, heart in mouth, she presented it to Reinhard.

'Dammit, Maggie, this is bloody good!' He slapped her on the back. 'I didn't realise you'd been listening to me all these months.'

He took her scraps of paper over to Bert Townsend, who scraped his comb-over back into place as he read her copy.

'Get some comment from the police and you've got yourself a front-page story, young lady.'

She took a few deep breaths, pushed the panic down. Slow and deep, slow and deep. She had to focus. She stood up, put her hands in her pockets and looked around. The familiar streets looked foreign, a wasteland of cars and shops and faces she didn't recognise.

Someone tapped her on the shoulder. It was Aslan.

'I just heard,' he said, his lively face and smiling eyes serious for once. 'I'm so sorry, Maggie.'

'They're throwing me on the scrapheap.' She pushed her hands deeper into her pockets, and scrunched her shoulders. 'I'm history. Nothing.'

Aslan shook his head. 'No, Maggie, that's where you're wrong. You're the best journalist I know.' His eyes shone and she looked deep into them, trying to find the conviction she needed.

He put an arm out to her, touched her shoulder. 'I don't know what it is you're up to. But I think you've got to finish it.'

She nodded and he turned, walked back to the office. In her pocket, her fingers touched something small and hard. She pulled it out – one of Grace's lucky beans.

Mbali.

Her life was on the line and it was her fault. Aslan was right. Even if this was the last thing she did as a *Gazette* reporter, it was a job she had to finish.

And this time, the deadline was real.

37

Saturday, 11am

She rubbed the lucky bean and tried to summon her senses. Ndlela was out of the question. He had not abducted Mbali. His face down the snout of that gun last night told her as much.

She had one last aveune left. Someone who until now had been silent.

She punched numbers into her cell and the old lady answered.

'Nkosazana, do you know where in Greytown Cora Ncube lives?'

Leaning her notebook against her knee, she took directions to eNhlalakahle and the bus station end of Jabula Road. She kick-started the Chicken and swung east. When she got to the group of farm signs that indicated the road to Oorwinning, she kept going. The wattles marched alongside her on the hills outside the town, but the road swiftly gave itself over to industry; used car dealers, a glazier business, peeling billboards for Home & Office Lighting. Shops were still open, but they weren't doing a roaring trade. Evidently people in Greytown took lunchtime seriously. She hoped she'd find Cora at home.

She parked and locked the Chicken under a single scraggly tree at the bus station. A little boy in shorts and an orange Joshua Doore t-shirt offered to watch it for her. She gave him two rand.

'I'll do a good job, Miss,' he called, giving her a thumbs-up as she waved and headed down Jabula in search of house number 1167. If only she felt that confident.

The township streets were alive with Saturday buzz: meat being grilled on open-air fires, music pumping from a hundred competing stereos and people talking, laughing, shouting.

Number 1167 was not spilling people out of its doors and windows in friendly chaos like its neighbour. It was shut down, door closed, windows tight and curtains pulled. She leaned over the iron gate to lift the lock. She stepped up to the front door and paused before she knocked. She had done this so many times before – knocked on doors for information – but this was the first time she was doing it without the framework of the *Gazette*, however rickety and unreliable, behind her. There was no Press card she could wave. She was just Maggie, trying to find out more about a dead person and looking for another person who was hopefully still alive.

She knocked. There was silence, but it was laden, the silence of someone holding their breath, wishing their visitor would go away.

She waited and knocked again.

The door creaked open, but there was no-one there.

'Hello.'

She looked down into the eyes of a tiny girl. She was not much bigger than Grace.

'*Gogo* sleeping,' she said.

She knelt down. The little girl's eyes seemed to hold the wisdom of the world.

'Tell *Gogo* Maggie's here.'

Half an hour later she rode the bumpy dirt road towards Oorwinning, with Cora Ncube riding pillion and wearing her spare helmet. Cora had answered her questions with terse replies. When Maggie told her she was going back to the farm, Cora said, 'I'll come with you' and deposited her granddaughter with a neighbour.

Cora tapped her back and she turned right into the plantation, where she parked the Chicken under a tree. They pulled the helmets off and left them with the bike. They would have to be unimpeded. Cora told her that from where they were parked it would be an hour on foot to the house.

The only sound was their crunching feet in the undergrowth. A natural forest should sing with life, but Meiring's fake forests were tree factories, soulless and empty.

'No,' Cora hissed and pointed. She looked up. In the branches way overhead she could just make out the shape of an owl. It wooed softly and swiveled its head, then settled itself back to sleep.

'Very bad luck,' Cora told her.

Maggie didn't believe in omens. She pushed on.

Cora's reckoning was right. It was an hour's walk to the house. Two days ago she'd snuck through the gate behind Claudine Meiring's car. Three dogs had greeted Claudine's arrival. She had to be careful not to alert them, especially not the vicious alsatian that had tried to bite her face off.

Cora gestured and she followed. They circled the house, keeping in the forest for cover.

The road itself hugged the fence around the house, rising steeply up a hill. From this side they could see the garden, dominated by the giant oak tree.

There was a sudden volley of barks. The dogs had sensed them.

'Ag, what's the matter now? Have you seen the monkeys again?'

Sanet.

She crouched down, Cora's breath on her shoulder and watched the dogs. One, an elderly labrador, gave the barking up on the sound of his mistress's voice, but two eager alsatians tried to batter the fence down. They knew something alien stalked out there.

'Okay, okay,' Sanet approached them, her tall girlish figure dressed in shorts. 'Let me finish my tea and I'll take you for your walk.'

One alsatian followed her, while the other patrolled the fence, growling in Maggie's direction. They were going to have to stay put until walk time. It seemed interminable, but it took only fifteen minutes until Sanet came into the garden, snapping leads and shouting for the dogs.

'We'll take the leads off once we're up the hill,' she promised the dogs, 'but you were so naughty last time, going into the kraal and scaring the children, that I have to do it. *Meisie, kom hier.*'

They heard the gate swing open and the three dogs panting. None of them turned towards Maggie and Cora, instead they raced off further up the hill. When Sanet's voice grew dim and they could no longer hear panting, they moved again.

Cora waved good-bye and headed behind Sanet and the dogs towards the kraal. She was going to search for Mbali there.

Maggie crept towards the gate. It had been left swinging open. She walked through and ducked right, behind the azaleas. They pointed their sharp green tongues at her.

The garage was now empty since Meiring's bakkie was out on the farm and Sanet had parked her small silver Opel outside the kitchen. She checked the rooms behind the garage once more. Still nothing but dust and the ARVs.

'They are not mine,' Cora had said in the Jabula Street house. 'But I know which one takes them.'

She combed the laundry room and workroom again, hoping that daylight would reveal any secrets hidden by the dark two nights before. Both still empty. She let herself into the art studio and stared at Balthasar's ghost.

She heard the dogs bark. Shit! She was trapped now. Through the dusty windows she could see Sanet giving them water. The old lab flopped down and drank supine, while the two alsatians stood and slopped their water. Sanet stood and watched them for a while and then went back inside. Maggie knew that once the dogs had her scent they'd be scratching at the door and whining, but for now they seemed intent on resting. She checked the door – there was an internal key, which she turned.

She sat on the floor, next to one of the deep windows, to wait until the dogs were either asleep or inside.

The frustration rose. Somewhere, somewhere on this farm, she believed that Lourens Meiring had Mbali, and she needed to find her fast.

She did some deep breathing to keep herself calm. It didn't work. She imagined Mbali tied up in a pit, or lying in some hovel where darkness had fallen. She thought of the hours she had spent chasing Msomi and Ndlela. It was quite possible that by now Mbali was dead.

As she sat there, her back against the wall next to Balthasar, she began to listen to the building. It creaked. This outbuilding, this disused art studio began to make itself heard. What stories could it tell? A tale of a talented woman who'd given up her art because it required her to be more honest than she was able to be?

With a start she realised the creaks she was hearing weren't the irregular sounds of a lonely building. The sounds were regular, a tap-tap-tap. She sprang up, throwing all the canvasses onto the table, no longer caring about placing them in order. Balthasar lay on top, staring at her.

'It's your fault,' she told him. 'If you hadn't left those children without proper protection, this wouldn't have happened. And it's also my fault, for telling your father about them.'

In the corner of the room was a big easel, also covered in a dust-cloth. She moved it to one side. The corner was empty. She looked at the floor. No trapdoors down there. She glanced up at the ceiling.

There it was. What she had been looking for.

What she'd missed.

A locked flap leading into an attic or crawl space above.

She grabbed a plastic garden chair. It wasn't dusty. Had it been recently used?

The tapping sounds grew louder and more desperate.

She scraped the latch to one side and pushed the flap up. The tapping increased and she could hear squeaks. She put her hands on either side of the opening and pulled herself up, legs flailing. She kicked the easel and it crashed to the ground.

'Mbali!'

Muscles straining, Maggie pulled herself into the gap, first getting purchase with an elbow and then with a knee. She found herself in a low attic room with no light except for that coming from the flap at her feet. The room had one central wooden pillar and it was there that she found Mbali. The child was gagged, her hands and feet bound, and tied to the pillar. Her eyes were wide and panicky.

38

Saturday, 3pm

Maggie quickly ungagged her.

'Don't worry, Maggie's here. Maggie's here,' she crooned, working to loosen the knots that bound the child's feet and hands.

Mbali didn't speak, but fresh tears came to her eyes and as her hands were freed, she wiped them away.

'Maggie's here,' she said, hugging Mbali to her. 'We'll get you away from this horrible place, make you safe, I promise.'

Mbali slumped into her body. Although she was small, the weight of her relief almost knocked Maggie over.

'Just let me make a phone call, Mbali, and then we're going to work out how to get you out of here.'

One arm around the child, she pulled off her backpack and scrabbled through it. She found her cell, but there was no reception. They were in a technology black hole. She pinged Officer Mathonsi a text message and crossed fingers that she would get it. Then she copied that message to Spike.

First she had to see if Mbali was strong enough to move. She propped her up against the pillar, stretched her legs out in front of her and began massaging them to try and get the blood flowing again.

'Have you had anything to eat?' Mbali nodded and pointed to a couple of apple cores and two empty chip packets. At least the bastard hadn't tried to starve her.

While massaging her legs, Maggie checked her over. She was still wearing her brown and white uniform and it appeared to be intact, if grubby. There were no indications of abuse or violence, but there was no knowing what the creature had in store for his captive.

The massage didn't seem to be doing much good. Mbali was floppy. Despite being propped against the pole, her shoulders drooped, her arms hung limply at her sides and her feet fell outwards. Maggie looked into her eyes. She was struggling to focus.

She lifted one of the juice cartons and sniffed it. Maybe he'd been lacing her drinks with sedatives to keep her woozy.

She had to get her out of the attic and to the Chicken, but how? Now she regretted parking so far away. There was no way she'd be able to walk the distance. Even if she did get Mbali there, would she be able to stay upright on the bike? There was only one option and it was not particularly good. But she would have to risk it.

'Listen, Mbali, I am going to go and get help.' She grimaced and tried to protest, scrunching up her eyes against the nightmare of being alone again.

'See, I'm leaving the door open here so that you have light. I promise I will be as quick as I can.'

Mbali's legs began to shake.

'I'll leave my backpack here with you. It's got my house-keys in and all my work stuff, so you know I'll come back.'

She put the backpack next to her, rested one of her arms on it, hoping that that would comfort Mbali a little. She pocketed her cell phone and let herself down the trapdoor. She took a deep breath and turned the key in the lock. Checking that the bakkie was still not there, she began to walk to the house. The alsatians set off a round of barking, which had the effect she desired.

Sanet came out of the house.

'What is going on with you two?' The larger of the beasts cantered towards Maggie, its mouth snapping open and revealing a set of scary-looking teeth. Sanet's eyes followed it.

'*Meisie!*' she called her dog to heel and held it by the collar. Maggie walked up to her as if hanging out in her garden in the late afternoon without her permission was perfectly normal behaviour.

'Hello,' she said. 'I need your help.'

'What? What do you mean?' Sanet looked puzzled and anxious.

'Come. There's something you need to see.'

Instead of rushing into the house and locking the door, Sanet followed her. She was good at obeying orders. The dogs swirled around them, no longer on defense mode and intent on a new game.

'Come in,' she said as they reached the art studio.

'What have you been doing in here?' Sanet saw that her paintings were all over the worktable and that the easel had been moved.

'It's not what I've been doing here that matters,' Maggie said, 'but what your husband has been doing.'

She pulled the chair into place under the door to the attic and indicated for her climb up. 'Take a look for yourself.'

Sanet climbed onto the chair. She put her head into the attic and screamed. She looked at Maggie with huge eyes, frozen on the chair. 'What is she doing in there?' she asked through her interlocked hands. Her eyes showed fear, a childlike look of terror that trouble was brewing.

'Claudine told you on Thursday night that she was missing. Did you really have no idea?'

She shook her head, eyes still large.

'I need you to help me get her out,' Maggie said. She's been in here for two nights and she's drugged and can't move. I'm going up and you are going to stand here and help her down.'

Sanet climbed mutely off the chair and watched as she clambered up. Mbali looked up at her with grateful eyes.

'I'm back, see,' she said, putting on her backpack. 'And now we are going to get you out of here.'

She helped Mbali crawl over to the trapdoor. The child lay on her stomach and let her legs down, which Sanet grasped. Maggie held her shoulders, then her arms and finally her hands as she eased through. When Maggie looked through the hole, she was sitting on Sanet's lap on the garden chair and the older woman was rocking her, crooning quietly. She allowed them a moment and then asked if they would let her come down too.

Supporting Mbali under the shoulders, Sanet stood up. Maggie eased down through the trap-door.

'How could he have done this?' Sanet looked at her, tears rising in her eyes, her arms around the limp child.

'Because he is a monster,' she replied.

Between them they helped Mbali out of the studio and across the garden. As they reached the house, Maggie said, 'I need your car. I have my bike in the forest but she's too weak to sit on the back.'

'But what will I say?' She was terrified. Mbali had been Meiring's captive for a couple of nights; this woman had been held hostage for over thirty years.

'You can come with us,' she said. 'No one says you have to stay here.'

Sanet Meiring looked at her jail, then at Mbali and made her decision.

'I'll just get some things,' she said.

'Okay, but fast. We need to get Mbali out of here.'

Mbali and Maggie leaned against Sanet's Opel. The afternoon sun glinted off the car windows but Mbali's skin was cold to the touch and Maggie could tell she was in shock. She needed to get to a hospital and they needed to get off Lourens Meiring's land. Fast.

It felt like Sanet was taking forever, but she came out, lugging a suitcase, which they put in the boot. Then she handed her the keys.

'You drive.'

She made her way to the passenger seat. Maggie was just strapping Mbali in when a bakkie roared up the driveway. It was Lourens Meiring. His wild eyes bore into her through the windscreen of the bakkie.

She froze, trying to decide whether to flee or to face him. Meiring made the decision for her: as he emerged from the cab of the vehicle, she saw he was holding a gun. She slammed the key into the ignition, started the car, turned a wild circle and aimed for the drive. It was time to get out of there.

They didn't get far down the driveway. Meiring shot out the two back tyres like a precision marksman. The Opel swerved to one side, narrowly missed a tree, and came to rest facing the azaleas and their pointed tongues.

Mbali hunched down in her seat, her hands covering her eyes, scarily silent. Sanet got slowly out of the car to face her husband. He walked down the driveway towards them, taking large strides like a colonist measuring out his land. Sanet trembled. When he drew parallel, she stood before him. Like a whiplash, so fast she hardly saw it, he drew his hand back and hit Sanet across the face. She crumpled to the floor, but he grabbed her by the arm and dragged her to her feet.

'When I get back from work,' he hissed, 'I expect my wife to be in the kitchen. Get inside and make me my food.'

Holding her bleeding mouth, Sanet stumbled back towards the house. Maggie watched her go.

'Get the child,' he snapped at Maggie, his eyes small and hard like pebbles.

Anger flowered in her chest, spreading through her body and chilling her, but she had to obey. He was pointing the gun at her. She had to keep calm for Mbali. She'd had a lifetime of adults failing her. Now Maggie was another one of those failures.

39

Saturday, 3.30pm

She opened the car door. Mbali was crouched down, arms and face buried in her lap, her breathing audible. The ragged panting frightened Maggie, even more than the man with the gun standing behind her.

'Mbali, we are going to get out of the car,' she said. She wanted to whisper something comforting in her ear, but Meiring was standing guard behind her. His body was centimetres from hers and his sweat smelled of resin and tar. He was breathing heavily.

She disentangled Mbali's arms and, as gently as she could, pulled her from the car. Her legs buckled and she flinched at the sight of Meiring, but she allowed Maggie to support her as they walked up the driveway to the house.

'Stop,' said Meiring, as he drew level with the bakkie. Still pointing the gun at them, he leant over the side and pulled out a coil of rope.

'Get inside the house,' he barked, indicating with the gun.

They went into the kitchen, where Sanet was holding a wet cloth to her mouth with one hand and stirring something in a pot with the other. Meiring pulled out two chairs and Mbali and Maggie sat. First he tied Maggie up, binding her body to the back of the chair and her feet to the legs. Then he started on Mbali. She was so limp he had to hold her body against the chair as he tied.

'There's no need to tie her,' Maggie said. 'That child's not going anywhere.'

'*Hou jou mond!*' he screamed. 'Shut up!' Spittle flew in her direction and she winced.

'You think I'm disgusting, do you?' His voice was quiet again. He bent towards her and spoke into her ear. His hot breath on her body was worse than his spit. 'Let me tell you what's disgusting. Wives who don't listen to their husbands. Sons who don't listen to their fathers. Loss of respect. That's disgusting.'

She glanced at Mbali. She didn't want her to hear this. Her eyes were closed and she seemed to be in some kind of trance. Her body was shutting out the horror.

Satisfied that he had made his point quite clear, Meiring moved away from Maggie and ambled towards his wife, still wielding the gun. He grabbed her by the arm and twisted it so that she winced. At the same time, he wiped a tendril of hair from her eyes. His voice softened.

'*Meisie,*' he said, 'You thought you could run away from me. How many times have I told you? That's never going to happen. What the *Here* has put together, let no man put asunder.'

Sanet gasped as he twisted her arm harder.

'What's cooking?' he asked, looking into the pot.

'*Hoendersop,*' she replied through her teeth.

He sat at a chair across the table from Mbali and Maggie.

'*Bring vir my,*' he said.

Sanet served him a bowl, with bread and butter on a separate plate.

'*Jy eet ook.*'

She obeyed, and sat down with a bowl. Holding onto his gun with one hand, Meiring filled the silent, heavy air with his slurping and spluttering. Sanet made tiny sips. She seemed to be sucking in air rather than food.

While she pretended, Meiring got up and got himself a beer from the fridge. Standing up reminded him that he had an audience. He advanced on Maggie again.

'Who do you think you are? Who do you bloody think you are?'

He grabbed her chin and she pulled her head away. He stuck his finger in her face. This was a finger she knew well, that of the self-important buffoons who ruled church and state for so many decades, who pretended that their cause was righteous and found justification for it in the Bible. It was the finger of the weekly sermons she sat through with her family, the pointed stick of damnation and hell.

He touched her nose, with that finger. She saw the remains of a blister on the back of his hand. The centre oozed and the edges were dry and cracked. Then he sat, opened his beer and drank.

'So here are the three little escapees.' His voice sounded amused. He downed the beer and passed the can to Sanet.

'Get another one.'

She began clearing the plates, but he grabbed her wrist. 'Get another one, *now*, woman.'

Sanet passed him a beer from the fridge and sat down again. Maggie tried to fathom her face but it was blank.

'You tried to run from me, *Meisie*,' he said. 'Why?'

The question was rhetorical. He wasn't interested in her answer. Maggie noticed he gave her the same name as she gave the dogs. Girlie.

'You thought you'd go with this so-called reporter,' he indicated Maggie, 'and the boy's little *kaffir*, and you thought what? You'd make a life without me?'

That old, hard word. It raked against her skin with all the hatred it was meant to convey.

He stroked his wife's arm. She looked down at his hand as if it were a new species; something that had not yet been named. Maggie saw fear ripple across her face. And something else.

He leant back and scratched his sides. 'You can tidy up now.'

Sanet got up like an automaton and began cleaning things away.

'I've had to make all the decisions in this family,' Meiring addressed Maggie. 'Running a family is like running a farm – it only works if there is one boss.'

Meiring paused, shook his head in disgust. He finished his beer, got up and fetched himself a bottle of brandy and a tumbler. He sat and poured himself a drink. He sniffed the brandy with appreciation and took a slug.

'The boss has to make decisions, sometimes hard ones. Sons are supposed to emulate their fathers, to admire them and want to be like them. Did he ever admire me? Did he ever ask about my work or show interest? Did he ever say, 'Pa, show me the farm'. No. He didn't. He hung about with his sisters and with his *friend*.'

Behind him, Sanet was still washing the dishes with her back to him, but Maggie had never seen a back so alert.

'Remember that time, Sanet?' Meiring hiccupped a laugh that was without humour. 'When he came in the bakkie with me for a week as punishment? The little *brak* spent the week in the cab listening to music on the radio. Twiddling the dials, just like he twiddled boys' *piels*.'

He hawked a mouthful of phlegm and spat it onto the table.

'Wipe, woman,' he rapped. Sanet wordlessly wiped his expectorate away.

Meiring picked up the gun and pointed it at Maggie. 'I know what you think about men who fuck other men,' he said.

She was not sure if this was another of his rhetorical statements. He got up, and began pacing.

'You think it is fine. You think it is a form of love, and the good Lord above is clapping his hands.'

He stopped near her, put one arm on the back of her chair and bent towards her, his gun-hand flapping in front of her.

'Well, I don't! I think it is degenerate and disgusting. I think they are pigs who deserve to die.'

He wiped his hands on the front of his shirt, all over his ample stomach. 'So I did it. I wiped the earth clean of the pig. I cleansed the earth and my family.'

He pointed at Maggie. 'And not once but twice.'

Sanet leant over the sink, her eloquent back still to the rest of the room. Maggie could hear her taking deep breaths. For the first time since Meiring began his rant, Maggie spoke.

'Why did you take Mbali?'

He leant one arm over the back of his chair, a study in casualness.

'Because it was easy.' He pointed a thumb in Mbali's direction. 'I told her Ouma had baked her a cake and she wanted to meet her. She got in the car, I gave her some mango juice and she fell asleep straight away. I put her in the studio for safekeeping.'

'You took her because you could?' Maggie could hear her tone rising.

'I took her because she is my grandchild, a child that my son chose to keep from me. He chose not to include us in his life. To keep us separate. I chose to undo his plan.'

He looked at Maggie, one eyebrow raised. 'I wasn't going to hurt her.'

Sanet's breathing grew louder.

'But now my plan has changed.' Meiring picked up his gun, holding it casually, like an extension of his body. 'Now, I am going to kill her, then you, and then this fucking traitorous wife of mine.'

'No! No more!' screamed Sanet, though to Maggie's ears it was a wail that started in pain and turned to fury and vicious rage, as she lifted the heavy-bottomed soup pot and battered her husband on the head with it, again and again, splattering blood over the table, herself, Maggie and the inert Mbali. He fell to the floor.

Sanet stood, looking at what she had done. '*God, versoen my.*'

'Sanet! Untie me!' Maggie screamed, but the woman was caught in a reverie of horror, staring at her bloodied, half-conscious husband.

Meiring grabbed her leg and with a last surge of strength, pulled his wife onto the floor with him. Maggie could hear the crunch of fist against bone as they wrestled in a ghastly grunting circus on the other side of the table from her and Mbali.

She struggled against her bonds, but Meiring had done a good job on the knots. She wanted to help Sanet. She started scraping her chair closer so that she could kick him. Meiring was on his knees now, blood pouring from the wounds on his head. His hands tightened around Sanet's neck. She hung limply as if she had given up. It was her strategy, one she had used before.

His hands began to tighten.

'Stop!' said a voice.

In the doorway, holding Meiring's gun, which had slithered to the floor when Sanet brained him, was Cora.

40

Saturday, 4pm

Meiring dropped his hands from around his wife's neck, but remained kneeling, like a penitent. His chest heaved and he slumped against the kitchen cabinets, legs sprawled in front of him. Blood ran in thick streams from his nose and stained his beard. He had a large wound on the side of his head.

Still pointing the gun at the prone man, Cora said, 'Sanet, untie the woman and the child.'

Sanet got up and limped around to Maggie. Her neck looked bruised and she could tell the woman would have a black eye the next day. Not the first black eye in her marriage, Maggie thought, but quite likely the last. She struggled with the knots, fingers slipping.

'Come and take the gun,' Cora said. Sanet obeyed Cora, who set about freeing Maggie. The knots were tight, but Cora's nimble fingers undid them. Maggie rubbed her wrists and watched Sanet.

She walked over to her husband and held the gun at his temple. Her hands shook. Maggie tensed her back for the report of a shot.

'Don't,' said Cora. 'His justice will come.'

Sanet closed down, her whole body drooping.

'You free the child,' Cora told Maggie, taking the gun back from Sanet who fell into a chair.

She untied Mbali and held her. She was still limp and Maggie hoped that in her woozy state she'd not taken in the gruesome events of the last few minutes. She placed her in her grandmother's lap and Sanet folded her arms around the child.

Cora still had the gun trained on Meiring. Maggie was in no doubt that if he moved she would shoot. He lolled against the cabinets, head on his chest.

'You killed Pontius,' Cora said, moving from her position in the doorway towards Meiring. 'You shot him because he was your son's lover.'

Sanet looked at Cora, aghast.

'Yes, Sanet,' Cora said. 'They were more than friends. Pontius was my little brother, the main earner of our family. How do you think it has been for us, living without him? For me, coming to work every day and seeing this murderer?'

'Why?' Sanet whispered, lifting her face from its leaning-place on Mbali's head.

Cora laughed, a dry sound that echoed in the still room. 'Why? the rich madam asks.' She turned and looked at Sanet with an expression of hatred. 'I am a black woman with a standard five. My parents took your husband's reparations for their retirement. How else do you think I was going to feed my family?'

She sat in the chair where Meiring had had his dinner. 'I had no choice. Either I carried on working for the killer, or sold my body, or let my children starve. I went to the sangoma, who cast a spell of protection over me. Then I came back here, to watch and wait.'

Her face grew vivid. 'I watched you, Sanet, but you didn't see me. What you don't realise is that I know everything about you. I know when he hit you and when you used make-up to cover the bruises. I know when he made you stop painting. I know when he forced you to have sex.'

Meiring lifted his head at this, like an old dog hearing its name called.

'Don't look at me!' Cora spat. His head sank down onto his chest.

'I'm sorry.' Sanet's voice was quiet but clear. 'I'm sorry, Cora.'

'Be sorry,' Cora retorted. 'You did nothing to stop him. You let him be who he was.'

'What could I have done?' Tears filled Sanet's eyes.

'You could have left, taken your children to safety, been a better mother. You could have left him when he threw your son out of the house. Or when he killed Pontius. But you stayed, like a coward.'

Cora leaned forward, over the table she had scrubbed and cleaned for many years, and looked into Sanet's eyes. 'He killed your son! And you still sit there. What kind of a mother are you?'

Sanet shook. She held Mbali's limp form closer to her body.

'The only person in this family who wasn't a coward was Balthasar. When he came back he gave me money for my children. He said he would always help me.' For the first time since she'd entered the room, Cora seemed hesitant. She had the burden of further information. Maggie could see that she was struggling with it.

'He knew –.'

'– that your husband is HIV positive,' Maggie said.

'What?' Sanet whispered, her arms tightening around Mbali, more for her own comfort than that of the child's.

'He's positive,' she repeated. 'Balthasar knew. He threatened his father that he would go to the police and tell them that Pontius's murder was no act of self-defence but a cold-blooded murder. Unless he admitted to you that he was positive. That's why Meiring killed him.'

'But how do you –?' Sanet was shivering.

'I found his ARVs. He keeps them in the room behind the garage under the bed.'

'And you, Cora?' Sanet turned to the tall woman, propping up the doorway with her former employer's gun in her hand.

'I found them. I was the one who told Balthasar.' Cora's face was set, lines scoring the paths from nose to chin.

'But where did he get it?'

'You'll have to ask your husband that question.' Cora's fingers tightened around the weapon.

'You are an evil, bad man,' Sanet said to her husband. His pale blue eyes opened. 'You tried to break our family apart and you nearly succeeded.' She pointed a finger at him. 'But I will do what I can to keep those of us that are left together.'

As if talking to herself, she continued, 'My beautiful boy. You died fighting for me. I am sorry for not helping when you needed help. I was a coward. I lived in fear.' She hugged Mbali tighter. 'But I will look after your children. God help me, I will do that. They are safe now, with me, and you can rest in peace.'

'Go and call the police,' Cora said to Maggie.

'Too late.' The voice came from deep inside Meiring's chest. 'You have killed yourselves with talk. Bloody women.'

Maggie's scalp burned.

He opened his eyes, the blue cauterized to white, and looked at his wife. 'On my way here, I set the farm on fire. You're all going to die with me.'

Maggie ran outside. Smoke filled her lungs and the hillsides around the farm were dark. Along the road towards the kraal she could see a ribbon of flame.

'Come!' she shouted to the others. 'We need to get out of here, fast!'

The only option was Meiring's bakkie. She grabbed the keys from the kitchen table.

'Cora, you get Mbali inside the bakkie.' Cora pulled the child off Sanet's lap and carried her out of the kitchen.

Maggie turned to Sanet, now paler than ever. 'Help me, Sanet.' She pointed at Meiring, still sprawled on the kitchen floor, blood from his head wound trickling into his neck. 'Help me pick him up.'

Each woman took one of his arms and pulled. It was like trying to lift a house. He was a dead weight. Lourens Meiring had no plans to leave his farm alive.

Maggie sprinted outside and climbed into the cab of the bakkie. She turned the key and the vehicle coughed. She turned it again and it choked into life. Looking over her shoulder she reversed the bakkie as close to the kitchen door as possible.

'Cora, we'll need your help.'

Between them the three women levered the giant man through the kitchen door. Grunting and pushing, they managed to shove his inert body onto the back of the bakkie.

'Sit with him, Sanet,' Maggie said and the woman climbed into the back with her husband.

'Do you have blankets?' she asked Cora.

'Hallway cupboard,' she replied. She pulled three heavy grey blankets out of the cupboard and with Cora's help hosed them down outside the kitchen door.

'We must go!' Sanet shouted from the back of the vehicle. She pointed at the hillside. The trees were burning now, each a candle of flame, blazing branches hitting the ground.

Sweat pouring off her body and, coughing, she threw the wet blankets to Sanet. Then she leapt into the cab and turned the key.

She drove towards the gate, pressing the remote as she did so. Sanet banged on the cab window behind her head. 'Stop, Maggie! The dogs!' She put her foot on the brake, while the three dogs jumped onto the back of the bakkie. Sanet covered herself, the dogs and the inert body of her husband with the blankets.

The iron gate swung open.

The road before them was a wall of fire.

Maggie looked at Cora, an unspoken question between them. Maggie judged that Meiring had set fires in a circle around the farmhouse. The only way to safety was through the loop.

'Just go!' Cora said.

She accelerated. Flames reached towards the bakkie. Ash swirled in currents. Branches collapsed around them and smoke rose metres above the canopy. Hunched over the steering wheel, she focused on the road and moving forward. Cora held Mbali on her lap, her arms tight around the child.

She pushed on. The heat was unbearable, her lungs full of ash and dust. She heard Cora cough and she spluttered, her lungs filling up. She had no more air left. They would suffocate, right here in the burning heart of Lourens Meiring's forest.

A whimper filled the cab. Mbali?

The whimper grew to a screech, an appalling ruckus of pain that scraped her eardrums. Maggie's teeth pressed together. She had to get them through, she had to.

Then water hit the windscreen. She braked.

Two fire-trucks were parked across the road, accompanied by three police vans and behind them, two ambulances.

Another car was parked there, an ancient Mercedes that she had seen yesterday, an entire lifetime ago. It belonged to Spike Lyall.

41

Three weeks later

She felt the caffeine rush into her veins. It was a wet, grey day and the mountains rose out of the mist. Later the sun would burn through the cloud and they would hike along the contour path, listen to the birds and look down into the steamy valleys below.

She took a deep, satisfied sniff of the folded newspaper in her hand. For a week after the ordeal at the farm, she had not been able to look at a copy of the *Gazette*. Just seeing the banner headlines posted on telephone poles in town had made her feel ill.

However, nothing was worse than going to Msizi's funeral. Nkosazana's youngest grandchild had spent his whole life being sick. He'd never crawled or tottered on his baby legs, never chased a gecko or a soccer ball. His coffin was hardly bigger than a shoe-box.

The funeral was held at Sanet's new place of worship, a non-denominational church only a short walk from Balthasar's house. Lindiwe spoke and Sanet read a passage from the Bible. Nkosazana wept and tore at her breast. Maggie, holding Mbali's hand, cried too.

Msizi was cremated. Nkosazana had not been happy about this departure from Zulu custom, but Lindiwe persuaded her that it was the responsible thing to do.

They scattered his ashes around the lucky bean tree. When Joyce and Busi grew stronger Sanet said they would be able to go outside, play under the tree and remember their little cousin. Nkosazana had raised her eyebrows. She didn't like to agree with anything her former employer said. The two women were engaged in a dance of power at the house, trying to negotiate new terms and every decision was a battleground.

Nkosazana phoned Maggie to complain. 'She is not my boss anymore.'

'Yes, Nkosazana, you tell her that.' Sanet had to learn. Nkosazana was her new partner in Balthasar's orphanage. Lindiwe had helped them to register it as an NGO, with both women as co-executives, and they had taken in two more AIDS orphans from Sweetwaters. Nkosazana seemed sprightly now – all the power play with Sanet had given her new life.

The only thing she did approve of was the sparkling new kitchen that Sanet had installed at the house. There would be no more cooking on an ancient stove or opening a leaky fridge for her.

Lindiwe phoned Maggie once to tell her that Sanet had agreed to test for HIV.

Another caller during her exile was Thandi Mathonsi. 'We'll need you to give evidence at the Meiring trial in April. Someone else from the *Gazette* will have to cover the story.'

She knew who that would be. Jabu. In her absence the cub was making front-page real estate on a regular basis.

Nzimande called her in for her disciplinary hearing one week early. He met her at the door to his office.

'We've cancelled it,' he said, 'in the light of what happened at the Meiring farm. You risked your life to save a child and stop a killer and, while you went beyond your jurisdiction, we can't punish you for that.'

He sat back down behind the acreage of his desk.

'However, you have lost your job. Jabu will cover crime and courts from now on.'

'What?' She slumped into a chair.

The smell of spearmint preceded Zacharius Patel, who stood in the doorway with a wry smile on his face. 'How's our new investigative reporter?'

She stared from one man to the other.

'You're being promoted, Cloete,' said Nzimande. 'Here's a bonus.' He pushed an envelope across the desk towards her. 'Use this money to have a holiday. When you get back we'll formulate a plan for your new job.'

She glowed. The relief shone in her belly like a sun.

'I think Maggie's got a story to write before we allow her to take leave. The cops arrested Lucky Bean Msomi today.' Patel was actually grinning. She made a mental note to save the image.

'Yes, yes,' beamed Nzimande. 'You'd better listen to your boss, Maggie. Get writing.'

That day she paid off Christo's hospital bills, paid Pete Dickson at Alpha Garage, wrote the Lucky Bean Msomi story and booked a cottage in the Drakensberg. In that order.

Now, surrounded by the mountains and with the smell of bacon and eggs making her stomach rumble, she unfolded the paper. The banner headline stabbed her.

Fraud suspect on the run

By Jabu Sibiya, Crime Reporter

Police launched a man-hunt last night after local businessman and fraud suspect, Lucky Bean Msomi, escaped from police custody.

Police liaison officer, Thandi Mathonsi, said that Msomi escaped under the cover of darkness. 'We are not sure how he managed to wrangle his way out of a locked jail cell, but we have launched a man-hunt. It is the duty of the law to protect the most vulnerable members of society from those who try to con them and the charges against Msomi are extremely serious.'

Msomi is facing fraud charges along with Sven Schloegel, a German national currently also the subject of a class action suit in the Pietermaritzburg High Court for selling a fake AIDS cure to families of people with AIDS.

Family members allegedly borrowed money from Msomi to pay for Schloegel's 'cure' and for the high cost of funeral expenses. Once in hock to Msomi, they had to find a way to pay the businessman back. In an undercover investigation by the Gazette, reporter Magdalena Cloete revealed that the grieving families all become Schloegel's Herbals operatives.

Msomi was arrested in February along with Schloegel and five other business associates, including Chief Siyabantu Phiri, whose son, local ANC member Dumisane Phiri, is facing charges of obstructing justice in the Vincent Ndlela serial rape case currently before the High Court.

Spike walked into the bedroom, and placed a tray on the bedside table. It was groaning with eggs, bacon, toast and fresh coffee.

'You won't believe this,' she said, shaking the paper. 'The shark's escaped! Msomi. He's on the run. I go on holiday and this happens. I need to get back to work.'

'Pass me the paper,' Spike said.

She ignored him.

'Magdalena Cloete, give me that newspaper right now. You're on holiday and under strict instructions to forget about the *Gazette*, about work and about any escaped crime lords, no matter how big or bad.'

Spike grabbed the paper out of her hands and threw it across the room. He knelt on the bed next to her, slid his arms around her waist and kissed her neck.

She found that it was easy to forget.

Acknowledgements

My grateful thanks to an array of authors whose sensitive and knowledgeable books have helped me understand both the complexity of HIV/AIDS and its social fallout. These include Edwin Cameron (*Witness to AIDS*), Kerry Cullinan and Anso Thom (*The Virus, Vitamins & Vegetables – The South African HIV/AIDS Mystery*), Adam Levin (*Aidsafari – A Memoir of My Journey with Aids*), Jonny Steinberg (*Sizwe's Test*), Stefanie Nolen (*28 Stories of AIDS in Africa*) and Rebecca Brown (*The Gifts of the Body*). Any errors of fact are entirely my own.

I am honoured by and grateful for the support of so many: family and friends, both near and far, in real life and online, who have cheered from the sidelines and given me the courage to keep going. You know who you are and how much you mean to me.

In particular, I am grateful to my agent Michaela Roell, who was the first person in the publishing world to see a spark of something in Maggie. My German publisher Else Laudan was the second, and I thank her for placing her trust in Maggie and in me. And a special, heartfelt thanks to Colleen Higgs of Modjaji Books for bringing Maggie to South Africa, where she belongs. Thanks also to my dear friend Angela Briggs, whose beautiful painting forms the cover of *Balthasar's Gift*.

Thanks also to Toni, Oliver, Andrew and my team at home – Thomas, Lily, Daisy and Ollie. You are the best and I love you.

CHARLOTTE OTTER
HEIDELBERG, MAY 2014

OTHER FICTION TITLES PUBLISHED BY MODJAJI BOOKS

The Blacks of Cape Town by CA Davids

Do Not Go Gentle by Futhi Ntshingila

Witchgirl by Tanvir Bush

This Day by Tiah Beautement

To all the Black Women We Knew by Kholofelo Maenetsha

Bom Boy by Yewande Omotoso

Shooting Snakes by Maren Bodenstein

Running & other stories by Makhosazana Xaba

Love Interrupted by Reneilwe Malatji

Team Trinity by Fiona Snyckers

One Green Bottle by Debrah Nixon

got.no.secrets by Danila Botha

Snake by Tracey Farren

The Thin Line by Arja Salafranca

This Place I Call Home by Meg Vandermerwe

The Bed Book of Short Stories edited by Joanne Hichens and Lauri Kubuitsile

Whiplash by Tracey Farren